SCREEN QUEENS

SCREEN QUEENS

QUEENS

LORI GOLDSTEIN

RAZORBILL

RAZORBILL

An Imprint of Penguin Random House LLC
New York

First published in the United States of America by Razorbill,
an imprint of Penguin Random House LLC, 2019

Visit us online at penguinrandomhouse.com

LIBRARY OF CONGRESS CATALOGING-IN-PUBLICATION DATA IS AVAILABLE
ISBN 9780451481597

Printed in the United States of America

1 3 5 7 9 10 8 6 4 2

Interior design by Corina Lupp

For Marc,
for making me believe in moonshots

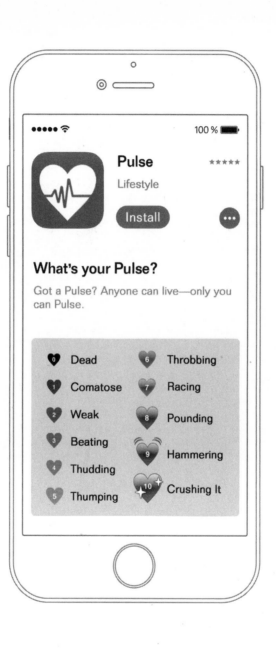

ONE

VALLEY OPTIMISTIC • *Silicon Valley's belief in new tech or ideas that engender doubt from those in the outside world*

FOUR. *STILL*. ONLY FOUR.

Lucy shifted in the hard wooden chair across from her mom's desk and clutched her phone tighter. She swiped up and down with such force that her Caribbean Blue Baby fingernails would have scratched the glass had she not been diligent about using a screen protector.

Twitter, Instagram, Tumblr, Snapchat, Facebook . . . *Swipe, swipe, swipe.* The likes, favorites, followers, friends . . . she had enough. Enough for her ranking on the Pulse app to be higher than four.

Four?

Swipe, swipe, swipe, swipe.

The pink plastic bracelet the bouncer had secured around Lucy's wrist danced up and down the same way she had last night, after name-dropping her way into the hottest new club in San Francisco's Tenderloin District. The fact that she didn't actually *know* Ryan Thompson, founder of Pulse, was a technicality that would soon be remedied.

Her ❤ OUR FINGERS ARE ON THE PULSE ❤ tee only given to Pulse employees opened doors closed even to most of Silicon Valley's elite. She'd snagged it from a hipster-preneur six months ago at a party in Fremont. He was so busy claiming he left Pulse of his own accord (*uh-huh*) because his eco-friendly (*read: non-profitable*) idea was going to change the world (*i.e., drain his bank account*) that he scarcely knew what he'd lost. All it took was a deftly spilled cocktail, an exorbitant dry cleaning bill, and Lucy's favorite tank (*note: pomegranate margaritas don't come out of silk*), but it was worth it.

Soon she'd have one of her own.

And she'd no longer be a 4.

Really?

The likes on her Instagram story from last night alone should have bumped her up to a 5. Thumping. But here she sat. Still at 4. Still Thudding.

She stared at the string of hearts on her Pulse profile, knowing that, somehow, this was all because she was wait-listed at Stanford.

And *that*, Lucy knew the exact "how" of: Gavin Cox.

Freaking Gavin Cox.

She shouldn't have done it, but her blue fingernail moved on its own, navigating to his profile.

Level 6. Throbbing. Gavin Cox was Throbbing and she was Thudding. If only she possessed a male member and a wing-span like Michael Phelps, she'd be Throbbing too. But now that high school was over, winning state would no longer be a crutch for Gavin, and his Pulse would plummet. He'd be lucky to be Beating—a measly 3.

Lucy was tempted to knock her mom's expansive cherrywood desk. But Lucy Katz didn't believe in luck. Lucy Katz didn't hope. Lucy Katz didn't dream. Lucy Katz did.

She knew what she wanted.

And it wasn't this.

Thudding and wait-listed and this drab third-floor office in this mud-brown building in this sad little Sunnyvale office park.

So it wouldn't be.

Tired of the edge of the chair digging into the soft underside of her knees, she scooted forward until her wedge sandals reached the floor.

Her mom was twenty minutes late.

As usual.

Lucy knew enough to show up for their scheduled lunch a half hour after its start time, but she was on time.

As always.

Lucy planned like other people breathed.

Which was why she wasn't nervous about Stanford. It was a blip. A minor inconvenience. Nothing that an internship at Pulse wouldn't wipe away like a hard reset on her MacBook Pro.

She stared at the gently tanned skin of her exposed ankles and wiggled her toes, enticing circulation to resume after being dangled two inches off the floor despite her heels. She pulled her pink-and-white-striped notebook onto her lap and leafed through the pages, refreshing herself on all the notes she'd taken thus far on ValleyStart, the summer tech incubator program she was about to begin. The five-week competition ended with one team winning an internship at Pulse. If she succeeded (*please*), she'd spend the rest of the summer at Pulse with Ryan Thompson. And Pulse, well, not even Stanford could ignore a pedigree that included Pulse.

Satisfied it was all already committed to memory, she closed her notebook and stared at the shiny gold *L* floating on the center of the cover—the only Hanukkah gift she'd received last year, sent in a FedEx envelope from her mom's assistant.

She tucked it under her arm and stood, passing by windows that looked out on row after row of blue, red, black, white, and green hybrid cars lined up like Crayolas in the parking lot, the closest the office came to having a pop of color. A four-by-six double frame propped beside her mom's three monitors was the only personalization in the room.

One side held Lucy as a baby, swaddled in her mom's arms with her dad looking off to the side, toward the London office he'd soon head. The second photo once again displayed the three of them, this time on graduation day, just a few weeks ago. Her dad had scheduled a week of meetings before and after in order to attend.

Two milestones in Lucy's life, as if nothing had happened in between, with the frame leaving no room for anything to come.

The graduation photo hung crooked in the frame. She could just see her mom hurriedly shoving it inside with one hand, typing an email with the other, while on a conference call with Singapore, Melbourne, and Dubai.

Lucy set her phone on the desk. She pulled off the cardboard backing to straighten the photo, and out fell the slip of paper behind it: a smiling baby—not Lucy, simply the picture that had come in the frame. How long had her mom kept that other child beside Lucy? Long enough to forget to print one to take its place, long enough to no longer notice that she should.

On the desk, Lucy's phone vibrated and lit up with a text.

ValleyStart: Team assignments are in! Meet Your Mates!

Lucy's arm shot out like a rattlesnake, and her notebook fell, knocking into one of her mom's monitors.

"Lucy!" Abigail Katz entered the room and rushed forward in her expensive flats.

"Got it!" Lucy's tennis-trained reflexes saved the monitor before it took down the others like dominoes.

Considering Lucy had read and reread the acceptance packet about a thousand times and been waiting for the past two months to see who she'd be spending the next five weeks with, her restraint in not jumping on the ValleyStart portal instantly was extraordinary.

It's actually happening.

Her pulse quickened, and she was almost dizzy as she circled one way around the desk, back to the hard chair. Her mom rounded the corner from the opposite direction, adjusted the tilt of the monitor, and sat down in front of it.

With the seven-inch height difference between them, Lucy could only see her eyes. And the tiredness in them.

Lucy would never deny that Abigail Katz worked hard.

But that was all she did.

"I'm sorry, Lucy." Abigail smoothed the ends of her chin-length bob. The barest hint of gray dusted the roots—a constant battle, waged every three weeks as she colored it back to brown. "They needed some guidance in a branding meeting that wasn't on my schedule."

"Right," Lucy said.

Abigail reached into the top drawer of her desk and pulled out two protein bars. "Just a quick lunch, then, okay?"

Peanut butter. Lucy hated peanut butter. "Sure." She peeled back the wrapping. Not even peanut butter could ruin her ValleyStart high.

"All set for tomorrow?"

"Packed the car this morning." She bounced (*just a little*) in her seat.

Abigail stopped chewing. "Not an Uber or Lyft?"

"It's ten miles."

"Right. *Ten.*"

Half the number of fender benders Lucy had been in. *Who has time to spend learning to be a perfect driver?*

"Fine. Whatever." Lucy pretended there was no judgment in her mom's question and forced a bite of the peanut butter. "I'll leave the car."

"Better plan. You won't need it anyway." Abigail set her own half-eaten bar down. "You have to focus. Palo Alto High School may have been competitive, but ValleyStart's in another league. The top startup incubator for high school graduates in the country with only sixty accepted out of—"

"Three thousand applicants, I know." An acceptance rate of only two percent. *Two.* Stanford's was four. The sole explanation . . .

Freaking Gavin Cox.

The only other applicant from her high school to make it into ValleyStart.

Lucy pushed her heels into the floor and all thoughts of Gavin where they belonged—in the past.

"I've been focused, Mom. I'm certainly not going to stop now." Top ten in her class, 4.8 GPA, tennis all-star, two marathons under her belt, and still a lecture on being "focused." Lucy regretted the bite as her stomach churned.

"Nothing wrong with reminders," Abigail said, just as one dinged on her computer and phone in unison, the sound as familiar to Lucy as the squeak of her bedroom door.

Lucy stood.

"Wait. It's just . . ." Abigail's eyes slowly drifted from her three monitors to Lucy's expertly draped off-the-shoulder tee and perfectly cuffed dark-wash jeans. "I've always given you freedom because you've shown that you can handle it. Up until now."

Now meaning not getting into Stanford.

"But with this, with this new world you're entering, well, I just want you to be aware of the pressures and the importance of how you present yourself."

"Present myself? I'm not a poodle in some dog show."

"That's not what I meant."

"Then what do you mean, Mom?"

"Letting off steam in high school is one thing, but now you're an adult."

"So I've heard." Her mom had repeated the same phrase ad nauseam since Lucy's eighteenth birthday three months ago.

"Believe me, Lucy, it's no secret how little you've wanted to heed my advice lately. If and when that changes, you know where to find me."

Right here in this same baby-poop-brown office you've lived in since I took my first steps . . . which, naturally, you missed.

Heat rose in Lucy's chest, and all she wanted to do was give her mom a reminder: that the phrase was "work hard" *and* "play hard." And the playing bit could yield the same—if not better— results as the working. Connections made things happen. Just ask her Pulse tee.

"Sure, Mom." Lucy brushed her hand through her long dark hair, forgetting she was still holding the brick of peanut but- ter. She picked a crumb off a strand by her chin and watched as her mom slipped on her computer glasses and turned the world right in front of her eyes crystal clear, blurring everything else beyond—including Lucy.

Lucy headed for the door. "Just one small thing . . . in order to give me freedom or anything else, you'd actually have to be around."

She didn't wait for her mom to look up; she simply wrapped her hand around the metal knob and closed the door behind her with barely a sound, making sure she "presented herself" properly.

How am I even related to her?

Lucy only made it halfway down the hall before she slowed, leaned her head against the crap-colored walls, and tried to stop her heart from racing.

Level 7. Seven hearts was Racing.

Like everyone her age, like everyone in the world, Lucy knew the Pulse levels as well as her home address. "What's your Pulse?" were the first words off anyone's lips upon meeting, the first background check determining worthiness for everything from friend to blind date to party invites, probably even job offers.

The brainchild of Ryan Thompson when he was only a year older than Lucy, the app amalgamated an individual's likes, favorites, views, thumbs-ups, and more from every major social media platform, translating it to a simple Pulse level, ranking you from zero, Dead, all the way to ten, Crushing It. Over time, as the app evolved, Level 10s became top influencers, the people everyone wanted to be or be seen with. Advertisers and the entertainment business soon realized that Level 10s' smiling faces could increase sales and media coverage. Now 10s got complimentary everything, from the newest iPhones to dips in Iceland's Blue Lagoon. To be a 10 was to live with all the perks.

Once Lucy and her team won the ValleyStart incubator, Pulse would be her second home for the rest of the summer. The prize of an internship at the most successful tech company in the past ten years was worth more than any amount of money.

She'd use it to her advantage. Starting now.

Lucy opened the Stanford portal and did what she'd wanted to do for weeks, since she was accepted into ValleyStart. She requested a second alumni interview. She knew it was irregular, but she explained that she had new information she was delighted to share—namely the incubator.

Lucy then lifted her chin higher and straightened her top. As she passed by the largest office—a suite—she ran her finger along the three little letters on the nameplate: *CEO*.

Pulse would secure that future.

At the elevators, Lucy logged in to the ValleyStart portal to find not just the names of her teammates but her assigned mentor: Ryan Thompson.

For the first time since arriving at her mom's office, Lucy smiled.

TWO

DESIGN HACKER • *A term that attempts to paint graphic designers as more "techie"*

THE ODDS OF FINDING a four-leaf clover are the same as being injured by a toilet. Maddie Li had yet to be the one in ten thousand to go toe-to-toe with a bathroom fixture, but she had come across a four-leaf clover. She'd plucked it from the green lawn of the expansive quad in Harvard Yard only six blocks from her Cambridge home when she was nine. It had hung around her neck, encased in a tiny glass ornament, ever since.

A constant reminder of what else came into her life that day: her little brother, Danny.

"Not a single pterodactyl. Defective, Maddie, I'm telling you."

Maddie watched as Danny ran figure eights with his spoon through his cereal milk. "I'm not so sure. I mean . . ." She made a show of checking if the coast was clear, glancing through the arched kitchen doorway to the hundred-year-old front door to the freshly wallpapered staircase. "Well, maybe I better not say . . ."

Danny tucked his feet underneath him, and Maddie's hand instinctually reached to steady the stool. He leaned across the marble counter. "You can trust me."

Maddie raised an eyebrow. "Hmm . . . I don't know . . ."

"Maddie."

"Danny."

Her brother sucked in his cheeks, folding his bottom lip into a pout that never failed to achieve its desired effect.

"Okay," she said, "but it's gotta stay under your hat."

"I'm not wearing a hat."

Maddie lifted her hand above her brother's red hair. Though empty of her stylus, her fingers automatically curled into position, and with a flourish she drew an invisible top hat above his head. "There."

He looked up and pretended to knock it off his head. "It's brown," he said matter-of-factly. "Green's my favorite color."

"How silly of me." With a fervent air scribble, Maddie abided by the wishes of her little brother. "There. Now, about those ptero-dactyls . . . my theory, and again, you didn't hear this from me, but I think they're the smartest dinosaurs in all of cereal land."

Danny's eyes widened, and a pang of sadness stole her breath. *Five weeks.* She wouldn't see him for five whole weeks.

She cleared her throat, lowered her voice, and pointed to the cereal box. "These guys . . . they're not going to become extinct. Not ever again. So each and every one waits and waits and waits and then flaps its wings a million miles an hour and zooms out of the box right before the factory glues it shut, and now they're all living together on a tiny island off the coast of Martha's Vine-yard."

Danny cocked his head. "That'd be nice." A wistfulness gleamed in his eyes, but not long enough. Growing up too fast was Danny's thing. Maddie's was hitting pause, whenever and however she could.

He slowly sat back on his heels and dunked his spoon in his bowl. "But it's just a story." His fingers swirled in the milk, and out came a tiny pterodactyl. He popped it in his mouth and chewed. "Gonna miss your stories."

Maddie's phone dinged with a text from ValleyStart. She flipped it over on the counter. But not before Danny saw it too.

"It's okay," he said. "I'm proud of you, Mads."

A hard lump formed in Maddie's throat, and she tried for the millionth time to convince herself that this was the right thing.

Which was hard to do with the way her phone continued to ding obnoxiously. She pushed it farther away. "I'm the one who's proud of you." She gestured to his sleepaway camp duffel on the floor of the living room, open and waiting for his favorite socks, which were still in the dryer. Maddie had had to pry them off his feet that morning. Probably the last time they'd be clean all summer, considering how he could barely stand to go a day without them. "That's one neat and orderly bag, kid."

"Learned it from you," Danny said, smiling his crooked grin. Then he burst out laughing at his own joke.

Maddie smiled. Even if she wanted to, she didn't have time to be neat, not when there was school and clients and a little brother to take care of.

As Danny read the dinosaur facts on the cereal box, Maddie reluctantly turned to the string of texts waiting on her lock screen. Ones not just from ValleyStart, but at least ten from a number she didn't know. The first message identified the sender as Lucy Katz, proclaiming herself to be one of Maddie's teammates and roommates. The girl had sent her Pulse handle and how excited she was to be at Thudding, whatever that meant, and as near as Maddie could tell, her life story since birth at five pounds, three ounces to . . .

Whatever.

"Packing a bag's easy," Danny said. "I can teach you . . . so long as a trip to J.P. Licks and a chocolate cone's in it for me."

Maddie shoved her phone in her pocket and put on her widest big sister smile. "Does this mean you've been snooping in my duffel?"

Danny shook his head. "Was going to help you get organized, but Mads, even that's too big a job for me."

"The creative brain doesn't have time to fold."

"Hope your new roommates don't mind."

Maddie felt her smile slipping and held on tight.

"It's okay," Danny said. "I already *know* how much you're gonna miss me. I mean, who wouldn't?"

They were both good at covering. A couple of nights, that was the longest they'd ever been apart. So, yeah, Maddie was going to miss Danny like she'd miss a limb—especially since she'd be spending her days at a technology incubator inventing another app people didn't really need.

"And you're gonna miss this." She hopped off her stool and plastered a kiss on his cheek. "When I get back, we're going to kick those pterodactyls off that island and claim it for ourselves!"

"Ew, Mads, that was all wet!"

Footsteps pounded the stairs, and Maddie looked up to see

her mom drop a leather satchel on the bench by the front door. Strands of her long auburn hair hid her eyes as Kelley Finnerty Li reached inside one of the galvanized steel baskets home to everyone's shoes, neatly tucked away by the cleaning lady. After pointing the toes of her stilettos toward the door, she stood and faced the kitchen, her wireless headset glued to her ear. Maddie was pretty sure her mom slept in the thing.

She gave a half-hearted nod to her children while simultaneously complaining about "him" and "joint assets." Swap out "him" for "her," and the conversation would be a replica of the one their dad had had less than half an hour ago. He'd breezed through the kitchen, side-hugging Danny, and on his way out, grabbed a muffin Maddie had made for Danny's ride to camp later that afternoon.

Maddie still wished she were driving her brother to New Hampshire. But she had a six a.m. flight to San Francisco the next morning, had to finish packing, and needed to finalize a project for her most valuable client. The client that would have been her *second* most valuable client had she landed the company whose proposal she'd worked on for weeks. Besides, the camp owners had assured Maddie that the bus ride with other campers was a great bonding experience.

Bonding was something Maddie had zero interest in doing with this Lucy chick. Her butt was still buzzing from the girl. *This is going to be a long five weeks.* Maddie made a mental note to pack her noise-canceling headphones.

ValleyStart offered Maddie one thing and one thing only: a rock-solid entry on her résumé. With the prestige of the program behind her, she'd never lose another client, which meant she'd keep growing her graphic design business, which meant, most important, she could forgo college and stay right here in Cambridge with Danny.

That hadn't been her original plan. But the allure of design school in Maryland had vanished four months ago when her grandparents, who lived in New York, were needed in Beijing more than they were in Cambridge. They'd been planning to move in to help with Danny after Maddie became a college freshman. But her grandmother's sister was sick, and Danny, after all, had two healthy parents.

Physically, that is. Because nothing else about her parents and their relationship could be called "healthy." At least not in the six years since their personal life merged with their professional one. Together, they'd founded an entertainment representation agency whose success consumed them—and who they used to be. Maddie had been taking care of Danny ever since.

Lately, things had gotten much worse. Not that they told Maddie; her only clue was that they now seemed to be communicating exclusively through lawyers.

Like her mom was doing right now, her freckled cheeks growing as red as her hair. Maddie wrapped her hand around her four-leaf clover and turned away. Her third-generation Irish mother and first-generation Chinese father meant the Finnerty-Li household was not devoid of superstition. Maddie didn't believe in most of them, but finding the four-leaf clover the same day her brother was born made this one an exception. Maddie's mom was the one who told her what each leaf represented. She'd let her nine-year-old daughter sit on the side of her hospital bed and set little Daniel in her arms. Even then he had a puff of red hair, taking after their mother and the complete opposite of Maddie, whose black shoulder-length hair and dark eyes were all her dad's.

Hazel eyes and round face strained from her long labor, Maddie's mom had smiled as bright as an August day when Maddie pulled Daniel close to her and showed her mother the clover.

"Faith, hope, love, and luck," her mother had said. "That's what each leaf represents."

"One for each of us," Maddie's dad, Jon, added as he stood on the other side of the bed. "For our family."

Maddie had believed it then.

"Profit share" and "my business" and "not in my lifetime" and more words Maddie didn't want Danny to hear came out of her mother's mouth. An eight-year-old should be protected from all this. He still believed in family. Or, at least, Maddie hoped he did.

Her mother snatched one of Danny's muffins and almost tripped over her son's luggage, momentarily surprised by the buzz of the dryer. She looked at Maddie, tipped her head to the laundry room, and continued up the stairs.

How am I even related to her?

Another vibration in Maddie's pocket, and she whipped out her phone to tell this Lucy person to give it a rest and saw that it wasn't this Lucy person but a notice to check in for her flight. California was so far away—from all of this. A wave of relief rippled through Maddie. And then she turned and saw the pout on her brother's face, this one very, very real, and all Maddie felt was guilt.

She pushed through it all, looked at her brother, and smiled.

THREE

GOING PUBLIC • *When a private company sells shares to public investors for the first time*

APPLAUSE HUNG IN THE air from the previous scene, and the soft notes of the solo began. Delia Meyer crossed her fingers. They immediately slid apart from sweat. Darkness shrouded the stage, and then, Delia sucked in a breath and flipped the switch.

A beam of light formed a circle on the wood floor, which showed its age in scuffs and nicks, all invisible to the audience because of the angle of the seats, because of the shadows criss-crossing the theater, but mostly because of Delia's mom, Claire Meyer. She took her mark center stage, and Delia peered around the curtain, her own feet filling the same space they had since she was a child, able to stand on her own.

Tight as a spring, Delia's body slowly relaxed as her mother settled into the first refrain. The voice that had lulled Delia to sleep her entire life transfixed every member of the audience, and Delia was reminded of how not everything could be boiled down to genetics.

She snuck a glance at the influx of messages from ValleyStart and her teammates. They crawled onto her phone, a hand-me-down from her dad, which she later realized meant he no longer had one of his own. "Your mother's the one they all want to talk to anyway," he'd said when she'd tried to give it back.

The one girl, Lucy, was a Pulse 4. A 4. *Wow.* And she lived in Palo Alto. She'd bring so much to the team, growing up right in the heart of the tech world. The other girl, Maddie, hadn't given her Pulse—a clear sign that she beat at the top end of the scale, at least according to Delia's best friend, Cassie. In fact, Maddie hadn't given much of anything aside from a simple text that read: *Arriving from Boston midday. —Maddie Li.* Boston, a real city girl.

Delia had taken the two-hour trip east from Littlewood, Illinois, to Chicago a few times to see shows with her parents and had gone to the science museum once on a field trip, but the labyrinth of streets and density of people were as unfamiliar as they were unimaginable. Delia liked trees. And the long shadows they cast.

Keeping an ear on her mom's lyrics for the next lighting change, Delia opened the messages app and typed.

Hi girls!

Great response if they were twelve. Erase.

I'm looking forward to meeting you both.

And now they're forty-five. Erase.

Delia considered saying something about Pulse, but what? She'd only signed up for the app a couple of months ago when she found out she was accepted to ValleyStart. She hadn't even told her parents she'd applied to the incubator until she'd gotten in. The odds were insane. As was the cost.

That was part of the reason for these early performances at the small theater her parents owned; the season usually kicked off at the end of June, but this year, shows had started before Memorial Day. Some of the newer actors still weren't up to speed.

Delia gave up on returning her teammates' texts and opened Delia's Den, the app she'd created when she was ten after burning through the free learn-to-code programs online and the ones available from the library. It began as a way to test what she'd learned and had continued as a sort of meditation. Tweaking and expanding the code and what she could create with it was as comforting as snuggling up with Smudge—more so sometimes. That dog was wiry.

"Dee!" Cassie said in Delia's ear, causing her to jump and nearly knock over the lighting board.

"Shh!" Delia held her finger to her lips. "Mom's almost done."

"I've seen this a dozen times, you don't think I know that? But Dee Dee, that's the problem. Her daughter's having a real intimate moment with a trash can."

"Her . . . what?"

"Let's just say the sun ain't shining for Little Orphan Annie."

Delia sighed. The play wasn't *Annie*. Cassie just liked to speak in riddles sometimes. All the time.

"Stage fright or Uncle Barry's Fried Bonanza, but either way she's not going to be hurling anything this audience wants to see."

"Understudy?" Delia said, knowing the odds were slim. Graduation was only last week, and school hadn't ended yet for most of the regular summer theater kids.

"Not cast yet. But your dad said you know the part."

Of course she did. Delia had a photographic memory and ran lines with her mom for every production—at home from the comfort of their floral couch, in front of their greyhound.

Delia caught sight of her father, preparing to stealthily change out the scenery behind her mom. He built every set piece himself by hand, had been doing it since her parents took over the production company when Delia was a toddler. He nodded to her, and Delia flicked another switch, moving her mom's light to the far corner of the stage.

It was almost time for her stage daughter's entrance. Delia couldn't let her parents down. The theater had been struggling over the past couple of years, ever since the giant fair that attracted tourists had downsized. The deposit at the local college Delia had insisted was her first choice was less than everywhere else Delia had applied but still more than they could really afford. Tonight the theater was only half full, and word of a snafu so early in the run would have a snowball effect.

That was why she'd applied to ValleyStart. Because with hard work and maybe a Pulse internship, maybe, just maybe, it might lead to a job that would make college unnecessary and mean her parents wouldn't have to worry that every seat in the theater wasn't filled. That *she* wouldn't have to worry. The theater was as much her home as the actual house she grew up in. She loved it, same as her parents did.

Delia tried to give her dad a thumbs-up, but her hand

trembled too much, and she lowered her arm to her side. She inhaled a deep breath and focused on her mom, trying to call up the first line that followed the end of the song. She couldn't. Her mind was as empty as her bank account. Spots flickered in front of Delia's eyes, and she couldn't take in enough oxygen. The theater was suddenly a thousand degrees, and sweat broke out on her neck and forehead. Still, she pleaded with her dingy white sneaker to lift off the ground.

"I got this, babe," Cassie said, putting a hand on Delia's forearm.

The dizziness clouding Delia's head began to recede, but her heart still knocked against her chest like Smudge's tail on the hardwood floor when she came home. "But do you know it?"

"What I don't know, I'll wing."

Claire Meyer's perfect pitch strung out the last notes of her song, and Cassie kicked off her clunky work boots and walked onstage barefoot.

Delia watched the furrow on her mother's brow ease and the gentle tip of her head as she quickly assessed the situation. Then Delia went back to work, adjusting the lights to mask her dad's set change, all the while hearing Cassie and her mom banter like mother and daughter—both of them improvising as they found their groove.

If she sprouted them out of her back, Delia still wouldn't be able to "wing" anything.

"How am I even related to her?" Delia whispered.

"Through your mind, your heart, and your pretty little mug." Jeffrey Meyer pushed aside Delia's corkscrew bangs—

a shade darker and, in Delia's mind, muddier than her mom's golden blonde strands—and kissed his daughter on the forehead. "Excellent work on the lights as always."

"Yeah, I'm a whiz backstage." She flicked her finger up and down in the air, miming her movements on the manual lighting board. They had saved up to buy a digital this year, but then ValleyStart happened and the money went to it. "How will you ever train someone to replace me?"

"We won't be able to. You are irreplaceable."

Delia knew a normal teenager should roll her eyes at corny dad behavior. Delia was happy to never play that role.

"Sorry I couldn't . . ." She pointed to Cassie onstage with her mom. "I wanted to. I just . . ."

"No apologies."

"But what if Cassie wasn't here? And Mom was relying on me?"

"But Cassie was here. And if she wasn't, your mom would have rolled with it. Can't be a performer for twenty years and not know a thing or two about adapting when things don't go as planned."

Claire and Cassie were entering into the final song of the act. Two women Delia had looked up to her entire life. Along with her dad beside her and Smudge at home, they made up Delia's world.

Delia had an image of stepping onto that plane tomorrow and not being able to step off. Mountain View was as far from Littlewood as you could get without leaping into the ocean and letting the tide take you where it would and felt just as out of her control.

But Mountain View was a place that valued what Delia could do. Because Delia could code. She loved it almost as much as she loved the people surrounding her on this stage—these people who'd be left behind in Littlewood.

"Maybe I shouldn't go," she whispered.

Her father silently watched her mother, reached around Delia, and made the final lighting change. She wasn't sure he'd heard her until he nodded.

"Hmm . . . maybe not. But you'll wonder 'what if' every day if you don't."

Delia swallowed hard. Her parents met as part of a touring company. They settled down in Littlewood when Delia came along. They professed to never regret it. But their business was putting on a show.

She tugged on a curl that had an extra spring thanks to the messy bob Cassie had given her yesterday and twirled it around her finger. "What if I can't . . ."

"Can't what, Delia?"

"I don't know. Can't . . . do it."

"Then you'll find what you can do. There's a role for every actor and for every actor a role." He winked at Delia. "Just make mine a cinnamon. Ba dum tss."

He then handed her a going-away gift—a necklace whose pendant was a small piece of circuit board.

Her throat tightened. She could see how tired he was; he'd worked so hard these past couple of months, traveling to Chicago to build sets for a couple of independent theaters to earn enough to cover what Delia's ValleyStart scholarship didn't. And still, he got her this.

"Description said it was perfect for fathers, sons, or your favorite tech lover," he said. "Since you're that last one for me, hope it's okay . . ."

"It's perfect." Delia threw her arms around her father, and when Claire and Cassie hurried offstage, before either said a word, Delia brought them into the hug, inhaled her mom's lilac perfume, and smiled.

FOUR

MEETUP • *In-person meetings of online groups made up of individuals with like interests*

USING HER SHOULDER, LUCY muscled her way through the heavy metal door that opened onto the third floor of the dorm. She did her best to ignore the cinder-block walls and tucked her chin to avoid the harsh glow of the fluorescent lights as she exited the stairwell, hauling her luggage behind her. Lucy quickened her pace, scanning the room numbers. *There.* 303. The door was ajar. Those fruitless ten minutes she spent searching for an elevator had knocked her off schedule. As project manager, she was the de facto team leader, and she needed to arrive first.

Thankfully she had. If only she hadn't arrived in *this* room.

Mountain View U was a far cry from Stanford's sprawling green lawns, but still, ValleyStart was the most prestigious summer incubator for high school graduates in the country—it should act like it.

But there were bunk beds. Rubber-coated mattresses. And linoleum tiles. *Linoleum.*

Lucy's shower flip-flops were just upgraded to full-time use.

She rested her bags on the floor, thought better of it, and set them both down on the single desk under the window. A fleck of paint chipped off the sill and onto her leather carryall. The last new coat probably preceded even her mom's attendance. Mountain View U was her mother's alma mater but not where she'd met Lucy's father. That was the software company where her mom still worked, though her dad had moved on years ago.

Lucy spied a cobweb stretching from the desk to the window and reached for her phone. She unlocked it and paused, her finger hovering over her father's number. It was after ten at night in London. He'd probably just left his office.

Lucy stood in the center of the room, trying to imagine five weeks of living in this dark, cramped space that smelled of gym socks and desperation. It wasn't like she expected a single or an en suite, but at least a proper wardrobe or a bed that wasn't pee proof.

At least it *was* pee proof.

Oh God.

Lucy dug her notebook out of her tote bag, searching for what she'd written down about housing, positive she must have missed the ability to pay more for a room that was, oh, *livable*.

Her finger kept flipping, landing on the page she'd filled in last night on Ryan Thompson. She already knew everything about him, but she'd organized it into categories for easy reference: likes and dislikes, hobbies, education, Pulse origin story, childhood, and family tree. Which was missing his dad. He died when Ryan was fifteen.

Lucy's father may not have been around much, but she knew what she could rely on him for: anything that could be accomplished with a wire transfer or the gifting of a stock option. It was how Lucy did everything from trading volleys with a former Wimbledon semifinalist at tennis camp to being the first to sport a limited-production sneaker from Nike.

But Ryan created Pulse all on his own.

And Lucy was an adult now.

And so Lucy extracted her lavender-scented hand sanitizer wipes from the side pocket of her bag and began disinfecting the pee-proof mattress.

A double rap on the door made Lucy jump. Her head collided with the underside of the bunk above her.

"Dammit!" she said, whirling around, sanitizer wipe in hand.

"Sorry, didn't mean to startle you."

A brown-skinned woman stood in the doorway. She wore a coral scarf over a crisp white linen shirt and wide-legged trousers, which made her already long legs appear even longer. Her dark hair pulled back at the nape of her neck accentuated her sharp cheekbones.

Nishi Kapoor. It was *Nishi Kapoor.*

Lucy stuffed the used wipe under the belt at the back of her sundress and smoothed her hair while simultaneously feeling for a welt.

"You seemed pretty focused there," Nishi said. "Is something wrong with the room?"

"How much time do you have?" Lucy gave a little laugh.

"Sorry, but it's pretty standard as college dorms go."

"Right, sure. I know. Just figured I'd spruce it up." Lucy fought the flush she felt creeping up her neck. "For my roommates."

"How thoughtful." Nishi stepped forward and extended her hand. "Nishi Kapoor."

"Lucy Katz."

"Welcome to the program, Lucy. And accept my apologies if I'm a bit starstruck."

Lucy exhaled a sigh of relief. "I know, I mean, Ryan Thompson's going to be here."

Nishi shook her head. "Oh no, I meant you. Daughter of Abigail Katz, if I'm not mistaken?"

"My mom? You know my mom?"

"What woman in tech doesn't?" Nishi said. "I'm excited to see what you have in store for us, Lucy. Our attendees never fail to astound me."

"It's amazing that you have time to mentor."

"Not so much 'have' as make. Three years running. My first year, the internships were at my company."

All facts jotted down in Lucy's notebook. "That was the daily planner app bought by Google for—"

"Enough to fund my second company. And my third."

"And steal this beautiful lady right out from under me." A man with tanned white skin, a swimmer's build, and a perfectly manicured five o'clock shadow poked his head in the doorway. He winked as he strode into the room, giving Nishi a peck on her cheek. "Good seeing you, NK."

Lucy froze.

Ryan Thompson.

In her dorm room.

Her dark, dingy dorm room that now smelled like lavender-coated desperation.

"Ryan," Nishi said. "I didn't think you'd be making the introductory rounds."

"Oh, I always enjoy mingling with the little people." Ryan turned and gave Lucy a playful smirk. "No offense."

Cement glued Lucy in place, but she took an imaginary pickax to her jaw. "Oh, oh, course not. I mean, it's no one's fault but my own that I'm only a 4, but I expect to be Thumping, or even Throbbing really soon."

Ryan laughed. "I meant the joke—a pretty lame one considering . . ." He gestured to their height difference.

"Of course." Lucy forced a smile, inwardly kicking herself for blurting out her low Pulse ranking to *Ryan Thompson*.

He stepped forward and offered her his hand. "And you are . . ."

"Lucy." That she omitted her last name had as much to do with Nishi's reaction to her being a Katz as it did with her inability to formulate a full sentence.

Ryan hummed the Beatles' "Lucy in the Sky with Diamonds," just like a lot of older people did upon meeting her, but somehow, this time Lucy didn't mind so much. "Let me guess . . . Cupertino . . . no . . . Palo Alto High."

"Go Vikings!" *Oh God.* "I mean, yes, 4.8 GPA, and I interned at Dropbox as a sophomore, and I'm about to start training for my third marathon, and—"

"And you're only Thudding? Clearly, we at Pulse have a glitch."

His mischievous grin sent Lucy's heart to a solid Level 8—Pounding. *Would it be inappropriate to ask him for a selfie?* She was about to reach for her phone when Nishi interrupted.

"Well, Lucy, we'll leave you to unpack."

"Aw, so soon?" Ryan said. "We were just getting to know each other."

"We've got five weeks, don't we?" Nishi said.

"That many?" Ryan said, and Lucy wasn't sure if he was joking or actually surprised. "Well, I'm game if you are, Lucy."

She was about to respond with an emphatic "yes" when the sound of someone clearing their throat made everyone turn to the door. A tall Asian American girl with straight black hair, dark eyes, and a smattering of freckles across her nose dropped her duffel bag to the floor.

"Hey," she said, kicking off her black slip-on sneakers and pulling her silver-rimmed aviators off the top of her head. "I'm Maddie."

FIVE

WYSIWYG • *What you see is what you get*

"UH-HUH," MADDIE SAID FOR the fifth or sixth time. She'd lost count. Some people's online personas differed wildly from who they were in real life.

Not this one.

Maddie was getting dizzy watching Lucy unpack. She buzzed around the room, spreading moisturizers and serums and tonics Maddie wasn't sure were for slathering or drinking out on the desk in size order. Then she began stacking her clothes by color on the top bunk on one side of the room.

"These will be mine," Lucy said of the two beds. A statement, not a question.

One look at her roommate's clothes, and Maddie knew they were expensive. She'd seen at least two of the exact same sweaters on the girls in her private Cambridge high school. It wasn't that Maddie couldn't afford them, it was simply that she didn't care to. Ripped jeans that didn't require a crowbar to get into, simple black tees that masked smudges from Danny's sticky fingers, and loose hoodies with pockets that hid everything from a few extra pounds courtesy of a Saturday Rib-It Festival in Inman Square to her tablet for spontaneous sketching were the extent of Maddie's fashion requirements.

Her computer was a different story. Her art translated to her business, which translated to Danny. Even state-of-the-art was a step behind.

She slid her ultra-sleek, mega-powered laptop out of her messenger bag, attached the extender cable to the charger, and plugged it into the wall before climbing to the top bunk on the opposite side of the room. For the first time since she crossed the threshold, she breathed in air that didn't reek of lavender.

She texted Danny at camp.

Maddie: Don't feed the sharks.

He quickly wrote back. *Too quickly?*

Danny: It's a lake. Sharks don't live in lakes.

Maddie: Because people don't feed them.

Danny: Maddie!

Maddie: Danny!

Maddie: Settling in okay?

Was he unhappy? Already?

Danny: I guess.

Danny: Someone smells like feet.

Maddie: Same here. Except feet doused in lavender.

Maddie: You'd think it makes it better. It doesn't.

Maddie: Mom call?

Danny: She texted. You?

She hadn't.

Maddie: Same.

"Don't you think?" Lucy was staring at her, awaiting a response to a question Maddie hadn't even heard.

Maddie gave a shrug and a head bobble, then returned to Danny.

Maddie: Gotta go before new roomie ropes me into designing an app for butt facials.

Maddie: Miss you.

Danny: 😆

Danny: Five, right?

Maddie: These weeks will fly faster than a pterodactyl.

Danny: ✌

"Because Ryan Thompson thought there was a glitch." Lucy's raised voice broke through Maddie's ability to tune others out, which she'd honed thanks to her parents. "He actually said that. Which means I totally look like someone at a higher level and . . ."

Maddie: ✌

She unearthed her four-leaf clover necklace from beneath her sweatshirt and held on tight. She should probably get off the bed, unpack, talk to this Lucy girl for a second—or at the very least try to get this Lucy girl to *stop* talking for a second. Instead, Maddie retreated farther into the corner of the bunk. Sharing a room was going to suck as much as she'd thought it would.

Maddie opened her laptop, connected to the dorm Wi-Fi, and responded to a couple of emails from clients. She'd been balancing her freelance work with school for the past year, and though she wasn't valedictorian or anything, she had held her own among the over-scheduled, overindulged, *over, over, over* kids in her high school and expected to do the same while at ValleyStart. Though if something had to give, it would be the program. She had no interest in Pulse or an unpaid internship or living three thousand miles away from her brother. This incubator was a box to check, one that would open doors not just to remote clients but to the host of tech startups and companies needing design work on-site in Cambridge, keeping her close to Danny.

Maddie was about to shut her laptop when a notification popped up for the private graphic design forum she'd practically lived on up until a couple of months ago. Taking care of her brother had narrowed Maddie's world, leaving little time for friends or extracurriculars, and that was okay. Most of the time. But when Maddie realized she could share her love of design with people and they'd actually *get it*, everything changed.

Their stories of successful freelance businesses sparked her own. First with chalk and crayon and then with graphite and colored pencils, Maddie had always loved to draw. She'd bring to life the characters in the books her parents would read to her at night. She'd re-create and eventually reimagine the covers—the wrappers, as she used to call the dust jackets. But it was the entertainment and literary agency her parents founded that brought graphic design into Maddie's world. She'd sat at the kitchen table with her mom and dad, listening as they spoke with a freelance designer, sharing their vision of the agency. Maddie drew as they talked, not fully realizing that she was translating their words into reality. The logo she'd doodled that day inspired the whole look and feel of their site. Her parents had sent Maddie's sketches to the designer. She could still picture the mix of pride and mischief on her parents' faces when they showed her the website for the first time and presented her with a brand-new drawing tablet. And that was it, Maddie was hooked.

But she didn't have a community to share it with until she found the forum. She liked the camaraderie and support, with everyone cheering one another's wins and commiserating over losses. She had one friend, a guy, who she relied on most. She valued his advice. So she'd thought nothing of him probing deeper and deeper into the request for proposal she was submitting to an about-to-blow-up virtual reality game startup. In their private chats, she'd written volumes about her ideas for the site and app, and he'd read every line, encouraging her.

Of course he had, right up until he slid his own RFP in to the company just before hers.

In his cover letter "explaining" how he'd learned of the startup, he "let it slip" that "M. Li" was not yet a high school graduate and also happened to be female, the opposite of the gamer's touted demographic. She lost the bid. Not because she trusted someone she shouldn't have, but because she trusted, period.

She'd been following him, torturing herself with what might have been for too long. If ValleyStart was anything, it was a new chapter, kicking off with lessons not just learned but seared into her skin. Maddie went into her profile settings and turned the notifications off.

If only she could do the same to Lucy. Not one pause in her babbling on about Pulse and *Ryan Thompson*.

"Listen," Maddie called down from her bunk.

Lucy extracted her head from the closet. "Sorry, what?" She swiveled her neck before looking up. "Did you say something, Madeline?"

"It's Maddie."

She bit her bottom lip. "Are you sure, because I think—"

"I'm sure."

"Well, if you change your mind—"

"Uh-huh."

"Then you'll think about it."

Lucy returned to lining up her shoes, and Maddie became

convinced that one of her new roommate's bags must have originally been owned by Mary Poppins. Maddie couldn't fit half of what Lucy had unpacked in even one of those pieces of luggage.

Lucy stepped back and assessed, then jotted something down in a pink-and-white-striped notebook.

"Retro," Maddie said, eyeing the notebook.

"Hmm, more classic with a hint of vintage and some surefire flair on club nights, but not really retro." She looked up at Maddie. "But maybe things are different on the East Coast? You should check out the online articles I wrote for *Teen Vogue* this season. 'California Style for Any Zip Code' and 'Optimize Your Closet in Six Easy Steps.' Happy to take you shopping anytime. You know, so you'll feel more . . . comfortable."

"I am comfortable."

"Oh, then, maybe, stylish?"

Maddie dug her fists into the mattress—and came away with something sticky, which she did her best to ignore. "And here I thought this was a *tech* incubator, not a fashion show."

"Why can't it be both? I swear, you should see what some of these startups let people wear. After Stanford, when I'm CEO, my company will have a proper dress code. Because like it or not, impressions matter, especially first impressions." Lucy grabbed something red off the top bunk. She affixed it to the wall beside her bed with beige putty from her Mary Poppins bag. A Stanford pennant. "Let's just hope I made a good impression on Ryan Thompson."

"He's just a guy, you know. Pisses standing up like all the rest of 'em."

"He's *Ryan Thompson.*"

A shuffling in the doorway drew Maddie's attention. A pale white girl with springy dark blonde curls clutched the plastic handle of an old metal suitcase plastered with stickers.

"Maybe you could show a little more respect," Lucy said.

Maddie whipped her head back to Lucy. "What's he done, truly?"

Lucy's eyes widened. "He's changed the world."

"Not in a good way." Maddie swung her legs off the top bunk, balanced on the bottom mattress, and dropped to the floor.

"He's the reason we're here."

"Not my reason," Maddie mumbled.

The girl in the doorway jostled from one foot to the other the way Danny did when he refused to admit he drank too much orange soda.

"Are you going to come in or not?" Maddie snapped—and immediately regretted it.

SIX

NOT READY FOR PRIME TIME • *When a product is not quite finished or is finished in such a way that will hinder its ability to compete in the marketplace*

"SORRY," MADDIE SAID.

Delia knew it was Maddie because she knew what Lucy looked like from her Pulse profile picture.

That.

Petite face, thick hair, a hint of bronzer on her cheeks . . . it was like she'd stepped out of a "Ten Ways to Get Fit for Summer!" spread in a magazine.

And Delia was sweating in the coat that had been too light when she woke up this morning back home in Littlewood.

Had she really left home?

Was this really going to *be* her home?

Delia clutched the handle of her mom's old suitcase tighter. "It's okay. I didn't mean to interrupt."

Lucy laughed. "Can't interrupt when it's your room too. *Entrez-vous,* dear Delia."

"*Entrez*," Maddie said.

"That's what I said."

"No, it's not. You said '*entrez-vous.*' You asked if she was coming in, when I'm assuming you meant to simply invite her in."

"I've had four years of French," Lucy said.

"I've had six," Maddie countered.

And all Delia had had were French fries and French toast. She forced herself to step into the room. "Uh, yeah, well, sorry I'm late. I missed my connection in Orlando."

"Orlando?" Lucy grabbed a fancy notebook off the desk and started flipping through. "I thought you were from Chicago?"

"Um, not exactly. But that's where I left from."

"Why not fly direct?" Lucy asked.

"Why not let the girl put her bag down before you ask twenty questions?" Maddie said.

Delia hugged the wall, missing Cassie, the only person she'd ever shared a room with until now. She shifted the weight of her suitcase from one hand to the other, waiting for her two roommates to challenge each other to whatever the Silicon Valley equivalent of a duel was.

Silicon Valley.

A place of myth and legend and dreams that became reality—not through wands and fairy dust but through innovation and iteration. From the back seat of the cab, signs with words Delia knew from "About Us" pages on websites and the back of product packages called to her: Bay Area, Burlingame, Menlo Park, Palo Alto, Cupertino. Silicon Valley, where every day people created things that didn't exist the day before, all from technology that didn't exist when her parents were her age. And she'd be a part of it.

She just had to figure out how to breathe here. Which may have been easier had the room not smelled like the theater costumes at the end of a hot summer's run.

"Settle in," Maddie said, pointing to the bottom bunk on one side of the room. "Unless you'd prefer the top?"

She would. It seemed like it might be a little more private. But she said, "Bottom's fine." She laid her suitcase on the rubber-coated mattress. *The introductory email didn't say anything about sheets, did it?* She turned to see Lucy opening a sealed package of silver bedsheets. "Uh, excuse me, but do you know if we were supposed to bring our own bedding?"

"Only if you have an aversion to lice," Lucy said.

Maddie rolled her eyes and walked to the closet. "Will these do?"

Delia nodded, accepting the stiff set of sheets and thin towel. Out of the corner of her eye, she saw Lucy cringe. It seemed she'd already settled in with double the number of items Delia had packed. Delia had gone over the checklist a dozen times but now worried that she should have taken it as a suggestion, not a mandate. Not that she had as much in her closet at home as Lucy had brought here. At least when it came to clothes. Cable-knit cardigans and corduroy jeans in winter, denim shorts and loose tees in summer were Delia's standard uniform. But if there was a market for a pop-up shop specializing in dissected computer parts and used programming books, Delia's room at home would be getting high ranks on Yelp.

"You're both unpacked, then?" Delia said.

"Almost." Maddie's eyes drifted over Lucy's careful stacks. She then opened the top drawer of the dresser across from her bunk and dumped the contents of her duffel, including her tablet and sketchbook, inside, followed by the duffel itself. She tossed a Red Sox baseball cap over the post at the end of her bed. "Yup, all done."

Lucy shook her head and tucked her own empty luggage away in the closet. "Take your time, Delia, but then we should probably start brainstorming. I heard one year they kicked things off at two in the morning."

"In the middle of the night?" Delia said. "That's crazy."

"Probably illegal," Maddie said.

"Just a way to challenge us," Lucy said. "Considering we all come from high schools that are more advanced than most colleges, they've got to do something."

"Sure," Delia said. Her own high school only had two AP classes, and as usual, Delia was one of two girls in them. She'd been on campus for ten minutes and already felt years behind. "It's just . . . the thing is, I didn't realize . . . and so, well, I have orientation."

"You? Why just you?" Lucy reached for her notebook.

"It's not part of the program. I have a part-time job."

"A job? But ValleyStart is your job—our job—all of us, together."

Delia focused on the Washington Monument on the "D.C." sticker at the corner of her mom's suitcase. "It won't interfere, I promise."

"But how . . . I mean, is this even okay with the program?"

Delia's eyes shifted to the Mardi Gras beads surrounding "New Orleans" before turning to Lucy. "They had a link at the bottom of the website for campus jobs. I'm used to working and going to school."

Lucy pursed her lips.

"Me too," Maddie said, glancing up from her phone, which was so new, Delia wasn't even quite sure what model it was. "Go, we'll catch you later."

Delia didn't wait for Lucy's reaction. She left her mom's suitcase on the bed, said a quick "nice to meet you both," and hurried through the doorway still wearing her too-heavy jacket beneath her equally heavy backpack with a heart that outweighed them both.

She nearly barreled into a girl in a cropped denim jacket carrying a guitar. Delia was so mortified that she couldn't even attempt to return the girl's "hey."

As soon as she reached the stairwell, Delia pressed her head against the cool brick wall and tried to breathe. She pulled her phone out to text Cassie and realized she'd be busy moving scenery just in time for her mom's solo. Delia was early for her orientation. So she sat on the top step and opened Delia's Den.

"Uh, yeah, we have Hot Pockets in Illinois," Delia said for the fourth time in the common room of the student center. Kiosks, including hers, lined the perimeter of an open space furnished with a brightly colored rainbow of beanbag chairs, couches, and even a couple of chaise longue chairs.

A guy with floppy blond hair and a sunburn that had turned his white skin the color of a red bliss potato eyed her skeptically—apparently completely unaware that *she* was the one who should be side-eyeing *him*. Delia was pretty sure that the ocean wasn't around the corner, and yet he was wearing jeans over a full-body wetsuit. The top half dangled unzipped around his waist, and his blue, red, and white plaid shirt hung loose, unbuttoned. If anyone needed food-service lessons, it was this guy.

"But these are *organic*," he said. "Let's go over it once more." He held up the rectangular Hot Pocket. "Unwrap this." He tapped the microwave. "Open this." He mimed punching the numbers. "Set it." He narrowed his eyes. "And don't forget it. But if you do . . ." He wiggled his phone. "Have the fire department on speed dial."

"Isn't that just 911?"

He cocked his head.

"For emergencies, don't you just call 911?"

He stared at her, raised a hand to each side of his head, and made a *pfft* sound. "Mind blown, Illinois. Mind blown." He slung a backpack over one shoulder and said, "Now go forth and feed."

Delia bit her bottom lip. She managed to contain herself until he was halfway across the room before she burst out laughing.

"Where am I?" she said to herself.

"Been asking myself the same thing," came a voice from behind her.

Delia turned to see a guy, tall and fit, with tanned white skin and light brown hair, buzzed on the sides, long and soft on top, smiling at her.

Immediately a warmth spread under her skin, and she knew she was glowing pink.

"That's the second dude in a wetsuit I've seen since I got here."

"Strange," Delia said.

"You want strange? Had two girls come by drinking pea milk lattes."

"I'm sorry, what?"

"That's what I said."

Delia knew she was now bright red, but she had to ask. "I really hope you mean the vegetable. . . ."

"Yup. Milk made from peas—the little green ones I realized my grandma would stop serving if they ended up in my nose more often than my mouth." He grinned. "And I thought Denver had its quirks. I'm starting to think I'm in for a bizarre summer."

"You're from Denver?" Was everyone from somewhere cool? And cool was probably not even the right adjective. Hip? Rad? Delia was going to have to study Urban Dictionary.

"Born and fed," he joked. "That guy . . . let's just say I'm glad you took over his shift. He was practicing surf stances for an hour before you got here."

"And the ocean is . . ."

"Not close. I double-checked. You know what he said?" The guy stepped out from behind the counter of his kiosk and jumped, ending in a squat with his hands straight out to each side. He lowered his voice and spoke slowly, "When the waves call, it doesn't matter how far, I'll hear them, and I'll heed them, bro."

Delia giggled. *Ugh. Laugh, don't giggle, Delia.*

He reclaimed his full height and hopped up onto the counter behind him. "I'm Eric Shaw."

"Delia Meyer."

"Lemme guess, ValleyStart?"

Delia looked down at her plain jeans and long-sleeved tee. "Coder. Am I that obvious?"

"Sure, but only because of that." Eric tipped his clean-shaven chin to her backpack. Her ValleyStart ID card and room key dangled off a carabiner on the side.

"Oh."

"And we coders need to stick together. Especially ones with part-time jobs."

"You're working too?"

Duh.

"Came in a few days ago and stayed with a friend so I could get in some extra hours before the program starts."

"And you like it?"

"More and more each day."

His grin made Delia's stomach flip. She pushed through the feeling—as she'd learned to do. Delia didn't date. Too many unknown variables.

Eric's smile began to fade, and his brow creased. "Oh, hey, hope I didn't sign up for too many hours and steal them from you."

It took Delia a moment to understand what he meant. "Oh no, I didn't apply. I only put in for—" She gestured to the sign above her.

"The Hot Pocket kiosk."

She nodded.

"You actually applied for the Hot Pocket kiosk? Instead of computer troubleshooting?"

She half nodded, half shrugged. His confusion made perfect sense since the computer kiosk job paid nearly double the Hot Pocket one.

He suddenly started nodding. "You're one of those."

"What?"

"Smart-smart. Figure you'll let your brain rest, is that it?"

Not at all. She didn't apply because she figured everyone out here would be smart-smarter than her.

"Smart-smart, Delia," he said again. "Because pea milk lattes may make you think otherwise, but this, this is going to get *intense.*"

Despite its name, the Mountain View campus didn't have a mountain in sight. The grounds were as flat as the farmlands around Littlewood. Except here there were palm trees. Everywhere. They hardly looked real. They looked like they were from another world. One Delia couldn't believe she was actually in.

The campus, compact yet filled with green space, revolved around the student center. It was the hub of the Mountain View wheel, with long white stone paths radiating out like spokes. Clearly marked with guideposts, each led to a cluster of buildings surrounding a grassy quad. A simple, easy-to-navigate design that eased Delia's stress level.

Her and Eric's shifts ended at the same time, and they walked to the dorms together. They discovered they were both at ValleyStart thanks to the scholarship program, which funded half the cost, had each only signed up for Pulse in the past few months, and shared a love of Python and skepticism for Swift, one of the hot new programming languages used by companies like Airbnb.

Just as they neared the two-tiered terra-cotta fountain in the middle of the grouping of white three-story dorms topped with red tile, Delia's stomach rumbled. She hadn't eaten anything since the fried egg and toast her dad had made her that morning. *Time change or not, could it have possibly just been that morning?*

She'd been too nervous to eat the packet of nuts offered on both legs of her flight, let alone attempt a Hot Pocket. Delia was twisting a lock of her hair, mustering the courage to ask Eric if he was hungry, when her phone buzzed, followed by his.

Her heart sank as she read the text.

ValleyStart: Welcome one, welcome all. And so it is time to heed the call! Hackathon, tomorrow, 8 am. Hack or Be Hacked!

"At least it's not two a.m.," Eric said.

Delia couldn't respond because a flurry of texts followed, all from Lucy.

Brainstorming time!

Followed by "brain" and "storm" emojis.

Let's bring our Level 10 game!

It's Ryan Thompson, ladies!

Then, finally, *Um, guys, where are you?*

SEVEN

THIS IS IT.

Electricity charged through Lucy's limbs like she was at a club in the Tenderloin. Music pumping, hips thrusting, rafters vibrating, the whole place one claustrophobic creature alive on artisan gin and Red Bull and sweat.

Her head bobbed to an internal beat as she adjusted the knot of her ValleyStart tee at her waist and crossed the quad with Delia and Maddie. The "Hackathon" banner beneath the yellow painted tiles beckoned her inside the Spanish Revival–style student center.

She had arrived.

They had arrived.

So what if Delia was a typical coder: all gray matter, practical shoes, and the social skills of beached kelp. From the little bit of code she'd shown Lucy last night, Lucy knew she wouldn't have to carry her.

And Maddie . . . well, yes, the girl had an attitude problem. But she also had a client list bigger than the population of Sausalito. No one would hire her for her personality, that was for sure. Which meant she must be a kick-ass designer.

That freed Lucy up to do what she did best. *Strategize, stylize, and socialize.* In other words, sell. The number-one component of any successful startup. And Lucy would be a success.

No matter what her mom thought.

CIO? *Pfft.* Lucy snorted. *Try CEO, Mom. Glass ceiling, my CrossFit-trained ass.* She couldn't help a snicker. Delia jumped beside her.

It's fine, it's going to be fine.

Lucy seized Delia's hand, which actually felt as wet and slimy as beached kelp. Still, Lucy pushed forth her most enthusiastic smile. "Isn't this exciting?"

Eyes downcast, Delia's head moved the tiniest bit, and Lucy took that as a yes.

It's going to be fine.

"Exciting, right?" she called to Maddie, who'd lagged behind since leaving the dorm, her fingers flying across her phone at four times the rate of her feet. And her words not flying at all. She gave an "uh-huh" without looking up.

Going to be fine.

Lucy pressed on, and she and Delia reached the entrance first. The "Sponsored by Pulse" on the welcome sign sent chills down her spine. She squeezed Delia's hand. "Let's all cross the threshold together."

Like newlyweds, beginning their marriage, which is what this would be for the next five weeks. It all started with this. The team whose app had the most functionality at the end of the twelve-hour hackathon would receive an advantage: a one-on-one session with last year's incubator winners.

They needed it. Lucy needed it. Because Lucy needed Stanford. And this internship was her ticket off the wait list and onto the perfect blades of grass that not even her mother's heels had sunk into.

As she waited for Maddie, Lucy craned her neck to peer through the glass door. Her pulse quickened. *There he was.* Broad shoulders that narrowed in a perfect V down to a trim waist and a butt as round as a peach and as tight as her mom's Spanx.

Ryan Thompson.

She'd recognize his behind—she'd recognize him *from* behind—even in a sea of Silicon Valley elite.

"Let's go! Early bird, and all!" Lucy tried to channel that bird and sound chipper, but she was growing impatient waiting for Maddie. Finally, they were all together, and a surge of energy propelled Lucy through the door. "I want to volunteer to present first, just in case Ryan doesn't stay for the whole thing."

"Ryan?" Maddie said in the harsh Boston accent that made Lucy cringe from her professionally plucked eyebrows to her Bikini So Teeny polished toes. "One five-minute convo and you're on a first-name basis?"

"Shh!" Lucy halted. She swore she saw Ryan's shoulders tense. When she was positive there wasn't a break in his swaggered stride through the lobby, she waved the girls forward. "This way."

Signs pointed them in the right direction, but Lucy had memorized the student center layout a week ago. Still holding Delia's limp hand, she moved through the stucco building, keeping her eyes on Ryan's muscular back. When she turned the corner, she increased her speed, fueled by the appearance of Gavin Cox.

Freaking Gavin Cox.

She'd successfully avoided him yesterday and was aiming to make that a two-day streak.

The drag on her forearm and the squeal from beside her caused her to fail.

Delia tripped. Indoors. On a flat surface.

This must be how Jobs felt around Woz.

Lucy shoved her butterfly-frame sunglasses tight against her face, but it was too late. She'd been seen. Which meant she'd failed. She hated failing. She never did. One of the few things she could credit to her mom, who'd taught her the only way to avoid it was by being in total control. But this incubator was a team program.

And one member of her team was currently holding the sole of her ratty tennis shoe in one hand and rubbing her coccyx with the other.

Gavin strode up to Lucy with a smug grin on his face. His wet mop of curls hung limp along his lightly sunburned cheeks and that patchy hipster beard his DNA knew he was too immature to grow.

"Li'l Lucy." He patted her on the head. "They relax the height requirement for this ride?"

She gritted her teeth. Being five feet nothing, Lucy was used to being treated like a dachshund or a two-year-old. But this was Gavin's paw on her fresh blowout.

On the floor, Delia narrowly missed being stomped on by smartphone zombie Maddie's foot. Her big . . . large . . . ginormous foot. Sasquatch had nothing on Maddie's hooves. At least Lucy wouldn't have to worry about either of her roommates borrowing her Louboutins. Being nearly six feet, Maddie had little chance of squeezing in more than her big toe, and being, well, *Midwestern*, Delia had little chance of telling a Louboutin from a leprechaun.

Fine. It's. Going. To. Be. Fine.

Gavin smirked. "Stellar cohorts you got there, Lucifer."

"Yes," Lucy said, eyeing the two tall, thin white guys behind Gavin, the three of them decked out in the Silicon Valley uniform of nondescript jeans, a white tee, and expensive sneakers. She reached down to grasp Delia's elbow. "In fact, they are. Don't be too intimated, Cox."

Blood boiling, Lucy marched down the hallway ahead of what she was trying to convince herself *were* her stellar teammates. She could feel Gavin's thick fingers on her scalp and the phantom tingle in other places she should have never let them go. She jammed a "delete all" on the memory, nuking it from her brain. Step by step, Lucy breathed, calming herself by visualizing the endgame. Which would start here, in the vast study hall turned hackathon headquarters. She paused under the arched entrance feeling very small.

Table upon table was filled with Gavin-esque seventeen-to-nineteen-year-olds in hoodies and those same plain white tees, all waiting to be emblazoned with a Facebook-Google-Apple-Uber-Lyft-Twitter-eBay-LinkedIn-Airbnb-Snapchat logo—or, better yet, their own.

The testosterone nearly choked her. Or maybe it was the stench of old french fries and Axe body spray.

"There," Delia's meek voice said. "Twenty-two. That's us."

Lucy searched the area surrounding their designated table. "Damn," she muttered. The judges' table—Ryan's table—may as well have been in Reno. She could barely see the top of his head, that sandy-brown "natural" tousle she was sure took an hour to achieve. (*And was so worth it.*)

"Does anyone notice what I'm noticing?" Maddie said, pushing her aviators back on her head. It was the first time she'd looked up from her phone all morning.

Finally. Lucy was relieved that at least one member of her team also realized what a complete disaster their placement was.

"What?" Delia said.

"The double X factor," Maddie said.

Lucy and Delia didn't respond.

"As in chromosomes?" Maddie said. "Girls. Chicks. You know, boobs."

Delia swiveled her head. "Oh, well, it's not that unexpected. And hey, at least there won't be a long line for the bathroom."

Maddie stared blankly, and Delia seemed to shrink. Maddie addressed Lucy. "We're all together."

"Yes!" Lucy said. "On this side of the room. How are we supposed to gauge Ry—the judges' reactions from all the way over here?"

Maddie's face twisted like the smell of french fry had finally hit her. "No, the teams. They assigned us—a coder, a designer, and a . . ." Her eyes floated to Lucy.

"Project manager," Lucy said.

"Uh-huh. The teams should have nothing to do with gender. And yet look at this. Is there even a single coed group here?"

Lucy searched. "There's one." She set her tote on the white

laminate table and pointed across the room to two guys and a girl with a heart-shaped face and smooth tawny-beige skin that made Lucy wonder if she'd remembered to pack her extra-strength pore cleanser. The girl rested something—*a guitar case?*—on the floor as she settled into a chair across from her teammates. Lucy squinted. "Hey, Delia, isn't one of those guys the cutie you were trying to hook up with last night?"

Sriracha-red painted Delia's cheeks. "I wasn't . . . he's like my coworker." Her usually soft voice dropped even further as she looked at him. "We were just talking."

"Tip for you, Delia: 'just talking' doesn't walk you to your door," Lucy said.

Maddie folded her tall frame into the seat. Her knees bumped the underside of the table as she extracted her monster laptop and her sketchbook out of her messenger bag. "They underestimate us."

Lucy stood on tiptoes to evaluate the room and the handful of girls in it, which included Nishi Kapoor as the only female judge. Her slight "I hope so" slipped out. Delia's head bobbed like she heard, but she sat down without saying anything.

What? An advantage is an advantage. The less someone expects of you, the more you can impress them.

Which got Lucy thinking back to the previous night's discussion about the app that would be core to their incubator startup project. Something they were passionate about.

She eyed the sketchbook, open to the logos Maddie had been working on last night.

How they had settled on an Uber-style dog-grooming service still eluded her. It was the only idea they could all agree upon, the most vanilla of all the concepts they'd floated.

And that was the problem.

Lucy was about to give Delia and Maddie the same real-world lesson her mom had given her when she was ten about average not getting you listed in *Forbes*, when something swept across her lower back.

Not something. Someone.

"Hey now, someone got their beauty sleep," Ryan Thompson said. "Feeling as ready as you look, Lucy?"

"More." Lucy smiled, quashing her body's reflexive flinch as his hand pressed into her in greeting, a stray fingertip accidentally gliding across the exposed skin between the bottom of her knotted tee and the top of her skinny jeans.

"That's what I like to hear. Because I'm counting on you." He lowered his voice. "These things are usually so boring, they leave me totally cached out. Just once I'd like a little wow."

"Well, you're in luck," Lucy said, determined to build on the rapport that had begun the day before. "Wow is our team name."

"Is that so?"

She raised an eyebrow. "Trademark pending."

Ryan Thompson chuckled. *Strategize, stylize, and socialize.* So far, so good.

"Did you see that?" Lucy said after he'd gone.

"Uh-huh," Maddie said.

Delia averted her eyes.

"Ryan Thompson thinks we can wow him." Lucy fell into her seat. "We have to wow him."

She watched her teammates disappear into their devices while the groups around them talked excitedly, huddling together behind a singular laptop or raiding the snack center's free chips, sushi, and energy drinks. She chewed on her lip—the bad habit she'd been trying to break since the third grade. She caught herself and grabbed hold of her wrist instead. Around and around she spun the pink plastic wristband from the club her Pulse tee had gotten her into two nights ago. Uber-style dog grooming was not a wow. It was barely a "wuh."

Finally, a bald man at the front of the room tapped a microphone. Lucy sat on her feet to see better. His zippered V-neck sweater marked him as a VC with a likely net worth greater than the output of a dozen small nations combined. He spoke into the mic, welcoming them all to day one of ValleyStart.

Lucy reached for her notebook and tuned out the instructions. She'd already memorized the five-week itinerary—from today's frantic race to lay down the skeleton of their app to the mornings of classes and lectures to the afternoons of "free" time to be spent getting their idea functional and scalable. They'd be going through the stages every startup did to take its product to market, leading up to the pivotal beta test where a small sampling of users would try the app, and ending in Demo Day, when they'd showcase their revolutionary creation and impress the judges enough to win the Pulse internships that would last the rest of the summer.

Impress the judges. Impress Ryan Thompson.

Lucy's mind whirled faster than her wristband. Then Ryan took the mic. She released the bracelet and sat up straighter. As did everyone in the room.

"Welcome, welcome, welcome. And now, the *p-i-i-i-tch.*" Ryan drew out the word. "Ah, nothing rattles to the core like that simple five-letter word. Nerves. Fear. Humiliation." Lucy was sure if she were closer, she'd have seen that same mischievous grin he wore in her dorm room. "But this is a no-pressure environment. And if you believe that, I've got a hip programming language called FORTRAN to sell you." He laughed, though, Lucy noticed, with less gusto than he had with her. "Okay, okay, seriously, this is easy stuff. Just get on up here, outline your team's project in sixty seconds or less, and you're good to go." He clapped his hands together. "Now let's get started. Hmm, you know, we usually go in numerical order, but let's just say that this morning . . . I'm feeling twenty-two."

Lucy's heart stopped. This was exactly what she wanted, and yet . . . was she actually going to do this? They'd brainstormed pet grooming half the night. She dropped her feet to the floor. But this was Pulse. She gently pushed back her chair, feeling all sixty pairs of competitor eyes on her.

This was Ryan Thompson.

She had to wow.

She quickly turned back to her table. "Do you trust me?"

"No," Maddie said.

"Yes," Delia said.

"Majority rules," Lucy said, inventing their team precept on the spot.

She brushed her dark hair over her shoulder and weaved through the tables to reach Ryan. Confidence was not something Lucy lacked. Today was no different. Still, after accepting the microphone, warm from Ryan's hand, she stood close to him, figuring it couldn't hurt to absorb some of his own three-comma-club, billion-dollar confidence by osmosis.

"Right," she said. "So you've heard of Uber. Lyft. Waze. They get you places. We aim to get you to the right ones." Lucy glanced at Maddie and Delia. They knew she was off message. But they had no idea just how far. *Yet.*

She cleared her throat. "Because nothing's worse than showing up first at a party." Now deliberately avoiding her teammates, Lucy surveyed the room and this lot whose last party probably had a bouncy house. "Or getting to a club that's more fossilized than a tyrannosaurus bone. Or a show where the band's dedicating the whole night to Barry Manilow covers."

Pulse. Ryan Thompson. And WOW.

Lucy placed one hand on her hip and pressed her heels into the floor, lengthening her torso as much as she could. "Like Waze, our app will rely on crowdsourcing, letting our users give you a heads-up if that party's a do or a don't. If the bar's full of hotties or hot messes. If the bouncer's particularly ornery. If it's an under-twenty-one night or a senior citizen early-bird dinner." Confidence brimmed with each sentence she uttered. Now, as she drew to a close, she paused and looked up. Exposed wood beams crisscrossed the vaulted ceiling. She smirked as the line that would clinch it came to her. Then she turned so she could see Ryan. "Uber, Lyft, they pick you up. We hook you up."

Ryan grinned as he took the microphone back from her. "And what are you called?"

He tilted the mic toward her, and she hesitated, distracted by a glimpse of Nishi looking a bit surprised. Lucy blinked and refocused on Ryan. Looking directly at him, she said, "Lit."

The way his lips stretched wider, Lucy knew she'd done it. She'd wowed Ryan Thompson. Adrenaline powered her feet back to her table. They may as well give her the noncompete now. The internship was hers. No one could deny what she'd just done.

Except, maybe, her teammates.

The moment Lucy touched her chair, Maddie attacked. "That's not what we agreed on."

"First, lower your voice." Lucy dropped into her seat and leaned across the table. "Second, where were you in the 'we' last night? You barely participated. You only care about the design. You said so a million times."

"I care because *she* cares." Maddie glanced at Delia, who was pastier than usual.

Her normally downcast eyes were staring at Lucy with shock and disbelief.

Raw, real emotion. A rarity in Lucy's world. It unnerved her. Almost made her want to take it all back. But even if that "almost" wasn't there, it was too late. Ryan liked it. Ryan expected it. And really, pet grooming? Poodle coifs and bowties on ferrets weren't going to get any of them into Pulse. Or her into Stanford.

"Listen," Lucy started slowly, focusing on Delia, knowing they couldn't do this without her. "I'm sorry. But we have to stand out. I mean, look at them." She jutted her chin to the room. To Gavin, even though she didn't intend to. "We have to be bold."

"But I don't go to bars," Delia said.

"You don't need to go to them to code them."

"But I'm only seventeen. . . . If my parents think they sent me here for this . . ."

"We'll extrapolate. Movie theaters, malls, the application's endless, really." Lucy realized her statement that was simply meant to convince Delia was actually true. She'd been thinking cities, sure, but college campuses, amusement parks, even that town fair thing Delia had fried cornholes or corndogs or whatever at for the past two summers. "This could actually work."

"Maybe," Maddie said. "But not without me." She scraped her chair against the floor.

"Wait. Just wait." Delia wrung her hands, eyes fixed on the table. "I never thought I'd get to a place like this. If this is what we're doing, then so be it. I'll code the crap out of it."

Maddie stayed in her seat, and relief began to regulate Lucy's hammering heart.

"But, Lucy?" Delia's voice was weak and strong at the same time.

"Yes?"

Finally, she lifted her head. "You put an 'i' in 'team' again, and I won't just let Maddie go. I'll follow her."

Eight hours later, and the only thing working was the shimmering effect at the edges of Lit's launch screen. It looked killer, Lucy had to hand it to Maddie. But it had taken her all day. The other teams were way ahead of them; she'd seen Ryan trying out the skeleton apps of at least a half dozen teams. He'd been at the table of Delia's cute coworker and the girl with the perfect skin three times. Apparently Ryan didn't share Lucy's contempt for bringing a guitar to a hackathon. He'd strummed what she'd only realized was the theme to *Jaws* after the girl corrected his notes. Lucy had looked her up: Emma Santos, a solid Pulse 5. One level higher than Lucy.

Not for long.

Maddie was a perfectionist. Obvious despite her silence. Apparently she'd used up all her words to condemn Lucy at the start of the day for forcing her to scrap the designs she'd sketched last night. The only word she had left was "no."

"No," when Lucy suggested a tiara icon for "dressy."

"No," when Lucy suggested a bicycle icon for "no parking."

"No," when Lucy suggested a faucet icon for "watered-down drinks."

No, no, no, no, no.

"Yes!" Gavin shouted, smacking the hands of his teammates for the sixteenth time. Sixteen in eight hours.

And all her team had managed to smack was one another. At least that was what it felt like.

"Delia," Lucy said. "Are you really sure you should be using Python?"

"Do you think I shouldn't?"

"Um, yeah, isn't that what I said six hours ago?"

"And four, and three, and oh, ten minutes ago," Maddie said. "Speed isn't everything."

"It's a hackathon. *Hack.* Hack implies speed."

"Really? I thought it was your middle name."

Lucy's jaw clenched just as Ryan circled to their table.

"Girls, how we doing?" he said.

"Perfect," Lucy said in a voice too shrill. She ran her hand through her hair, cringing when it came away sticky and purple. Hour seven was when the jelly donut fiasco had occurred. She'd told Delia it was fine.

It wasn't.

"Have you seen that dude Gavin's app? He's using Swift. Even I learned something today." He mouthed, "just kidding," and flashed a grin. "His teammates sure hit the lottery."

Lucy would have never imagined wanting to be paired with Gavin. Until now.

"Delia's using Python," Maddie said.

"I told her not to," Lucy said.

"I told you not to tell her what to do," Maddie said.

"Somebody has to push the schedule forward. We only have five weeks."

"Don't remind me."

By the time Lucy realized Ryan was inching backward, he was almost out of reach. And then Delia popped up and spun her computer around. "Look!" she cried.

"Lit" flew onto the screen, light bulbs flicking on around the word like an old Hollywood dressing room mirror. All three girls stared as each bulb fizzled out, along with Lucy's hope of a Pulse internship.

"This is all your fault," Maddie hissed.

"Me?" Lucy said. "I told her not to use Python."

"Along with a million other instructions. You're micromanaging us both, while you sit there and do what? Paint your nails?"

Lucy's face flamed. She'd fixed one chipped nail. *One.* "At least I care about what we're doing."

"Yeah, your passion for 'hottie havens' is inspiring."

"Stop," came Delia's barely audible plea, but Lucy and Maddie continued spitting blame at each other until finally Delia slammed her laptop shut, clutched it to her chest, and bolted out of the room.

Everyone was staring at them. Snickering came from Gavin's direction. But the only thing that threatened to steal Stanford from Lucy was the pitying look on Ryan's face.

She plastered on a smile, smoothed her hair, and said, "So, Ryan. Can I ask . . . do you have any pets?"

EIGHT

RIDESHARING TENSION • *The discomfort experienced by carpoolers who feel an obligation to chat with fellow riders*

MADDIE PARKED HERSELF AT breakfast with a plate of zucchini-flour pancakes, which seemed as ill-conceived as her decision to come here. She'd steered clear of the cereal station, but it didn't make her miss Danny any less.

Delia was already under the scratchy comforter when Maddie and Lucy had returned to the dorm last night.

After Delia had peeled out of the hackathon, Lucy's face paled and she flattened her hands on the table. Maddie shut her laptop and opened her bag, figuring Lucy's own sprint from the room was imminent. And then she saw Lucy's hands ball up tight.

Lucy had marched to the snack center, loaded her arms with iced coffees and kale chips, and then carefully arranged them on the table beside her. She pulled out her laptop and said, "Should we try Swift, then?"

She punched letters on the keyboard, and Maddie learned two things: that this Lucy chick could code, and that so far the only thing they had in common was a stubborn streak. They may have had the worst app, but they *had* an app by the end of the hackathon.

They were there when Ryan Thompson announced Gavin Cox and his teammates as the winners. They were there when Gavin Cox stood on the table, pumped his fists in the air, and shouted, "Boom!" And they were there when the team attempted to crush Red Bull cans with their chest bumps. One can must have been mostly full, and when Gavin Cox received a shower of sticky liquid, Maddie and Lucy both cracked up—the first time they were in sync all night.

BFFs and Maddie went together as well as her dad's bean soup and her mom's Irish soda bread. This was simply a professional partnership. Except so far it was anything but.

Maddie had lain in bed, exhausted but wide-awake—from jet lag and the thoughts running through her head. She'd listened to the faint sounds of a guitar echoing from somewhere down the hall, figuring it was that Emma girl Lucy had been creeping on during the hackathon. She'd checked the flights to Boston and had almost booked one. But then she pictured herself alone with her parents and without Danny.

Maddie would stay, but not like this.

"I think we should see Ms. Kapoor," she said after Lucy and Delia took seats across from her at the breakfast table. "She's my mentor and—"

"And we need mentoring," Delia said.

"Doubt that'll be enough," Maddie said. "Face it, we're just not compatible. I think we should consider splitting up. Maybe there are other teams looking to make a change, or maybe we can work alone."

Delia's face showed her shock, but Lucy simply finished chewing her bite of scrambled tofu.

"Fine by me," she said. "I was going to propose the same thing."

Delia lowered her eyes and pushed her bacon around her plate.

They ate in silence.

When they got up to leave, Maddie noticed Delia's plate was as full as when she'd sat down.

An awkward silence hung in the air as they stood in front of Nishi. They'd arrived early to the class on functionality that she was leading that morning.

"There's precedent," Nishi finally said. "Team members leave for all sorts of reasons—job offers, emergencies, illness. We've had two-person and solo teams in the past. We don't like to, but really the disadvantage is yours, so if you all agree . . ."

Maddie and Lucy said "yes" at the same time. Delia, still, was silent.

Nishi studied them. "Tensions were high yesterday, certainly. I firmly believe competition yields excellent results, but so does collaboration. And that can take time to develop. So all I ask is that you think about this decision a little longer. Because I'm a big fan of firsts."

Lucy tapped her notebook, which she was clutching against

her chest. "You were the first Indian American woman to receive nearly all of your Series A funding before leaving YC."

"Translation?" Maddie wouldn't be intimidated by this pretentious startup world, with its own language that kept outsiders out.

Nishi smiled. "YC, Y Combinator. What ValleyStart strives to prepare you for. And Series A . . ."

"First round of significant venture capital funding," Lucy said condescendingly.

"Cash," Nishi said. "And lots of it. Firsts gain attention—sometimes good, sometimes bad. And you young women would be the first all-female team to win ValleyStart."

Win ValleyStart? This was a box to check. A line on Maddie's résumé. Nothing more.

Nishi pulled a brochure out of her blue-and-white quilted bag. "My company—"

"Write Me," Lucy said. "Pen pals for the next generation, connecting people around the world, encouraging the sharing of cultures, religions, and ideas to broaden horizons and smiles."

"Word for word from my mission statement," Nishi said. "Which makes me realize something's missing: kids—connecting kids, especially. That's what I was doing on my last trip to India, visiting schools and pairing them with ones around the world. A classroom in Delhi sent me this as a thank-you after I mentioned I might need treatment for my obsession with Indian fabrics." She held out the end of her coral scarf and gestured to her bag. "Working with kids is my passion and why my company sponsors a free tech day camp for middle schoolers at the old science center on campus. It's now a rec space." She gave Maddie the brochure. "All the counselors are volunteers, and their tech skills vary. Do me a favor and help out today, together. If you still want to break up the band after, I'll facilitate it for you. Deal?"

Maddie got one glimpse of the day camp's redbrick building, and her shoulders relaxed. Stucco and cement and concrete may fare better in earthquakes (*strictly a guess*), but buildings should be made of the more aesthetically pleasing brick, like they were back home.

No one said much on the walk over, and as soon as they spoke with the head counselor, Delia and Lucy set out in different directions. Maddie leaned against the wall and checked her texts. Danny had sent a thumbs-up and a canoe emoji earlier but nothing else all day. He must be busy, having fun. Good. Great.

She scrolled through her email, pissed at herself for the pangs of jealousy that accompanied her relief.

"That's it, I'm out!" someone cried.

Maddie looked up. One of the day campers, a young girl with red hair, a shade darker than Danny's, flopped across the table beside a desktop computer. She hid her face with a box of cereal—dinosaur-shaped cereal. A hint of a smile tugged at Maddie's lips. She pocketed her phone and crossed the room.

"Dramatic much?" she said as she stood over the girl.

"Yes, in fact, I am."

Maddie laughed, sat beside her, and moved the cereal box. "I'm Maddie."

"And I'm done. *D-u-n*, done."

Maddie had barely parted her lips when the girl held up her hand. "I know, I know. But I'm too exhausted for four letters."

She slowly turned her head to Maddie. "But you can call me Sadie," the girl finally said. She grinned and sat up straight. "Sassy Sadie, if you want. That's my Pulse handle."

She knew she'd heard right, but still Maddie had to ask, "You have a Pulse account?"

"*D-u-h*," she spelled. "For three years."

"How old are you?"

"Eleven."

Eleven. "What's an eleven-year-old need a Pulse account for?"

Sadie eyebrows shot up. "What doesn't an eleven-year-old need a Pulse account for? I mean, do eleven-year-olds not wear clothing, drink cherry soda, and read amazing books about Gumberoo?"

Maddie shifted in her seat.

"Oh no, no, no. If you tell me you haven't read the Gumberoo books, I'll spit splinters right now."

Sadie's cheeks puffed and her eyes grew so wide that Maddie nodded, fearing the girl might otherwise spontaneously combust.

Maddie had not only read the series about the mythical, splinter-spitting, bear-like creatures—hairless save for their bushy eyebrows and the bristles on their chin—that had more weeks on the bestseller list than any middle-grade fantasy in history, she'd split the last apple tart with the author across the dinner table at her house.

The agency founded by Maddie's dad, an MBA, and her mom, an attorney, owed its existence to Gumberoo. The author, Esmé Theot, was their first and still most profitable client. She was the reason Maddie lived in a single-family, Revolutionary War–era home in Cambridge and had attended top-notch private schools. But she was also the reason Maddie grew up without many friends.

Maddie's tendency to disappear into her sketches started early. When she was younger, she'd ask to have "playdates" at the Harvard Art Museums. Her circle of friends had always been small. And honestly Maddie preferred it that way—one or two close friends were enough. But as each book in the Gumberoo series sold better than the last, sparking movie deals and a rabid fandom, the circle around Maddie widened.

Though unfamiliar, the invitations to birthday parties and movie nights and sleepovers gave Maddie the attention she was missing at home as her parents became as in demand as their famous author.

So what if her new friends asked for free swag at the lunch table or to tag along to book talks and signings? It was fun, and friends had fun together. And then, one day, in the girls' restroom, Maddie overheard the two Kimmys—the alphas of the popular clique—talking.

"We keep this up, we'll be at the premiere," brown-haired Kimmy had said.

"It's not as bad as I thought," blonde-haired Kimmy replied. "I mean, she's as boring as a goldfish, but at least she doesn't talk all that much."

"True. But I was hoping to get her to do my math homework. Sucks she's just as bad as I am. That's like false advertising, you know?"

Maddie had been only a little older than Sadie. Unable to

discern if the tightness in her chest was more from the stereotype or being used. She didn't tell anyone. She'd wiped tears she vowed never to let fall again and retreated into herself, her art, her family, knowing they were the only ones she could trust. Until her parents took that away from her too. They'd promised to be better, to not let differences over how to run the business, be it client relations or expansion or travel, spill into their home life. And yet still the hostility spread like a virus, poisoning them all.

"Look!" Sadie shoved her phone into Maddie's face. "Pulse 10! Double duh. Of course she's a 10, she's Esmé Theot. But it's not like she needs all that stuff."

Maddie shook off the ache unfortunately now entwined with Gumberoo and said, "What stuff?"

"You did come from ValleyStart, didn't ya?"

Maddie nodded.

"And *you're* asking *me* about Pulse?" Sadie squinted. "You messing with me?" Clutching her phone, Sadie asked, "Handle?"

"Don't have one."

"How is that possible?"

"I decided the only pulse I need is the one that keeps my heart ticking," Maddie joked the way she would with Danny.

"Don't let Ryan Thompson hear you say that." Sadie jumped. "Oh my God, you've met him, haven't you?"

"Unfortunately" almost slipped from Maddie's lips.

"He's, like, *soooo* hot," Sadie said.

"Eleven-year-olds shouldn't know who's hot."

"Eleven-year-olds have eyes, Maddie. So, yeah, he's hot just like all the Level 10s. Because triple duh, of course *he's* Crushing It! Here, look."

Sadie handed Maddie her phone and showed her how to flip through all the Level 10s. A black woman sporting a fancy watch in the front row at Wimbledon, a dark-haired white guy pointing to a TV the size of a car, a blonde woman smiling and holding a first-class airline ticket, another woman at a runway show, one more turning on a fancy stove, more and more and more, each 10 more beautiful than the last.

"Aren't they amazing?" Sadie whispered. "My goal is two years."

"For what?"

"To be a 10! That's why I'm here, so I can get some SEO tips and skyrocket to the top." Maddie stared blankly, causing Sadie to explain, "Search engine optimization, you know, increase my Web traffic."

"I know all about SEO. It's just, you're eleven. Shouldn't you be hunting for pterodactyls or—"

"I'm eleven, not five. Future's online for the taking, Maddie. Now, want to help me with this interface or not?"

Maddie sighed and hit the space bar on the keyboard in front of them, returning to the world she knew, the world she understood, the world that made sense.

She walked Sadie through the components of a graphical user interface and set her up to try implementing a drop-down menu on her own. As Sadie worked, Maddie sat back, searching for pterodactyls in the cereal box, listening to Delia quietly explaining the pros and cons of the different programming languages to a black boy two tables over—the most words Delia had spoken since she'd met her. She was showing him a coding game on her phone, guiding him through the basics of how to play. Even though she was talking to a middle schooler, Delia wasn't talking down, and Maddie was impressed with her knowledge and enthusiasm. All the way on the other side of the room, Lucy rattled on about demographics and marketability, citing stats on the readership of her *Teen Vogue* articles as an example. Maddie turned to see her commanding a crowd of kids, getting a glimpse of what she'd bring to Demo Day.

By the time they'd finished their session, Sadie was prepared for the next step in the learning-to-code program: getting a pixelated mini porcupine tap dancing. She was about to toss herself over the table in despair, when Maddie stopped her.

"If you need help, you could just ask."

"Then . . . *ask, ask, ask*."

Maddie liked this kid. "You come every day?"

"So long as my annoying brother remembers he's supposed to take me. He's home from college and hasn't played soccer or Minecraft with me once. All he does is stream Netflix and text his girlfriend. Mom's a super-important employment lawyer at a big software marketing company. *She's* busy. Still, she wants to be the one to take me, but I told her my brother could get off his duff."

Maddie had spent her whole life making sure Danny knew he always came first. The bravado failing to cover the sadness in Sadie's eyes was the reason why. "Then I'll be back."

"Sweet . . . and bring a list of the incubator teams. I want to keep tabs. See what it does for their Pulse."

Seriously? But Maddie nodded.

As the counselors started collecting the campers and leading them to their parents' cars, Sadie asked Maddie, "So you gonna win or what?"

"You care if I do?"

"Do porcupines tap dance?" Sadie held up her hand. "Don't answer that."

"Can we settle on a 'we'll see'?"

"Ugh, you sound like my mom." Sadie turned and sashayed to the door.

Maddie watched the back of Sadie's red-haired head disappear from sight, realizing how much fun she'd had and hoping someone back on the East Coast was feeling the same after being lucky enough to spend the afternoon with Danny.

Delia wrapped up with her student, promising to give his counselors links to websites for him to learn more, and Lucy stood among her admirers—most of them as tall if not taller than she was. But Lucy would never fade into the background.

They gravitated toward one another, each of their wide smiles growing more tentative as they studied one another's faces, trying to discern what each was thinking. Pulse and Ryan Thompson and the internship hadn't budged from the bottom of Maddie's priority list, and yet . . . Lucy and Delia, their passion and talents, they were rising. Maddie wasn't entirely sure what that meant, but one thing kept repeating on a loop in her mind: *win ValleyStart.*

NINE

TEAMVESTING • *When an investor offers a startup financing because of a belief in the team more than the actual idea*

DELIA HAD SPENT HOURS talking about coding. The only other time she'd done that was when she was ten and she and Cassie had watched *The Shining* even after Cassie's mom had said it was too scary for them. She'd been right.

Cassie had begged Delia to tell her a story so she could fall asleep, but Delia didn't know any stories. But she knew programming. Despite Cassie groaning from boredom, sleep only came with the morning light. Yet that night inspired her to create Delia's Den. The first iterations, the ones she shared with the boy in the day camp, featured a character eerily similar to the wild-eyed Jack Nicholson that had scared the crap out of her and Cassie in *The Shining*.

"Those kids were pretty great," Delia said as she and her teammates (*were they still?*) walked from the edge of campus back to the dorm. They passed the semicircular two-story gym and the dozen women and handful of guys balancing on one foot in front of it—either an outdoor yoga class or flamingo training.

"So were those programs," Lucy said. "My summer camp had the best—"

"Naturally," Maddie said, but followed it with a head nod that encouraged Lucy and a wink that made Delia stifle a laugh.

"And still those were way better than the ones we had at their age," Lucy continued. "Don't you think, Delia?"

"I, uh, guess," Delia said, pressing her hand to her neck and feeling the coolness of the circuit board pendant against her skin.

"Which ones did your instructors use?"

"I'm mostly self-taught, actually."

"Really?" Lucy said.

"Really?" Maddie said.

Delia shoved her hands in her pockets and focused on the ground, wondering if she could get a counselor's job instead of heating up Hot Pockets if she gave up on ValleyStart.

Going home and telling her parents she'd failed, here, the one place she could possibly succeed, would end with her folded into their arms, listening as they said how proud they were of her for trying, knowing she'd never feel the same about herself.

Especially after the sacrifices they'd made for her these past couple of years—from her dad's long drives to Chicago to forgoing theater improvements like the new lighting board to her mom taking on everything from catering to costume repair to save more for Delia's college fund. Delia helped as much as she could.

But seeing those kids, helping those kids, for once Delia didn't feel ashamed of who she was and what she could do. All the while, she'd snuck glances at Maddie and Lucy, who seemed to be enjoying themselves as much as she was. When they were all volunteering, they'd seemed almost like equals.

Delia couldn't believe she'd actually thought they could be a team, that she'd found girls who were like her, that they could all be part of the same club.

She'd never been part of anyone's club but her parents and Cassie's. Her town was small, her schools even smaller. Her computer was her second best friend, and her classmates knew it. Everyone liked Cassie and would never have said out loud that Delia couldn't tag along—at least out loud in Delia's presence.

"That's amazing, Delia," Lucy said.

Delia stopped walking. "What?"

"I said . . ." Lucy looped her arm through Delia's. "That's amazing. That you taught yourself. You're a true unicorn."

Maddie snorted. "Is that supposed to be a compliment?"

"It is," Delia said shyly. "A unicorn's a . . ."

"Programmer or startup that is too incredible to actually exist." Lucy's tone had a bit of awe in it.

"A unicorn?" Maddie mimed a long pointy horn on her head. "Pink and blue and swirly?"

"Whatever color you want it to be," Lucy said. "And horns might only be for the male unicorns."

"Hmm," Delia said. "Yeah, I'm not really sure."

"Are we seriously debating the anatomical correctness of a magical creature that doesn't exist?"

Lucy looked at Delia and smiled. "I guess."

"I guess," Delia repeated.

A lightness in the breeze wafted over them as they crossed beneath an arbor covered in a purple flowering vine and continued on the path that would lead them back to the dorms. Delia had the strongest urge to text Cassie, like she should be here with her, with them.

After a while in silence, Maddie said, "Really? Self-taught, Delia?"

Delia nodded. "And . . ." She sucked in a breath and felt Lucy tighten the hold on her forearm. "I—I know what we're up against, all these kids who had so much more than me, who started at these types of summer camps like Lucy, so I'll understand if you want to still split up, it's just . . . did you see how few girls were in that day camp?"

"Yeah," Maddie said. "I did."

"Me too," Lucy said.

"First all-girls team . . ." Delia started.

"To win," Lucy said.

"Sounds pretty unicorn-y to me." Maddie's face was unreadable, and then her freckles lifted as she grinned. Delia was pretty sure it was the first time she'd seen her smile around Lucy.

"Going on record that I want that horn though," Maddie added. "Better to ram up Gavin Cox's—"

"Aha, yes, no need for visuals," Lucy said. "But I for one think that's a brilliant idea."

They all laughed, and Delia realized how much weight she'd been carrying, about their team, about staying in the program, about not getting to go to work anymore. Because she just *loved* heating up Hot Pockets.

Uh-huh.

It had nothing to do with a certain boy.

Nothing at all.

They spent the rest of the walk talking about their ideas for Lit. Lucy even let Delia speak some of the time. Though when Delia questioned if they really needed a "sticky floor" rating, Lucy chuckled.

"Delia, I think you need to see—and feel—the inside of a club."

"Like research? For work?" Maddie said.

"And play." Lucy raised an eyebrow. "Fortunately, Ryan Thompson and I think alike. Next weekend's field trip? Who's in for a recon bonding night?"

TEN

THE DAVE RATIO • *The gender imbalance in startups and tech, where the number of Daves is often greater than or equal to the number of women*

THE MUSCLES IN LUCY'S arms quivered, but she gripped the handle tighter. It had been nearly an hour, and she wasn't giving up now.

"Hold on," Lucy said as she tugged the hair straightener through Delia's surprisingly resilient curls. "We're nearly there."

"I appreciate this, I do," Delia said, recrossing her legs for the zillionth time. "It's just . . . that was a lot of matcha. Delicious—you were right about the tea—but just . . . a lot."

"The grande colossal. Your body's flying so high on antioxidants it's devouring free radicals like Maddie eats zucchini-flour pancakes."

"Who would have thought?" Delia said.

"I know," Lucy said. "Every morning this week."

"She even saved some for lunch."

"Huh. Maybe this California sunshine is finally starting to thaw our dear Madeline."

Delia simply crossed her legs—again.

In the past week, Lucy had begun to understand the differences in Delia's silences. There was the head down, immersed in code silence Lucy wouldn't dare interrupt. The texting with a certain coder who was a hottie haven all unto himself silence. And this, the nonconfrontational confrontational silence.

"Sorry," Lucy said. "I love Madeline, you know that."

Delia silence.

"Fine. *Maddie*. But Lit—"

"Is behind. We're lagging behind where the other teams are." Delia hugged her arms against her chest, knocking her necklace to the side. "It's my fault. That real-time reaction is our core, and all week I've been following what should work, it's just . . ."

"I know." Lucy centered Delia's computer chip. "And I'm confident you'll get us there."

She patted Delia's shoulder, but truthfully, she was concerned about their progress. Delia cared too much about the other teams, and Maddie didn't seem to care enough about theirs. While Lucy didn't exactly regret their decision to stick together, she did feel the burden of being the glue.

"I was more talking about Maddie. Pieces of Lit do look stellar . . ." Lucy tipped her head toward the designs for the Lit logo and site icons wallpapering the back of their door. "But they're scattered." *Like everything of hers*, Lucy restrained herself from adding, despite the tees, jeans, computer cords, charging cables, and who knew what else—dirty or clean, alive or dead—piled on the floor and lining the wall of Maddie's bunk like a body pillow. "And she hasn't entirely abandoned communicating with me via grunting. Sometimes, doesn't it feel like . . . like she's only half here?"

Delia remained silent. But she nodded. Then, she put her hand around Lucy's wrist and yanked.

"Sorry," Delia said. "I'll be right back."

Lucy sighed, rested the straightener on the edge of the desk, and sat down on her feathery comforter. Maddie's distance worried Lucy. Because Lit needed all three of them to not just *be* here but to *be here*, to eat, sleep, dream, walk, run, think, breathe *here* here, every minute of every day. It was the only way to win.

On the desk, her phone lit up with a text.

ValleyStart: Week 2, we are in. Go ahead and grin. But don't forget: the beta test approaches like a shark fin!

Every day ValleyStart sent a pithy rhyme—whether to psych them up or out, Lucy still wasn't sure.

She doubted any of her ValleyStart competitors needed the beta test reminder. Though it wouldn't arrive until the fourth week of the program, it loomed over every class and lecture, every brainstorming session, every mentor meeting. And every program deadline—like the one coming at the end of the week: submitting their in-progress apps for review. They'd only have a few days to implement the feedback before the beta test, and they had to do it right. The team with the most successful beta test had an eighty-five percent chance of winning on Demo Day. *Eighty-five.*

The beta test was the domino that would set off all the rest and end with Lucy strolling under the palm trees at Stanford. It would be here before Emma Santos mastered the song she was singing—singing *again*. The same one she'd been practicing since the day they all arrived. Her voice spilled through the door, and Lucy once again wondered how she had the time.

Then again, she'd been straightening Delia's hair for the past hour. All the while looking at the necklace Delia always wore, same as Maddie and her four-leaf clover—gifts from their parents. Lucy had one too.

She opened the desk drawer and reached for her jewelry case. Inside was the silver Star of David her mother had given her for her bat mitzvah when she was thirteen. It had originally been her mom's, given to her for her own ceremony. Lucy hadn't worn it in years.

She left it where it was and instead hooked a black choker around her neck. She then stroked the felt of her red pennant for luck, picked up her phone, and logged in to Stanford's online applicant portal, checking on her request for a second interview. Now that she'd actually *met* Ryan Thompson, if she happened to get the chance to slip his name into the convo, all the better.

No response, still.

Lucy entered the date and time of the check-in into her notebook right below the last one, two days ago, the same day Lucy had heard from her mom.

Any news from Stanford?

That was the only text her mom had sent since Lucy first arrived at ValleyStart. That maybe there'd have been more had Lucy responded was irrelevant.

"Still analog, huh, li'l Lucy?"

Her spine stiffened. Freaking Gavin Cox.

She closed her notebook. "Studies show writing things down increases our memory and allows us to process information on a deeper level."

"Huh, you don't say. Wait, sorry. What was that again?"

"I said, studies show—"

He grinned, and Lucy hated that some part of her actually still thought he was cute.

"So this is the home of the dream team behind Lit." His big feet clomped into the room, leaving a trail of dirt behind him. "Surprised it's not covered in rainbows and boy band posters."

"That was last week. This week's theme is feminine hygiene. If you want to join us, we're making tampon garlands later."

"No one ever said you weren't quick, Katz."

Lucy's eyes flitted from Gavin's to below his waist and back again. "Unfortunately same holds true for you."

"You never complained."

"You never listened."

"No need. Always another customer waiting to be served."

That Gavin was arrogant didn't mean he was wrong. Gavin's father was one of the first VCs with a history of betting big and right. With Gavin's Mercedes convertible, partying prowess, and, yes, dammit, those floppy curls, he did have a line of girls waiting outside his bedroom door.

She'd never been one of them.

Until the night her ride to the after-after-homecoming-game party drank too many seltzer wine coolers and accidentally flushed her car keys down the toilet. Lucy had called AAA and sat on the curb to wait, once again regretting the last fender bender (*was that her seventh or eighth?*) that had put her car in the shop. That's when she'd heard Gavin talking behind a tree at the side of the house.

"I know my times were slower than the last meet, Dad, but we still won. By a—"

Silence.

"I'm not making an excuse, it's just—"

Silence.

"I know."

Silence.

"Yes, I remember. Pissing in a tin can. Got it."

Gavin hung up, reared his arm back, and hurled his phone across the front lawn. Right into Lucy's tote. She cried out in surprise before exploding in laughter. When Gavin peered around the tree and she pulled his phone out of her bag, his eyes narrowed before he began laughing too.

"Now if only someone had recorded *that* and shown my dad," he said with a sheepish grin, knowing she must have heard the conversation.

Gavin walked to Lucy, and she handed him his phone, never expecting him to take it and sit down beside her. They were in a couple of classes together, went to most of the same parties, but they weren't really friends. But, honestly, in their ultra-competitive high school, was anyone truly just "a friend"? See and be seen, give a little, get as much as you could, everyone equally as good to party with as to use to your advantage—the best being when both could happen at once.

That night had been different.

From beneath her bunk bed, Lucy grabbed the dustpan she'd "borrowed" from the janitorial closet and swept up after Gavin. "Why are you here?"

"Can't a friend stop by?'

"Yes, a *friend* can."

"Oh, come off it, Lucy, there was never anything real between us. You know that."

Lucy knew it.

She knew who Gavin was.

But somehow she'd let him in. For weeks—the longest relationship either of them had ever had. Which happened to include the night before her Stanford interview.

He'd texted, upset about the latest thing his ass of a father had done.

Gavin's parents were at Pebble Beach for the weekend—his dad knocking around golf balls and terms like *valuation* and *hockey stick growth* and his mom marinating herself in seaweed wraps and aloe martinis. Back at home, Gavin had been checking their travel itinerary after realizing that the credit card he had on their account had expired. He'd noticed his father was signed up for a father-son golf tournament, party of two.

Gavin was an only child.

He'd asked her to come over. She went. And she listened as his venting about his father transitioned into something else: the reason the itinerary had affected him so much. He'd been eleven the last—and only—time he'd played in a father-son golf competition with his dad. His first off hit had led to more, fueled by the strain on his father's face and Gavin's nerves. Knowing he'd disappointed his father, he was shy and self-conscious at the luncheon afterward. He made excuses and explained to his dad's friends how he'd work to improve for next year. His dad nodded right along, and then, first chance he got, he dragged Gavin to the men's locker room.

"I don't give a rat's ass if it's golf or pissing in a tin can; you don't have to be the best, you just have to act like you are," he'd spat at his son.

"I'm sorry I'm not," Gavin had said.

"Not what?"

"The best."

"You and me both, kid."

Lucy had comforted Gavin, and they'd shared a bottle of red from deep in his dad's cellar. Things spiraled that night. The drinks, the people, the party, her life.

She lied. She never told her mom she missed the Stanford interview entirely, sleeping off all she'd imbibed the night before with half a dozen classmates on the floor of Gavin's basement. His basement. Not even his room. She'd opened his bedroom door before leaving and slammed it shut so quickly she didn't even know who it was in his bed. All she knew was that it wasn't her. And she'd given up Stanford. *Stanford.* For this? For who? And how? *How? How? How?*

"Listen, Luce," Gavin said, sauntering deeper into the room. "I missed this morning's lecture. And I know how diligent you are about taking notes."

"And you thought I'd let you borrow them?"

"Why not? I'd do the same for you."

Lucy snorted. "Only if you had something to gain."

"Backs and scratching, you know that, Luce." He leaned in so close, she could feel his hot breath on her cheek. "And believe me, I do, from firsthand experience. Those pretty little nails digging in every time I—"

"Um, excuse me?" Delia hovered in the doorway. "Lucy, do you want me to wait in the common room? I owe my parents a call anyway."

"No, absolutely not." She backed away from Gavin and told him, "Sorry, I forgot my notebook this morning, so in fact, I didn't take any notes."

Delia looked like she was about to offer up her own, and Lucy said, "Neither did Delia. None of us did."

"Considering what I heard, you might think about starting."

"Heard? What? From who?" Lucy said. *People were talking? About them?*

Gavin ran his fingers along his mouth, zipping it shut.

Fine, whatever. Underestimate us. We'll show you. The Stanford portal was still up on her phone. She clicked it shut. *We better.*

Maddie came up behind Delia. She leaned against the doorjamb, and her brow creased. "Why is there crap on our rug?"

The turquoise-and-white diamond shag rug Lucy had ordered after the first time her bare feet hit the linoleum.

Gavin pursed his lips. "It's not crap, it's dirt. They ran the sprinklers too early on the golf course."

"That's not what I meant." Maddie slid off her sneakers and added them to the pink canvas basket Lucy had also ordered and set by the door for their shoes.

Lucy's jaw clenched both at the clumps now on her rug and at Gavin. "Some nerve, Gavin. Coming to me for notes because you were golfing."

His shoulders rounded, not much, but enough for Lucy to tell. "I thought you'd understand. My dad called at the last minute. Needed a fourth."

Maddie snorted, but Lucy stayed silent, searching Gavin's eyes for a truth she was surprised to see was actually there.

She said in a soft voice, "You tell him about the hackathon win?"

Gavin nodded. "Got a whole chin lift out of him. But if I 'stay the course' . . ." Gavin used air quotes. "Well, then he might put Demo Day on his calendar."

Lucy bit down on her lower lip, chewing, until she realized she was doing it and stopped. "Fine. I'll take a photo of my notes and send it, okay?"

Maddie tossed her tablet and stylus on her bunk with a huff.

"Thanks, Luce." Gavin winked at her.

Maddie stared at him. "What's your team's app, anyway?"

"It tracks the development of new apps."

"How meta of you."

"Can't hurt to have a little self-awareness in our lives, now can it?" On his way out the door, he nodded to Delia's half-curly head. "Way to rock the asymmetry."

"Goodbye, Gavin," Lucy said in a voice more high-pitched than she liked. *We* will *show everyone.* "Now, Delia, sit, before this thing overloads the fuse box."

Delia grabbed her laptop and reclaimed her seat. "I've just got to figure out what's breaking this line of code."

"No," Lucy said, reaching around Delia to shut her computer. She refused to let Gavin under her skin—under any of their skins. "We worked all week. Tonight's for fun." And letting everyone see how unified they were because, turns out, Lucy's mom was right about the importance of presentation.

Lucy looked up at Maddie, who was sitting on the end of her top bunk, her long legs dangling well into Delia's bed underneath. "I'll do you next, Maddie."

Without lifting her eyes from her phone, Maddie replied, "Got straight covered, thanks."

"I have a curling wand. Three, actually. *Teen Vogue* asked me to do a review. And you can borrow one of my tees. It'll be like a crop top on you, and it's always good to show a little skin and—"

"I'm good," Maddie said.

Strategize, stylize, socialize.

Tonight needed all three. Lucy yanked the straightener through Delia's hair.

But then Delia asked, "You're coming though, right?"

Maddie stared at them, twirling her stylus in her hand. "He really rented out the whole place?"

"I heard he tried," Lucy said. "But the club donated it. Way better deal for them with all the attention they'll get from Ryan walking through the door."

"Unbelievable," Maddie said.

"Pulse is the only way to live," Lucy said with a wink.

"Is it though?"

"Come on, Maddie, it'll be fun," Delia said. "I've never been."

"To San Francisco?" Maddie asked.

"To a club?" Lucy said.

"To anywhere." Delia's eyes flickered to her makeshift nightstand, the metal suitcase plastered with tourist stickers.

Maddie swung her legs back onto her bed. "Just let me finish texting my brother."

"Way to go, Delia," Lucy whispered in her ear.

"I wasn't trying to manipulate her or anything. It's just the truth."

"Huh, really? Well, how about that."

There was a cooler on the bus. Cans of cane sugar soda and organic coconut water, courtesy of ValleyStart. What surely wasn't provided by the program were the koozie-covered PBRs and metal bottles full of premixed mojitos, margaritas, and rum and cola. Lucy wasn't sure who'd snuck the alcohol on, but the drinks surreptitiously made the rounds. She and Maddie each had some, but Delia barely even tasted the sippy box of sangria before passing it off to Lucy.

She held it in one hand as the soft, warm sounds of an acoustic guitar filled the bus. Emma's rich alto overlaid the notes, drowning out the excited chatter.

"Wow," Delia whispered. "If she's half as good a designer, we're all in trouble."

The song was the same one Emma had been practicing earlier. But this time, her voice played with the inflection, the ballad more sultry than before, as if Emma was finally honing in on her strength, letting the music accompany her instead of the other way around. Exactly what Lucy needed to do with ValleyStart. As the rest of the bus became entranced by Emma, Lucy sank deeper into the seat, mentally rehashing the past few days while sipping the sangria.

So by the time they walked through the door of the same club Lucy had been at little more than a week ago, she was well on her way to floating to the rafters above. Half the busload had partaken of the refreshments, but Lucy was the only one aiming for the dance floor instead of the buffet of free food. Even Delia and Maddie were heading toward the taco station, forcing Lucy to reluctantly trudge along behind them.

She leaned against the wall, surveying her competitors.

Unfazed. That's how she wanted to be seen.

Which is why when Gavin passed by, she grabbed his shirt and tugged him all the way to the dance floor. Gray jeans, a white shirt with the sleeves rolled to his elbows, he was dressed not like a Valley wannabe but the way he had in high school. Part of what had attracted her to him then. And that she hated still did now.

It only took a second for Gavin to kick into gear. His hands cradled her waist, and he flung her low into a dip. She giggled— purposely, loudly—as she righted herself. He held her close, using their bodies to shield a can of PBR in a red koozie.

Lucy tucked herself into Gavin and accepted the can. She took a swig, gave it back, and he polished it off, circling their fused bodies to the side of the dance floor where he stashed the empty. Gavin had showered since he'd been in her room, and he smelled like the redwoods like he always did. . . . *Why does he have to smell so good and why does his hair feel so soft against my skin and why, why is he such a good dancer?*

His arms were strong and her feet were quick and they were both so damn cocky that they didn't care if they were the only ones dancing. The song ended and another began and they dug in deeper. Their rhythm was smooth and effortless, and anyone watching should have been able to see this was not the first time they'd moved in sync. Lucy's eyes shot open. She jerked back, searching for Ryan.

He was at the end of the buffet, talking to Eric's group. His head shifted and his eyes met hers. She slowly backed away from Gavin. He cocked his head, and she tilted her own toward Delia.

"Girl bonding." Lucy wasn't sure why she said it—like she cared if Gavin thought she was dissing him.

He shrugged and pulled an airplane bottle from his back pocket.

Lucy and Gavin's dancing had enticed a few more to join. The night was sponsored by Pulse, and Ryan had made it a mixer of sorts, including some of the newer Pulse hires. Thankfully. Because the Dave ratio was strong at ValleyStart. A few more girls in addition to guys in those tees only given to Pulse employees began circulating through the crowd.

All of ValleyStart—and a few of the Pulse hires—were underage, which meant the bar was locked down for the night. But it was still a club. And so the lights dimmed further and the music pumped louder.

Lucy found Delia and Maddie. "Come on, I love this song!"

She knew the only way she'd get Delia out there was if Maddie came, so she locked eyes and silently pleaded with her.

Maddie's eyes were unreadable, and then, finally, they softened. "One song," she said, moving past Lucy and to the center of the growing crowd.

Lucy mouthed a thank-you before clasping a hand around Delia's wrist and dragging her to the floor. Maddie was a decent dancer, her height and confidence making up for her lack of innate skill. Delia wobbled beside them, as unsure on her legs as a newborn fawn.

"Just let it go!" Lucy cried over the music, but Delia only shifted from one foot to the other, and so Lucy wrapped her arm around her waist and led her in an exaggerated tango.

Delia's hands were clammy and her face glowed pink, but by the third time Lucy spun to lead her in the opposite direction, Delia was giggling. They zoomed past and through Maddie, trying to get her to join them, but Maddie simply snuck away after the song ended.

"Your loss," Delia shouted, surprising Lucy by grabbing her and leading what was probably the worst tango in history. But Delia was finally showing confidence, leading, and Lucy, knowing everyone was watching, let her.

Until a super cute guy in a Pulse tee cut in. Another planted himself in front of Delia, and Lucy gave her a thumbs-up.

Lucy then followed her own advice and let everything go—Gavin and no news on Stanford and her mom's voice in her head and her constant worries that they weren't bringing Lit to the next level. She commanded the floor, moving from Pulse employee to Pulse employee and eventually landing in the arms of one of Eric's teammates.

"Marty, right?" Lucy said.

"Marty Martinez," he said. "And, yes, it was on purpose, and, no, my parents aren't crazy, they write sitcoms, and, yes, I've considered changing my name."

Marty spun Lucy, but the dizziness didn't stop when her body did. After a quick peck on Marty's cheek, she pushed through the sweaty pack and to the buffet, where she downed two mason jars of hibiscus water. The only tacos left were labeled beef tongue and Cowgirl Creamery goat cheese, and she ate one, cold, as her eyes searched for Maddie and Delia. Head still swimming, she started down the hall to the restrooms, remembering the door that led to the private patio area on the roof of the club.

She climbed the stairs, flung the door open, and breathed in the crisp night air, for once grateful for the microclimate surrounding the city. Lights from buildings in the Financial District glimmered in the distance, none more than the top floors of Salesforce Tower, which had edged out the Transamerica Pyramid to become the tallest building in San Francisco when it opened. Each night, fleeting images moved across the aluminum panels that formed the crown at the top—a public art installation visible from twenty miles in every direction. Lucy watched as a lone cyclist, a black shadow against the white lights, pedaled around the side of the building and out of view. When she stepped forward and turned to try to get a glimpse of the lights on the Bay Bridge, she realized she wasn't alone.

Ryan was here. With Emma. Eric and Marty's teammate. Ryan and Emma were so deep in conversation, his hand on her forearm, that they didn't even notice her. She considered quietly leaving, but if Ryan was dispensing advice, Lucy wanted in.

"Hey," she said.

Ryan's head jerked back, and Emma averted her eyes.

Is this more than a tip or two? Is Ryan actually helping Emma's team?

That if Lucy's Pulse were higher, maybe he'd be helping her raced through her mind. *Damn you, Gavin Cox.*

Ryan handed something to Emma and she nodded. He then sauntered over to Lucy. "Someone's been having fun."

Pissing in a tin can, right? Just because Lucy wasn't a 10 didn't mean she couldn't act like it. "How could I not? Especially when it's this very club that inspired Lit."

"Really? So you've been before?"

"A couple of times."

"Isn't it a shame we didn't run into each other?"

"Tragic, really," Lucy said.

He laughed and placed a hand on her shoulder, just past the skinny strap of her tank top. "Keep enjoying yourself, Lucy."

His fingers pressed into her bare skin, giving a gentle squeeze. It wasn't until he'd reentered the club that Lucy realized she'd basically admitted to using a fake ID and he hadn't even blinked.

He's so cool.

Emma barely looked at Lucy as she moved past her.

"Care to share?" Lucy said.

"Share what?"

"The intel on ValleyStart. Us girls gotta stick together, right?"

"Oh, we weren't talking about the program."

Lucy eyed her skeptically.

"We weren't. Ryan's into music and so am I and—"

"Got it. Keep it to yourself. I can get my own intel."

And with a determination to do just that, Lucy marched into the club. She wormed her way back onto the dance floor, gathered as many Pulse employees around her as she could, and took a selfie, immediately posting it online.

As a baseline to test the photo's traction, she double-checked her Pulse. Still a 4. *Thud, thud, thud, thud.*

Below, in her recents, was Emma. Lucy clicked on Emma's Pulse profile and almost dropped her phone.

And for the first time since she sent in her application, Lucy knew Stanford was hers for the taking.

ELEVEN

BUY-IN • *Gaining support for an idea or project, often from management or the full team*

THE THREE-HOUR TIME DIFFERENCE between them didn't stop Maddie from checking if Danny had texted back. She shifted on the hard barstool where she'd been since leaving Lucy and Delia on the dance floor and logged in to her email. While she wasn't taking on new clients during the program, she still had to field requests and answer questions from existing ones.

"This seat taken?" Nishi Kapoor asked.

Maddie looked up. "Feel free."

"Me and my blisters thank you. Aren't new shoes the worst? Damn cute though. That's how they get you. Like babies."

Though Maddie's closet full of slip-on sneakers made her unable to relate, she nodded.

"Go ahead." Nishi gestured to Maddie's phone. "Don't let me stop you from checking your Pulse."

"Please. I don't even have an account."

"How refreshing. You have single-handedly restored my faith in the next generation, Maddie."

"Don't get too excited. I'm an anomaly."

"Change always starts with one. One idea, one person, one chance, one risk. Without anomalies, life would forever be status quo. How boring would that be?" She smiled, and Maddie put her phone away. "Now, tell me why you're here and not out there." Nishi glanced at Maddie's feet. "It's not because of improper footwear."

Maddie shrugged. "Not really my scene."

"What is your scene?"

"I don't have one, but if I did, it wouldn't be this."

"I'm familiar with the culture shock. Took me three months to realize 'ramps' was just a fancy word for onions. Though you do get used to the sunshine."

Maddie leaned in to better hear Nishi. "You're from the East Coast?"

"New Jersey. Tell me, is it drinking out of mason jars or adding a 'preneur' to every noun that gets you?"

"Both. It's all so surface."

"Not what you expected?"

Maddie sighed. "No, it's exactly what I expected."

Across the room, Lucy was standing on a chair, shining the flashlight on her phone over the crowd. Maddie lifted her hand and gave a halfhearted wave.

"Maybe not everything," Maddie qualified, surprising herself.

They both watched as Lucy weaved her way through the dance floor to reach them.

"She's performing well," Nishi said. "I suspect she doesn't exactly relish the idea of following in someone else's footsteps."

Maddie cocked her head.

"Of course she hasn't mentioned her mom. Well, Abigail Katz was in tech before someone told her she shouldn't be." Nishi looked at Maddie, considering her words. "Navigating the Valley takes some adjustments, more for those of us who don't look like Mark Zuckerberg. I won't deny the heavy level of self-importance and the frat boy mentality. But there are smart people with some great ideas here. We just need more of them."

"Ideas?"

"People. Especially ones that bring new perspectives. Like your team."

Maddie gave a derisive laugh. "Yeah, Lit's going to change the world."

The edges of Nishi's lips gently curled before she forced them back into a straight line. "Maybe it will and maybe it won't. But the *people* behind it can."

"Hey!" Lucy said to Maddie. She nodded to Nishi. "Hip place, right?"

"It's very Ryan. You'll see during the Pulse field trip at the end of the program. You seemed to be having fun, though?"

Lucy tilted her head. "You aren't?"

"CEOs don't dance."

They could all see Ryan twirling Emma Santos.

Nishi corrected herself. "Different rules for the gents. It is Silicon Valley, after all." She gave her seat to Lucy. "Just about time to start loading up the bus. Remind me never to chaperone again. And when I don't listen because I've got a memory like a sieve and a heart like a Disney character, remind me not to do it in heels." She slipped off her shoes and swung them in her hand as she headed toward Ryan.

"Have you been here the whole time?" Lucy asked.

"Mostly."

"Come on, Maddie. Don't you want to get to know people? Tonight was supposed to be about having fun."

"And by fun I assume you mean kick-starting a summer fling?"

"Summer what?"

"An incubator boyfriend. Looked like you were testing out candidates."

"Dancing's just dancing, Maddie. No one has time for dating."

"Don't tell Delia that."

"Where is she? I've been looking all over for you both."

"She's out front."

"You didn't leave her alone, did you?"

"She's an adult. But no, she's with Eric."

"That's what I need to talk to you both about."

"Delia's love life?"

"No, not directly anyway. And since when does Delia have a love life?"

Maddie shrugged.

"We have to be more proactive." Lucy climbed up on the stool and spun Maddie's seat to face her. "Look, you know Emma Santos? Eric's teammate?"

"Of course. She's really talented."

"More importantly, she's a 7." Lucy held up her phone, open to the Pulse app. "Last week she was a 5."

"Well, good for Emma?"

Lucy tucked one leg under her to sit up higher. "Good for all of us. One week into the program and she shot up two whole Pulses. *That's* how important ValleyStart is. Just think what it can do for us."

What Maddie knew about Pulse came from Sadie, and she didn't really think getting free iPhones and tickets to football games would matter this much to Lucy.

"It's not really my thing, Lucy. I'm sorry I can't share your enthusiasm. I just think there are more important things to worry about than Pulse."

"It's not just *my* thing, it's everyone's thing." Lucy sucked in her bottom lip and spat it back out. "Listen, I get it, you're not from here, you don't want to be from here, so you don't realize just how huge this incubator is. Or what it can do." She paused, and when she spoke again, her voice lacked its usual bravado. "What *I* need it to do. Because I'm wait-listed, Maddie. Wait-listed at the place that's been my dream since before I knew what the word 'college' meant. If simply *being* at ValleyStart can make Emma's Pulse—our Pulses—rise, then just think what a successful beta test . . . what a *win* can do. If we win ValleyStart . . . if we intern at Pulse . . . there's no way Stanford doesn't let me in."

Maddie wasn't sure what to say, and in the time it took for her to decide, Lucy straightened her spine and reclaimed her authoritative tone. "Your design skills are sick, sure. But you don't care about any of the rest of it. You're not in it like me and Delia."

Maddie pulled back in surprise. She'd laid the foundation, the typography and color scheme. She had designs for the logo and buttons. Maybe she wasn't pulling all-nighters, but the user interface was easy stuff. "Because I don't need to be. You don't have to worry about my part."

"That's where you're wrong. I do have to worry, because your part is my part, my part is Delia's part, Delia's part is your part, it's all connected. Or it should be. We're a team. It's like you don't want to be. Makes me wonder why you even bothered applying in the first place."

Maddie had seen Lucy angry, and this wasn't that. Anger Maddie could handle. Disappointment was something else.

Part of her wanted to explain to Lucy why she was here, what Danny and his future meant to her—that it meant more to her than her own. But Lucy didn't have siblings, didn't seem to have any real friends beyond those she'd partied with in high school. How could she understand doing something that wasn't entirely self-centered?

"Why did you help Gavin?" Maddie suddenly asked.

Lucy once again began chewing on her bottom lip. "Why not?"

"Because he's the competition. And an ass."

"It's just lecture notes. He could get them from anyone."

"But he didn't. He got them from you. Which seems out of character for you both. Unless he's messing with your head. Or you, his."

She shrugged. "We have history. Sometimes people act the way they do for a reason. Besides, I help him, and down the line, he helps me. It's how things work. It's business. It's life."

"Not mine. I don't use people."

"I didn't say I did. Or was. Give and get isn't the same as using people."

"Says the person who's doing the 'getting.'"

"Are you speaking hypothetically or from experience?"

"Does it matter?"

"Yes. Because people act the way they do for a reason, and I can't understand your reasons unless you tell me."

Maddie laced her fingers together on the table in front of her, a tiredness that she could no longer blame on jet lag weighing her down. The energy it took to be here was sometimes more than she thought she had.

"Fine, whatever," Lucy said. "But you said yes to us, and this may not be important to you, but it is to me and to Delia. You hopped on board this train; there's no getting off now." Lucy tossed her leg out from under her and dropped down from the stool. "Don't make me regret staying with you."

Maddie sighed in frustration. Sharing her feelings alternated between a quick retort and a well-placed eye roll. She and Danny were different with each other, but her parents . . . her dad's preoccupation with the business left less time—literally and figuratively—for hugs and *I love you*s. And her mom . . . her distance increased in direct proportion with her success, as if displays of affection even at home translated to weakness. If it weren't for Danny, Maddie may have turned out even more like them.

She reached for her four-leaf clover, holding it tight, missing Danny and her bed at home and the way her family used to be before her parents turned into people she no longer recognized—ones she didn't really even like anymore. She suspected their juvenile behavior of late, badmouthing each other and jockeying to be seen as the true force behind the agency, was a precursor to a split—personally and professionally. Maybe it was for the best. But telling someone wouldn't change anything. So she didn't. She just watched the now-angry version of Lucy that she was familiar with get smaller and smaller as she walked away.

TWELVE

EARLY STAGE • *When a startup's product or idea is undergoing development or testing and not yet ready for release*

FOR THE FOURTH TIME, Delia regretted letting Lucy straighten her hair. Because every time she reached for a nonexistent curl to wind around her finger, she must have looked ridiculous—like she was swatting invisible flies.

The dress she let Lucy talk her into wasn't just three inches too short and so tight it was bruising her ribs; it didn't have pockets. She'd spent the past ten minutes trying to concentrate on what Eric was saying all the while wondering what to do with her hands.

Eric leaned on his, clasped behind his back, which rested against the side of the building. He'd opened the door for her as they'd exited the club. Delia coming out second meant he got the building to support him while she only had the sidewalk under her feet and not even a curl to fiddle with.

"Turns out," Eric said, finishing a story he was telling her about his last customer of the day, "he didn't realize he had the wrong power cord. Guy was trying to jam his roommate's adapter into his laptop. Took a damn drill to the thing."

"Did you say a drill?"

"Yup. Figured all he needed to do was make the opening bigger."

"He's lucky he didn't fry the whole motherboard."

"And that he had enough juice for me to transfer all his files since he doesn't own a backup drive and doesn't believe in the cloud."

"Meaning he doesn't believe it exists?"

"Oh no, he believes. And if you've got twenty minutes and nothing better to do I can tell you all the things he believes, like how it's an alien planet's way of infiltrating our minds."

"He really said that?"

"Nah, just doesn't understand how it works." Eric grinned, and something fluttered in Delia's stomach. "But my story's better, isn't it? Keeps things interesting, at least. 'Don't count the days, make the days count.'"

Delia stared at him.

"Smooth, Shaw." He hung his head, and some of the long brown strands casually swept across the top fell over his ear. "Real smooth, quoting your grandmother."

"No, I, uh, I like it." Her hand lifted toward her hair and she forced it down, somehow perching it on her hip and inciting a true battle over whether it looked or felt more awkward.

"Then you'll have to come to dinner, because she can't take two bites before she's spouting another one."

Delia inched her hand down her side. She'd never been so conscious of her body before and couldn't help wishing this preoccupation had struck earlier—like when she was dancing. How had she danced? How had she danced *like that*?

When Eric had begun talking to her at the edge of the dance floor, she'd been grateful for the darkness that hid her bright red face. But the volume made it hard to hear, so he suggested they go outside. The instant the cool air dried her sweaty forehead, it was like she'd come back from another world. To the Delia who would never set foot on a dance floor, let alone tango on one, in front of strangers, in front of her peers, her classmates. Eric.

Heat again rose in her cheeks, and she clutched the dress fabric between her fingers, willing the flush not to spread to her neck. She turned and looked down the block, comparing San Francisco to her memories of Chicago. She imagined the sheer number of streets lined with endless buildings, big and small, were indicative of any city. But the river she and her parents had walked along was missing, as were the trees. In their place were, as far as Delia could tell, deathtraps Lucy had called "hills." She'd been convinced the bus was going to topple over headfirst more than once before they pulled up to the club.

Even now, she couldn't see a distance greater than a couple of blocks before the steepness concealed what lay beyond.

"How's Lit going?" Eric asked.

Delia faced him. "It's still early, but we, uh, we think it's viable. Slack's helping us share ideas and links and keep track of questions, which is good since Lucy seems to have as many as the lines of code we'll ultimately need. For the prototype, it's just, well, the crowdsourcing aspect's new for me, but I'm making headway on the—" She stopped. "Sorry. You shouldn't let me do that."

"What?" Eric said.

"Ramble. You were just being nice, and I'm going on and on about details you couldn't possibly care about especially since you've got your own app you're working on, and how's that going anyway? And I'm not just asking to be nice, and, oh boy, I'm doing it again."

Eric's smirk meant Delia was definitely turning as red as the beets her dad grew every summer. The ones Delia wished she could taste now, even if—especially if—it meant watching Cassie eye them with suspicion no matter their form, including fried like potato chips.

"I *was* being nice," Eric said. "But I also care about the details."

"No one actually cares about the details."

"Were you at the same hackathon I was? Caring about the details is how we all got here." He pushed himself off the wall. "Still crazy to me sometimes that I'm actually here."

"I know. I go back and forth between what's crazier: that I'm here or that here actually exists." She rolled a rock under her sneaker—the one she'd glued the sole back onto with Lucy's surprisingly strong fake eyelash glue. "Silicon Valley. As mythical as—"

"Gumberoo School." When Delia didn't respond he said, "You know the series, right?"

"I know the name, but I'm not much of a fiction reader."

"This cannot be. Hanging with a girl who hasn't read the Gumberoo? Impossible!"

The way Eric's hazel eyes widened followed by a toss of his hair infused the flutter in Delia's stomach with the strength of a hummingbird.

"You know what else is impossible?" he said.

"What?" Delia hoped her voice was louder than the thrumming of her heart.

"That we're here in this amazing city and seeing nothing but the inside of a pretentious club and this one little street corner." He pulled out his phone, and Delia wondered if he was as relieved as she was to be able to break eye contact.

She and Eric talked all through their shifts and had been texting a lot too, mostly about how traitorous she felt to their beloved Python since Lucy had forced her into using Swift. Even Delia could admit their shared interest in coding and ValleyStart and aversion to pea milk lattes meant she might be slightly more interesting to Eric than the guy taking a drill to his laptop. They were friends. She liked him.

Except she might *like* like him.

"Okay." Eric looked up from his phone. "What do you say to some sightseeing?"

"Now?"

"No better time, as my grandma would say."

"But, I mean, it's just . . . can we?"

"Who's gonna stop us, Ryan Thompson?"

Delia's foot found that rock, and she pressed until she could feel the edge through the bottom of her shoe. She wanted to say she wasn't sure if they'd be breaking any ValleyStart rules and that she couldn't be tossed out of the program because her whole plan of helping her parents save their theater relied on her not just being in the program but excelling in the program. She wanted to say she'd never walked in a city without an adult's supervision and even if Eric was technically an adult because he was eighteen that wasn't the same thing and what if they got lost or missed the bus back or—

And then he took her hand.

And all she said was, "Okay."

Which she came to regret with . . . each . . . huff . . . and . . . puff . . . up . . . this . . . godforsaken . . . "hill."

This city needed a pulley system. With each street they climbed, Delia lost more and more feeling in her toes. Which maybe she could tolerate if Eric's long, soft fingers were still entwined with hers, but he'd only held on long enough to encourage her to start this trek up Mount Everest.

The sightseeing so far had mostly been of cement as Delia carefully watched her every step. Her occasional upward glances caught boarded storefronts that transitioned into empty storefronts and finally some actual storefronts. Though now closed, the shops sold things like fair-trade clothing and gourmet coffee and organic dog food—sometimes all in the same place. Scattered in between were a few restaurants with stark white tables, light fixtures that looked like artichokes, and plants cascading down from living walls. Most of it cool, all of it requiring more funds than she had to enjoy.

They approached the corner just as the traffic light turned red and Delia gave a silent thanks. "Maybe we should turn back?"

"Just a little farther." Eric's breaths were also labored, which made Delia feel better. "I promise it'll be worth it."

"Where are we going?"

"It's a surprise."

The light changed and the hand signal beckoned them forward. Though Eric had slowed his pace, Delia's thighs still screamed.

"You never said how your app's going," Delia said. "Did you settle on a name yet?"

"EatSafe," he said.

Eric's team was developing an app that tracked and rated restaurants on their ability to handle food allergies. They were hoping to incorporate a feature that facilitated easy communication between restaurants and patrons, since those cooking at home adapted recipes and used workarounds every day.

"EatSafe," Delia said. "That's good."

"Yeah?"

She nodded.

"Awesome—and thanks. Marty seems like he'll be great when it comes time for hustling, but he's a bit all over the place with his ideas. And Emma's cool, and I don't mean to rag or anything, but I'm not really sure of her skills. She knows HTML, and she's got some great sketch art she's put to music. She writes her own lyrics and everything, but even she said she's not really a designer."

One thing Delia didn't have to worry about was the skill of her teammates—she knew she was the weak link.

"Though her Pulse is going through the roof, so there's that. Gotta help us when it comes time to beta test."

"Will it?" Delia hadn't thought of that. None of her team was anywhere close to Crushing It, not even Lucy.

"I hope so. I really want this to work. Yelp's a great model for us, but ours has to go further, plus be safe for kids to use, because it's when they're on their own that they're most at risk."

"And the idea came from your sister?"

"Yeah, she's allergic to peanuts. Like even breathing in the dust can be a problem."

Delia remembered the bags of peanuts she didn't eat on the airplane and was glad she'd been too nervous to open them. "That must be hard."

"Her teachers are great about it, but she had a serious scare a couple of years ago. She was out with her friend's family, and she and the mom alerted the server. But the guy in the kitchen was a sub for the usual chef and didn't know what was in the sauces he was heating up. A tablespoon of peanut butter in a gallon of sauce. That's enough. If she didn't have her EpiPen . . ."

Eric's voice faltered at the end, and all Delia could think was if Cassie or her parents were in that situation, there was no way she'd be coding an app like Lit.

"So I'm here, and I'm doing my best for her, you know?" Delia nodded, and Eric continued. "My grandma was so proud when I showed her the acceptance email. She said, 'dreamers dream, doers do.'"

Delia smiled, but her mind clung to Eric's "doing my best"— the thing she was doing and realizing wasn't enough. She was dragging her team down, no matter what Lucy said. She had no hope of helping them with her Pulse ranking, and she was even failing at the code. Had she actually thought she could be some superstar and get a job out here? She should be home, *actually* helping her parents, not here. She was a little fish in this big pond and she knew it—everyone knew it. She was certain that she was the one everyone at ValleyStart was talking about.

She hadn't realized she'd increased her speed until a red

light stopped her and she saw that Eric was half a block behind her.

"Damn, Delia," he said. "Though what better way to finish than with a sprint." He pointed across the street. "We're here."

The light turned green, and once again he took her hand.

Soft and smooth like Lucy's comforter, which Delia had secretly napped under once—okay, twice. As they crossed the street, Delia seemed to let go of everything but the feel of his hand and . . . *Oh no, the street's not wide enough and don't let go and . . . he let go.*

They kept moving, but now through a park that seemed to appear out of nowhere in the middle of an area that had become increasingly residential, with three-story homes nestled in among more squat ones made of concrete. Though it was dark, Delia's fears of being alone in the city were less than she'd imagined, thanks to the abundance of streetlights, the groups of people walking along the paths, but, mostly, thanks to Eric.

The comfort of the grass and trees now mixed in gave the neighborhood a charm she'd have almost said was worth the climb. Then Eric stopped walking and turned around. She did the same.

"Oh, wow," Delia whispered.

Directly across from them was a row of tall Victorian houses with pitched roofs and scalloped trim across the front like loops of icing. Up a flight of stairs from the street, fairy-tale-like arched doorways adorned each house. Along the sidewalk stood short trees with cotton ball puffs of greenery atop a single, thin trunk. Lights glowed in some of the windows, casting yellow hues on the exteriors, each painted a different color, from baby blue to deep red to pink and more. And beyond the row of homes, brightly lit squares shined out of windows and from tops of skyscrapers soaring into the dark of the night, the skyline of the city stretching before them.

"That climb was so worth it." Delia stepped forward, as if she could get close enough to not just see what was before her but become a part of it.

Eric moved behind her, holding his phone in front of them both. The image on his screen was of the same houses in the daytime, and the rainbow of colors brightened the photo even more than the sun.

"Painted ladies, they're called," he said. "One of the must-see sights in the city."

"One of?" Delia said. "What could be better than this?"

Eric's hand brushed her shoulder as he pocketed his phone, and a spark of electricity suggested the answer to her question.

Just as she was about to turn to face him, a bus came roaring down the street, a voice calling from the window even louder than the roar of the engine.

"*A-a-nd*, there she is," Lucy called, waving her phone. "Looks like we found my friend."

THIRTEEN

FAST TRACK TO UNICORN STATUS • *Startups or individuals seen as so smart and on point that they're on their way to instant success; high rate of false positives*

THIS WAS LUCY'S WEEK.

Sure, she could handle some amount of code. She knew enough to be entry level (*okay, more than*) at most organizations. But *this* was her domain.

"Can anyone tell me three elements of a business plan?" Nishi asked.

Please.

Lucy's hand shot up. "Executive summary, business description, products and services, marketing strategy, management team, funding requirements, financial forecast."

Beside her, Lucy sensed Delia fidgeting. She caught her eye, and Delia mouthed, "market analysis." Lucy couldn't believe she forgot. She tipped her head to defer to Delia, but instead of giving the answer, Delia shrank lower in her seat.

Lucy shrugged and announced it herself.

"Spot on. Even if it was more than three," Nishi said.

"Aw, leave the little lamb alone, Ms. K," Gavin called from the back of the room. "Can't expect a pretty face and a head for numbers."

From beside Delia, Eric spun around. "In some cases, neither."

Gavin snorted. "See what happens, boys? A chick on your team makes you soft. Oh, well, not everywhere, right, Shaw?"

Emma sucked in a breath.

"You entitled piece of—" Fists balled, Eric shoved back his chair. Delia set her hand on his forearm, and he turned to her, sat back down, and clamped his mouth shut.

Well, would you look at that.

Nishi locked eyes with Gavin. "I won't tolerate this in my room, and neither will this program, Mr. Cox. You're not in high school anymore, and we don't operate on a warning system. If today's guest lecture didn't make this an excellent teaching moment, you'd be out the door already." His lips parted, and Nishi added, "And yes, I know who your father is. I turned down his funding offer for the second company I founded. I'm on my third, so that was probably an okay decision, wouldn't you say, Mr. Cox?"

Gavin crossed his arms against his chest.

"Now, benefits of crowdfunding versus those dear VCs like Mr. Cox Senior?"

Lucy's hand shot up.

"Anyone other than Lucy?"

No one spoke, and Lucy sat up straighter in her chair.
This was her week.

Lucy paused outside the entrance to the auditorium to check her Pulse.

Thudding. No movement. Even after all those likes on the club pic. And there was Emma.

Crushing It. Level 10. Up from her 7 at the club.
How is that possible?
She logged in to the Stanford portal. Nothing.
You've got to be kidding me.
The ding of an arriving text sent her into her messages.

ValleyStart: At the close of your second week, we assess
the strong and the weak, the tortoise and the hare, the
apps proceeding with vigor and care. Take a look, see
where you stand, then grab your code with both hands!
Lest you forget, Week 4 kicks off with the beta test!

The intensity of the program had ramped up these past few days, as teams focused on improving functionality before the deadline to submit their in-progress apps for review. Believing competition yielded better results, just as Nishi had said, ValleyStart planned to rank the apps. And the results were in.

Lucy squeezed her phone. Her team was tenth. Ten. Out of twenty.

What?

The middle of the pack. Average.

What? What?

Lucy was many things, but average was not one of them. She scanned the full list. Gavin's team was tied for first.

What? What? What?

No. *No, no, no.* They'd fix it. *She'd* fix it. This *was* going to be her week. She flipped her ringer to silent and dug her notebook and favorite polka-dotted pen out of her tote, desperately trying to ignore the *thud, thud, thud, thud* in her temples; it was like her heartbeat was mocking her.

She pressed her hand against the carved wood of the door leading into the auditorium, crinkling the edge of the A DISCUS-SION: WOMEN IN TECH sign attached to it.

A groan Lucy hated that she recognized came from behind her, and she gritted her teeth.

"*Women* in tech. And I have to go to this, why?" Gavin grumbled. "Luce, do me a favor and tell them about my big—"

"Mouth? Attitude? Chauvinistic tendencies? We all got it, Gavin, no worries." Lucy sped through the doorway, knowing there wouldn't be room enough for her, Gavin, and his ego when he checked his ranking.

She hurried down the gently sloped aisle, catching sight of Delia on the other side of the crescent-shaped room, next to Eric. Lucy waved, but Delia was talking with such excitement and intensity that she didn't even see. The girl was downright peppy. A state Lucy had yet to witness.

Maybe *this* was the problem. Eric and Delia were spending a lot of time together, had even coordinated their kiosk shifts, which Delia insisted was only so when things were slow, they could work on their programming together. Either Delia was that naïve or somehow thought Lucy was.

Yet all the time Delia was spending with Eric hadn't affected his team—it was fourth. Was Delia helping Eric so much that Lit was suffering or was he not helping her enough? Lucy fought the urge to wedge herself between them and instead made a note to talk to Delia about her "give-to-get" ratio.

She found Maddie up front and took the seat beside her. Before Lucy could speak, Maddie held up her hand. "I saw."

Lucy pushed through the clench in her jaw. "I've been canvassing my contacts. My editor at *Teen Vogue* knows a designer at Waze. I'll set up an interview. Should give us an edge."

"Okay," Maddie said.

Things had been strained between them since the club last week.

"Appreciate it," Maddie added. "And don't panic. We'll step it up."

But Maddie, to Lucy's surprise, had been trying. Well, the Maddie version of trying, which involved fewer eye rolls and an increased tolerance for Lucy's fashion advice.

And more work on Lit. She'd stayed up late twice in the past week, coordinating with Delia to ensure the larger design elements wouldn't increase load time. She'd presented three different options for the overall color scheme and, after Lucy steered them toward a darker, ultra-modern palette (*obviously*), had begun working on some of the more complex elements, like buttons.

She was good. Great. They all were. Which is why . . . tenth place?

No freaking way.

From somewhere above, partially hidden from the audience by the thick, ebony beams that traversed the ceiling, lights shined on the stage. This auditorium was used for lectures like this as well as performances—and Demo Day. Lucy imagined herself looking out at the creamy white walls, her voice echoing off the wood panel insets, her feet flat against the floor. She pictured herself holding the microphone, just as Nishi was doing as she walked to the center of the stage.

Lucy uncapped her pen, determined not to miss a thing.

"Everyone, please take a seat. We're about to get started." The coral scarf around Nishi's neck hung perfectly, and yet her hand kept lifting to fiddle with the ends. Nishi Kapoor didn't fiddle.

"Yes, well, okay, then." Nishi cleared her throat. "As an administrator of ValleyStart for the past three years, I can honestly say that we have never had a more impressive panel of speakers." *Fiddle, fiddle, fiddle.* "Our guests have generously donated their time to be here, so let's be considerate listeners and thoughtful in our questions."

She introduced two women, a CEO of her own social media company, who was black and in her early forties, and the other, a principal engineer at a software business, who was white and in her early thirties. And then Nishi yanked so hard on that scarf, it almost dropped to the floor. She adjusted it back into place and cleared her throat again. "And our final guest is a woman who has seen Silicon Valley become Silicon Valley. She has been here long enough to know which garage origin stories are fact and which are myth."

Gavin's "old," barely masked by his fake cough, made Maddie spin around and growl, "Shut it, dumbass."

"Now, please welcome Abigail Katz."

Abigail Katz? Lucy's quick reflexes plastered a smile on her face though her stomach flipped with nerves.

"Wait," Maddie whispered. "Is that your mom?"

An efficient nod.

"Why didn't you tell us?"

Why didn't she tell me?

"Surprises are more fun, right?" Lucy clasped her hands together in her lap, feeling more and more eyes on her as her classmates began to make the connection.

Had her mom even for one singular second considered what this would be like for her? A nasal snort escaped. That would require her remembering where Lucy was, and the only thing her mom had an elephant-like brain for was where Lucy wasn't.

"Any news from Stanford?"

Nishi finished reading the bios of the first two women and settled her eyes on Lucy's mom. "Ms. Katz—"

Her mom's nod mirrored Lucy's. "Abigail."

"Of course, yes, Abigail." Nishi's voice wavered, and her hand rose to her scarf. "Okay, I'm going to deviate here for a moment, because this is my first time meeting Ms. Katz—Abigail. And the little girl inside me clearly won't be satisfied unless I do this. So, here goes." She looked at the audience, her eyes meeting Lucy's and holding her gaze, before facing Abigail. "While it wasn't all that long ago when I could have been out there, in the audience, tech years aren't like normal years. Things move fast, even faster now. I grew up with a mom who stayed home wrangling my three brothers and me, while my dad was a professor of history. Like many families, including Indian American ones like mine, family and education were the priorities. But for me that didn't include anything related to computer science. Then, one day, I was at my cousins' house when my uncle came through the door with one of the first iMacs, and I just wanted to wrap my arms around it and hug it."

Abigail laughed, a sound strangely unfamiliar to Lucy. "It was adorable."

"And blue! Computers weren't blue."

"Bondi Blue. Gosh, I can still picture it perfectly."

Nishi motioned to the audience. "Phones down, everyone. You can google it after." She faced Lucy's mom again. "My uncle was so proud of acquiring one. We all followed him as he walked through the house, ending in my cousin Sanjay's room. They turned it on, and I barely saw the screen flicker when my mind started racing, wondering how it worked."

"Because you could see inside. Genius idea. Made computers approachable."

"Coveted. Changed everything. Especially for me."

"What did you do first?"

"That day? Nothing. My cousin Nadia and I were shooed out of the room. We weren't allowed to touch it. I remember going home and falling into my mother's arms, crying. She couldn't understand what I was so upset about. But the next day, when I came home from school, an empty iMac box was on the dining room table. I searched the house, all my brothers' rooms, the basement, even my parents' room—and we didn't go in my parents' bedroom. But I couldn't find it anywhere. When I sat down defeated at the kitchen counter, my father was smirking. He asked if I'd checked everywhere, and I said I had. He then said I may as well go start my homework. I trudged into my room and screamed."

"He put it in your room."

Nishi beamed. "My mother and I were on it so much, my dad had to buy a second for the boys."

Abigail nodded and clasped her hands in her lap. "Thank you for sharing that, Nishi. Especially since, while a personal story, I believe it's representative of the tenuous relationship between girls and computer science then as well as now." Abigail shifted to better see the audience, her lecture face firmly in place. "Fifty-one percent of professional occupations in the workforce in this country are held by women. That number drops to twenty-five percent when it comes to computing."

Nishi nodded to Abigail as she added, "And only twenty percent of Fortune 500 CIO positions are held by women. You are one of that twenty percent. And it all started with that iMac, which I didn't learn until years later. You were on the team."

Mom worked at Apple? Mom worked with Steve Jobs?

"For a short time. Intense doesn't describe it. But it was a dedication that I internalized. I knew when I was in the position I am now, I'd be grateful."

"When, not if," Nishi said.

Abigail smiled. "Always."

Nishi went on to her first question, and Lucy simply stared at her mother.

"*She'll never be me,*" Lucy once heard her mother say to

her father. Was this why? Why Lucy's achievements were never enough? How could she compare to the woman who helped launch the product that made Apple Apple? And how had Lucy never known this?

Lucy shifted in her seat, wanting to be anywhere but here.

Maddie leaned in and whispered, "Are you okay?"

Lucy shook her head and blurted out, "Sometimes I feel like I don't even know her."

"Or don't want to," Maddie said quietly.

A lump swelled in Lucy's throat, and she found herself reaching for Maddie's hand. Maddie patted Lucy's quickly before tucking both her hands under her thighs.

It wasn't much, but it was enough.

"Women in tech," Nishi started. "It won't come as news that the gender imbalance is huge. Even in our own incubator, despite our efforts to recruit more female participants. Studies estimate that women make up only a quarter of tech employees and eleven percent or less of executives. And those numbers plummet when we narrow them for women of color. My question for you all is why?"

The engineer answered first. "Anyone can found a tech company, right? Anyone can change the world with a single great idea. Drop out of college and still become a billionaire. Facebook is the model, right? The genius comes from within, so that means tech companies can hire based not on education or background but on merit—a meritocracy, that's what Silicon Valley is purported to be. But the truth is that's a myth. Because studies have shown that we are biased to think that this important tech trait—

this innate genius—is a male trait. A white, male trait. As this plays out, it indicates that you don't necessarily have to be biased against someone, you can be biased for someone, meaning reinforcing what you see around you, which is predominately white and male. That's who gets hired."

The CEO chimed in. "Tech is all about the future, with meditation rooms and juice bars and collaborative spaces, and you think it's all very liberal, but it's also very male and young. Which unfortunately can and does lead to some of the worst frat boy stereotypes you can imagine. And when the behavior comes from the guy leading the company . . . well, employees follow their leaders in terms of what's accepted."

Lucy whispered to Maddie, "This isn't a discussion, it's venting."

Maddie's brow furrowed. "Shouldn't you be interested in this?"

Lucy shrugged. It all seemed so . . . stereotypical.

Onstage, Nishi probed further. "I know what I've seen. But I'd like you to share any experiences you feel comfortable with."

The CEO started. "There are the things most people would call small. Things like being the only female in the room at the same level as everyone else, or higher, and being asked to take notes. Or leading a presentation and having potential investors direct all the questions to the male at the table."

"Then there are the big things," the engineer said. "Not being given credit for our ideas, being the most reliable programmer on the team but consistently overlooked for promotions. Things that affect our career and earning ability."

Nishi nodded to encourage Abigail, but her face was stoic as she sat back, listening.

The CEO looked at her fellow panelists. When no one else spoke, she began. "And if you want us to go there, which I absolutely think we should precisely because of the gender imbalance here before us . . . Imagine being told the substance of your pitch is irrelevant because you're hot. Being asked to show pictures from your beach vacation—and not of the sunsets. Being sent a link to a sexy costumes site at Halloween. Being told that your very hiring, especially as a woman of color, was due to a lowering of the bar. And then, of course, there's the 'handsy' factor—in elevators after a night at a retreat, under the table during dinner, back rubs at a meeting."

The engineer snorted. "Just once I'd like to see a male colleague try to deftly brush off a coworker's wandering hands and then be told he's not being a team player."

The CEO gave a commiserating nod. "Skills in diplomacy are a prerequisite for women in tech. Startups in particular are a tough place, with investors dangling money in exchange for drinks and dinners, holding hot tub parties—as if most women want to pitch their company in a string bikini—and, well . . . the point is once we get in the door, there are impediments to staying and succeeding. Women leave tech at twice the rate of men. We need to be open about why. It's the only way it's going to change."

"And is it?" Nishi asked.

"Diversity training and commitments for hiring are happening. But I believe real change will come from us. Programming was seen as unglamorous and rote when Silicon Valley was emerging in the forties and fifties, and so it was relegated to women. Once its profitability was revealed, the guys came and suddenly coding became a male realm. If as a woman you look around at your team and no one looks like you, you may feel like you don't belong in that job. And that's a problem not just for the women who want to be in this space, but for the women who use the products we create. Apple's first health app could track sodium intake but not menstruation. Phones with ever-growing screen sizes may be welcomed by men, but their usability for women who have smaller hands decreases with each centimeter gained. We can no longer fit our phones in our pockets or type or take photos with one hand unless we choose an older model that, interestingly, comes without all the bells and whistles. One of the newest, most advanced artificial hearts fits more than eighty percent of men but only twenty percent of women. Would this happen if more women were on these development teams? We need to find out. We need more women and women of color to start their own companies, like you've done, Nishi."

The conversation shifted to education, Abigail Katz took the lead, and Lucy tuned out.

After the discussion ended, Lucy sprang out of her seat. She had her weekly mentor meeting with Ryan Thompson and she wouldn't be late. But Delia and Maddie flanked her, expecting to meet her mother. She was stuck.

Abigail stepped down from the stage with Nishi, while the other panelists spoke with a few students, including Emma. It was the first time Lucy had seen Emma engaged in anything other than her guitar.

Lucy's mother had donned a pair of black kitten heels for the event, as if she needed the extra height. Both of Lucy's parents were tall, as was everyone in this grouping, save for Delia, though even she had a few inches on Lucy.

Lucy straightened her spine as awkward introductions were made. Awkward because Lucy refused to be the one making them. She listened, waiting for an indication from her mom that this invitation was last minute, a fill-in for someone else perhaps, but it didn't come.

Fine, it's all fine.

Nishi was the one to explain the premise behind their app, saying how impressed she was with the ideas they'd come up with so far.

Not impressed enough to rank us higher than tenth though, right?

While Delia delved into the technical portion and the bug she'd been unable to fix, Abigail listened with interest, and Lucy tapped her Pick Me! Purple nails against her notebook.

Maddie shot her a look, and Lucy stopped, instead saying, "I've got a meeting." She made sure to catch her mother's gaze. "With Ryan Thompson."

"Of course," her mom said. "Important things await us all. But a moment, Lucy, before you go?"

Lucy just managed to stop her eye roll and stepped to the side with Maddie and Delia.

Her mother thanked Nishi, who seemed to go in for a hug—twice. Lucy could have warned her that her mother was an expert at deflecting. Nishi's awe perplexed Lucy. Nishi was way more successful. Apple was a feather for sure, even Lucy could admit that, but it must have been a nanosecond in her mom's career.

"CIO?" Delia said with the same excitement she'd displayed with Eric. "And the iMac team? Your mom's amazing, Lucy."

"Uh-huh." Shocked by the hot prick behind her eyes, she pulled in her lower lip and averted her eyes—but not before Maddie's face softened.

"Come on, Delia," Maddie said. "I've been thinking about upping the amount of white space and could use your help."

"Ooh, great, Eric and I were just talking about that," Delia said, reaching for the round, gold-rimmed sunglasses Lucy had helped her pick out at one of the kiosks in the student center (*not bad for something on the clearance rack*). Maddie pulled her aviators down from her head, and the two started toward the exit, leaving Lucy alone, waiting for her mother.

After saying goodbye to Nishi, Abigail placed her leather briefcase in her hand and approached her daughter. "Walk with me?"

Resentment simmered at the surface, but Lucy moved her feet.

"Sounds as though things are going well," her mom said.

No one mentioned tenth, then?

"I'm glad I decided to accept this invitation to speak, otherwise I would have no idea what you're up to."

"And that's my fault? You're the tech guru, but I'm pretty sure cell phones can now make as well as receive calls."

"Interesting."

"What?"

"I interpreted our last encounter in my office to mean you wanted space. I gave it."

Right, and what's your excuse for the eighteen years before that?

"Your team seems competent. Are you getting along?"

"What is this about, Mom? We don't do chitchat."

Her mother sighed. "Believe what you want, Lucy, but I am encouraged to hear how well things are going. However—"

"And there it is! Do I win a prize?"

"However," Abigail said, unfazed, "before the panel Nishi mentioned she chaperoned a field trip to San Francisco—"

"Oh, God, Mom, *please*. And what? Did she say I was dancing? In a club?" Lucy fake gasped. "I was having fun, which I deserve, because Lit *is* going well, so, so well, because I'm working my ass off to make sure it does. I'll never understand why you can't trust me even the tiniest bit. You don't think I'll ever be you? Good, because I don't want to be."

Lucy quickened her pace, as if the pounding in her feet would help her ignore the tremble in her hands. She thought about canceling, but she didn't have a way to get in touch with Ryan and she wouldn't be a no-show.

She followed the path to the student center and breezed through the glass door. Under the arched entryway to the study hall, site of the hackathon and now ValleyStart's collective workspace, she steeled herself with an image of sharing her Demo Day win with Stanford. So long as she stayed on the wait list, she was fine, everything was fine, *fine, fine, fine.*

But nothing was. And now even the table in the corner dedicated for mentor meetings was empty. Had Ryan forgotten?

The lecture had only just ended, and already teams were tethering themselves back to tables and chairs, walling themselves off with laptop screens, immersing themselves in their work. Maybe ValleyStart was right about the rankings spurring competition.

Lucy scanned the tables, hoping to see Maddie and Delia. Instead all she saw was everyone training their eyes on her. They probably thought she didn't belong here—that she was only here because of her mom.

Light-headed from her brisk walk and realizing she hadn't eaten anything all day, she stared down as many of her competitors as she could as she headed to the snack center in search of spicy tuna rolls. It was there that she found Ryan.

He and Gavin were facing each other, both clasping a Red Bull sideways in one hand. Standing beside them were Gavin's teammates. On the count of three, each teammate plunged a knife into a Red Bull, and Ryan and Gavin flipped the cans upright, shoved their lips to the hole, and popped the tops. Shotgunning. Ryan Thompson was shotgunning Red Bulls with Gavin Cox.

This was supposed to be her week. But since leaving class this morning it was like she'd entered an alternate universe.

She spun on her heels only to hear, "Lucy? You're here! Finally got my excuse to ditch these losers."

The slap of a high five and Ryan's resulting laughter made Lucy feel like the only loser in the room was her.

She gave Ryan a hesitant smile and started toward the mentor table. She was halfway there when Ryan caught up to her, placing a hand on her elbow. She turned, trying to hide her disappointment at seeing Ryan and Gavin so in sync. But Gavin was tied for first, after all, so why shouldn't they be?

"This way," Ryan said. He led her to a door at the back of the study hall space, opening it and ushering her inside first. "Don't need those brogrammers hearing your killer ideas."

A metal desk with a chair on either side was crowded

by floor-to-ceiling shelves stocked with buckets, mops, and industrial-sized jugs of soap. That they were in the janitorial office/closet couldn't have mattered less to Lucy.

Because . . . "Did you say 'killer ideas'?"

"Totally." Ryan smirked before holding his finger to his lips. "But don't tell the others I said so. Can't appear to be having favorites, can I?"

Lucy's mind returned to the night of the club and the way he and Emma were talking. But Delia hadn't mentioned anything about Eric's team getting any tips. Maybe Emma had been telling the truth when she'd said they weren't talking about the program.

Good.

Lucy sat up straighter and read from her notebook, where she kept track of everything Lit and life related. She updated Ryan on her team's progress. The intensity of his eyes and the bobbing of his head as she spoke signaled how impressed he was.

Halfway through their session, she let herself take in what was happening: not only was she having a meeting with Ryan Thompson, but Ryan Thompson thought her ideas were killer. *Ryan. Thompson.*

She held back her grin but couldn't stop the bubbly feeling inside. This was what ValleyStart was about. This was not just going to be her week but her summer. And she wasn't going to let anyone or anything take it from her.

So their app was ranked tenth. Tenth meant nothing. Tenth was fine, great even. *Strategize.* Tenth was how they'd sneak past the other teams.

"Good stuff, this is all good stuff, Lucy." Ryan sat back and raked his hand through the front of his hair without disturbing a strand. "I'm debating something here. Give me a sec."

"Uh, okay, sure." Lucy's pen hovered over her notebook. Ryan closed his eyes and breathed deeply. Lucy waited. And waited. Eventually, she thought he'd fallen asleep. Should she wake him or leave quietly? Just as she was about to slide off her chair, his eyes popped open.

"Okay, I'm doing it. But this has to remain between us. Mentors are under strict rules to encourage, answer general questions, and point our students to ways to solve problems on their own. One thing we are forbidden to do is offer guidance for what the judges will be looking for on Demo Day." Ryan's eyes widened. "Oops. They should know I live to break the rules. So, Lucy, this one's for you: it's not so much what you present but how you look doing it."

Lucy's pen slid across the page. *Was he giving her fashion advice?* "Uh, look? You mean—"

"Confident. Commanding. Owning the room. You must exude it. Believe me, I know from personal experience how much it can mask. Not that your app won't be there, for I firmly believe it will be, but if it's not . . . Own. It. Combined with a Pulse of 7 or higher to demonstrate your influence, and, well, I think I may just be sitting across from my next Pulse-tern."

Pulse-tern. Pulse intern. That might just be the cutest thing Lucy had ever heard. And yet, she was only a 4. Racing was 7.

She licked her bottom lip, resisting the urge to suck it in. "Since you bring it up, I've been hoping to get a chance to ask, and I hope it's okay that I ask, but I just—"

"Lucy, Lucy, Lucy. I saw you at the club. Shy isn't in your lexicon. Out with it. Consider me a Reddit AMA."

"Well, the thing is, I seem to be having trouble with my Pulse. I'm doing all the right things, at least I think I am, but I can't seem to get any traction."

"And you're looking for a tip?"

Lucy nodded.

"It's easy, Lucy. You want to raise your Pulse, just be seen with me."

FOURTEEN

SOCIAL PROOF • *When investors fund a company based on the prominence of existing investors, i.e., keeping up with the Joneses*

MADDIE COULDN'T STOP THINKING about the time her little brother became best friends with a turkey. As tall as baseball bats, wild turkeys roamed the streets of Cambridge like it was a ten-acre farm. Loitering outside the subway station, pecking the glass of the bike shop, meandering down the brick sidewalks in her neighborhood. Where, one day, Danny saw a male with its red triple chin (Maddie later learned it was called a "wattle") and reddish-brown fan of tail feathers and declared him George, his new best friend, there to play with him after school.

Smiling and steering Danny away from the giant creature, which gave her newfound respect for turkey farmers, Maddie had explained that this was a wild animal and therefore unpredictable. Not a month earlier a wild turkey had chased a girl and her dog down a Cambridge street. Maddie had made Danny promise to never approach one.

"Sure," he'd said.

The next day, she'd found him trying to feed a turkey popcorn. She asked why he'd broken his promise.

"Because that wasn't a wild turkey, it was George."

Maddie thought Lucy had the same inability to distinguish Ryan Thompson from an ass.

And like those turkeys, Silicon Valley asses ran rampant thanks to a lack of natural predators.

"I'm not signing up for Pulse," Maddie said, "and I'm not trekking to Sausalito to crash some Pulse loser fest."

"Pulse-a-palooza," Lucy corrected.

"Uh-huh. For 10s. What makes you think you can even get in?"

Lucy was checking her phone.

"Lucy?"

"Yes?"

"What makes you think you can get in?"

"Just something Ryan said the other day."

"Seriously? Is this why you didn't want an incubator boyfriend? He's twice your age."

"He's not, and it's not like that."

"Then what's it like?"

"He's helping us." Lucy held up her phone, open to the Valley-Start daily message:

ValleyStart: As we begin Week 3, next week's beta test should be all you can see. For if you excel, it's no secret we tell, that your Demo Day may just be child's play!

"Things are moving fast," Lucy said. "And Ryan's giving us advice for Demo Day and—"

"That's cheating!" Maddie said. "He's not allowed to do that. I know you like to push the envelope, but I never thought you'd actually break the rules." She stared past Lucy at the redwood tree in the center of the *S* on Lucy's pennant—the school had a tree for a mascot, seriously? "Don't you think Stanford frowns upon cheaters?"

The color drained from Lucy's cheeks. "I didn't trust you with that so you could throw it in my face."

Maddie hadn't meant to; it just came out. But if that was what it took to make Lucy see reason—

"Besides," Lucy said, pushing her shoulders back and trying to grow taller. "I'm not cheating. A tip or two isn't cheating. You're just jealous that he's giving them to me and not you."

"Not in this lifetime," Maddie sniped, immediately wishing she could take back the words that could have and did come out of her mother's mouth. "Whatever. Do what you want, Lucy, but I'm not having any part of it."

Maddie grabbed her bag, plucked her canvas sneakers from the pink basket, and left before Lucy could try to convince her to stay, to hear her out. But Maddie wasn't Delia, easily convinced to straighten her hair or have a Demo Day prep session while on a three-mile run.

Shoving open the door to the dorms, Maddie stepped outside, where the warmth of the sun hit her face—again. Every damn day. She tossed her head back, glaring at the constant blue sky and cheery puffs of pure white clouds, wanting to scream.

Rain, one day. Just one day. One day where the sky swallowed all color, painting everything gunmetal gray with murky clouds that hung low enough to touch and humidity that clung to your arm hairs . . . and maybe then she wouldn't feel the three thousand miles so much.

Aimlessly, Maddie passed by summer students lying on towels on the lawn in front of the student center, reading everything from *War and Peace* to the Gumberoo series. She trudged down the spoke leading to the ValleyStart headquarters but turned around when she heard two teams having a heated debate on Objective-C versus Swift. She kept going past the rounded gym and park at the far edge of campus. All the while, she had to keep unclenching her fists.

She hadn't been this upset since her parents charged into the living room two years ago, shouting loud enough to wake Danny and scare away the only friend Maddie had dared to make since she was twelve. The girl was newly transferred and into art, and Maddie was lonely. But she'd have never tried, never invited her over, had her parents not sat in that same living room with her at the family meeting she'd called and promised they were going to do better, be better—better parents, better spouses, better people.

They'd lied. The yelling about infidelities started out marriage-related, transitioned into the agency, and back again, a loop Maddie didn't care to figure out.

She'd walked her almost new friend out the back door and read *From the Mixed-Up Files of Mrs. Basil E. Frankweiler* to Danny, all the while fighting the burn behind her eyes at the memory of her parents reading the book—her favorite at his age—to her.

Though she'd stopped drawing book covers years ago, that night she drew one for Danny, featuring the scene he loved most: the kids bathing in the fountain, scooping up coins.

Thoughts of Danny led her to the tech day camp and to Sadie.

"And she lives!" Sadie cried when Maddie walked in the door.

Some of the weight she'd been carrying immediately lifted. "Watch it, squirt, or I won't open up my bag of designer tricks."

"Speaking of . . ." Sadie eyed Maddie's messenger bag. "Might want to think of being humane and leave that for the rats to nest in full-time. Carrying that will make you tumble from 10 as fast as Emma Santos."

Maddie plunked her bag right in Sadie's line of sight. "Emma Santos? From ValleyStart?"

"One and the same."

"How do you know Emma?"

"I don't. But I've been following her on Pulse." Sadie made a face. "No thanks to you. Had to get the roster list myself."

Maddie's eyebrow lifted. "Did you hack into the system?"

"I could have, surely." Sadie tossed her red hair. "But I just asked Ms. Kapoor. She said it's on the website. Who would have thought to look there?"

"Who'd need to?" Maddie said.

"Anyone with a *Pulse*." Sadie smirked. "If only they had an incubator for kids my age. It's not right, I tell ya. Because, I mean, ValleyStart and Ryan Thompson and Pulse—it's like all the best Gumberoo books combined." Her smile faded and she spoke softly. "You know I almost met her?"

"Who?"

"Esmé Theot," she said with awe that Maddie was glad to hear wasn't reserved just for Pulse and Ryan Thompson. "My mom promised to take me to her signing in San Francisco a couple months back. We were gonna have dinner after—and not at one of those places with a lame kids' menu."

"What happened?"

"Avocados."

"Avocados? I didn't know you could get food poisoning from avocados."

"No, not food poisoning. Runaway avocados. Some truck headed for Napa Valley got in an accident. No one was hurt, but the road was covered. Took so long to clean up that we missed the signing. Mom was really upset, saying she should've taken the whole day off, not just half. She took off the next day though, and we watched all the movies together with a big bowl of guacamole."

Maddie could barely remember a time when her mom would have done that for her. She knew she'd never done it for Danny.

As Sadie settled back into the coding program, Maddie helped, getting lost in it, enjoying the break from Lucy and the incubator and all things Pulse. When the counselors announced it was time to start wrapping up, she was surprised at how much time had gone by.

Sadie grabbed her phone to text her brother about pickup and then dove back into Pulse.

Maddie groaned.

"Right?" Sadie said. "So you see?" She spun her phone around. "Emma's down to a 4! She was a 10 a couple of days ago."

"Okay."

"Don't you get it? A 10 doesn't fall to a 4 in a matter of days unless they've been, like, arrested or something—and not even then depending on what they were arrested for."

"That's disturbing."

"I know, I mean, what could she have done?"

"That's not what I meant—"

Sadie talked over Maddie. "She's on hiatus everywhere—every social media account. Like 'later, alligator.' And look what she wrote on her Pulse profile: 'Can there be a Pulse without a heart? Discuss.' Weird, right? She was supposed to perform at Pulse-a-palooza, but if she's not a 10 . . . Crush it or be crushed."

Maddie stood and slung her bag over her shoulder. "Forget it, and while you're at it, maybe forget Pulse too? Just for a bit?"

She laughed. "You're funny. Standup, really, Maddie, totally gotta go for it." An incoming text made Sadie sigh. "My brother's gonna be ten more minutes."

"I'll wait with you," Maddie said.

"Yeah?"

"Why not? I've got a thing for porcupines."

"If that's true . . ." Sadie dug something out of her knapsack and held it out to Maddie. "We're doing a presentation thing, so if you want to see my porcupine dance and meet my mom and brother or anything, you can."

Maddie accepted the flyer. "I'll be there."

"Yeah?"

"Yeah." She reached for her sketchbook, flipping past the pages of potential Lit icons she'd been working on—a flickering candle for "romantic," a coffin for "dead," a sardine popping out of a can for "packed." Paper was the medium she'd started drawing with, and she still tended to brainstorm that way. Though she'd often transition to her tablet, there was something about the feel of the light texture against her skin that released her creativity.

She focused on Sadie. "Now, let's sketch some mockups of moves for our spiky friend."

When Maddie returned to the dorms, she saw Delia and Eric sitting on the edge of the fountain in the center of the quad. He looked upset, and Maddie wasn't sure if she was intruding, but Delia waved her over.

"Did you hear?" she asked.

"Hear what?" Maddie said.

"Emma left the program."

"She's gone?" Maddie realized she hadn't seen Emma since the talk on women in tech a couple of days ago.

Eric nodded. "She missed classes and our prep sessions the past two days. Said she was sick. And then, today, she texted from Stinson. Family emergency and she's out."

"Stinson? Is that a hospital?"

"Beach. North of San Fran. Summer home. Her dad's a big Google guy." He stuffed his hands in his pockets. "Sure hope everything's okay."

"How bad could it be to spend the rest of your summer on a beach?" Maddie said.

Delia looked horrified. "We don't know what's wrong, which is awful for Emma."

"Of course, I didn't . . ." Maddie was frustrated at how poorly her East Coast sarcasm translated. "Awful, sure."

"And now Eric's team's down to two," Delia said. "That's not fair. There should be a provision in the rules—"

"It's okay, really," Eric said. "She was always more into her guitar than the program anyway. I mean, I wish she didn't have to go, but we'll make it work." His words were full of more confidence than his voice, but still he smiled, for Delia's benefit, Maddie couldn't help thinking.

Then Maddie remembered what Sadie said about Emma's Pulse rating falling quickly. Because she left ValleyStart? Because she had a family emergency and took a social media break?

Pulse was exactly what Maddie thought it was. A complete and utter load of crap.

FIFTEEN

MVP • *Minimum viable product: the most basic version of a product that functions just enough to prove that the concept works; often used in beta testing*

THE GOOD NEWS WAS Delia had figured out what was breaking her code. The bad news was she was baffled by a half dozen more "snags," as Lucy called them. Snags were for her fancy sweaters and tights, not code, but Lucy continued to brush them off as if Delia could wave a magic wand and make Lit ready for the upcoming beta test, which was now mentioned in every daily ValleyStart message. Like that morning's:

> **ValleyStart:** In the alphabet of Greek, it is the second letter. But for what you seek, it is the trendsetter. In less than a week, the beta will test your mettle!

Delia sighed. It wasn't like she didn't wish for that wand—she did, every day and every night as she lay awake, playing games on Delia's Den, hoping for a eureka moment. She'd created nearly a dozen games over the years. The first, not-so-loosely based on *The Shining,* where the caretaker of an English manor battled ghosts and zombies, was the most straightforward but great for problem solving. From the Smudge Fudge Factory to the Sassy Cassie Studio, all the games she'd created were inspired by something in her life. The later, more complex ones featured people—women, specifically, female coders.

She'd almost given up being one, and she would have if it hadn't been for her mom. Delia was in sixth grade when an "incident" she still didn't know the details of occurred, and the principal found himself in need of a tutorial on the difference between "reply" and "reply all." While explaining it to him in his office after school, a call came in from the mother of the twins—a boy and a girl—in her class. She had a flat tire and would be late. Delia said her dad, who was coming to pick her up, could drive them home.

The twins were waiting by the front entrance. As Delia headed down the hall, she heard them arguing about their separate birthday parties scheduled for the upcoming weekend.

"You take her," the boy had said.

"No, you. It's your turn. I took her last year," the girl said.

"Dull Delia will ruin everything," the boy said. "She'll win all the points at the arcade with her stupid robot brain and everyone will be mad at me."

The girl countered, "She'll flinch every time the manicurist touches her toes, and besides, do you really want me to have to see her toes? Forget about the sundaes after."

Delia's shoulders rounded and her backpack, perched on one shoulder, fell to the ground. They heard. They turned. They saw her. She saw them. No one uttered a word.

And then her dad arrived, and they all drove home together. The only words spoken were by him. He told them of the new way he'd discovered to make a two-legged chair that would be so much lighter to move onstage and yet still could sustain the weight of three people.

At home, Delia sat on the floor in her dad's workshop in the garage, smiling as he demonstrated the chair and put her, him, and Smudge in at once. And then she cried into her pillow until she fell asleep.

On Saturday morning, she feigned a stomachache and sequestered herself in her room, playing on her computer. But all the while the boy's "stupid robot brain" looped through Delia's mind. She shut her computer and unplugged the cords from the back.

Her mom found her in the closet, burying the monitor under the stuffed animals she no longer played with.

"Delia?" her mom had said. "I'm all for improvisation, but there's not even an outlet in there."

"I don't need one," she'd said. "I'm done with it. All of it."

"If it no longer interests you, I'm all for finding something that does." Her mom sat on the floor in front of the closet. "But first, I'd like to understand these." She brushed her thumb across Delia's face, drying her tears.

Delia couldn't hold it in anymore and told her what the twins had said, but she didn't stop there. She told her about the looks the boys gave her when she joined the mathlete team, the ones that turned into glares when they realized she knew more than they did; she told her about the sleepovers Cassie was invited to that only turned into invitations for her when Cassie intervened. She told her that it didn't really matter—that Cassie and her mom and dad and Smudge were enough.

Her mother listened, dried her own tears, and then pulled her daughter into an embrace. Delia curled into her, breathing in her lilac perfume, shielded by her light blonde hair, desperately trying to fit into the space of her mother's lap, but she couldn't. Not anymore. She pushed herself back, so tired of not fitting in.

"I wish I were like you and Dad," Delia said. "Everyone loves you, the way you sing, how you make them feel. Numbers don't make anyone feel anything."

But numbers didn't care if you "fit in" either, Delia had thought, and she'd begun to reconsider relegating her computer to the stuffed animal graveyard.

Her mom took both of Delia's hands in hers. "I'm going to tell you something that my mother told me the day I insisted on wearing my Cinderella costume to school and came home in tears, searching for a pair of scissors. She said, 'Some people are just plain mean, but it's up to them to change, not you. Never stop being Cinderella, Claire.'"

Delia shrugged an understanding.

"I know." Her mom gave a soft smile. "I thought it was corny too."

"But did it help?"

"Some. Especially when I realized that if I were going to be someone for the rest of my life, it was going to be Princess Leia. Wore that costume until it shredded on its own. Hair buns and all."

Delia laughed. "I hope there are pictures."

"Sure are, I was a ham from birth." She squeezed Delia's hands. "And you, you were exactly this from birth. You started reprogramming the clocks after daylight savings time when you were four. I was so proud. I still am. But you need to be too."

And that day, with Delia by her side, her mom researched Delia's version of Princess Leia.

The end result was an expansion of the games on Delia's Den, ones inspired by real-life women who made breakthroughs in computer science, like Ada Lovelace, whose writings from the 1840s led to her being credited as the first computer programmer.

Delia's eyes drifted to the Ada quotation taped to the bottom of her bunk—the one that used to live on the corkboard above her desk at home.

Imagination is the Discovering Faculty, preeminently. It is that which penetrates into the unseen worlds around us, the worlds of Science.

The power of imagination.

Maybe for Ada.

Delia wished she could channel Ada's brilliance now as she listened to Lucy talk about the problems with Lit. She'd followed every protocol she knew and more she'd had to learn. And still she couldn't break through. The problem wasn't in the user interface or the code layer but had something to do with the database. It was responding slower and slower with each request, even when the requests were the same. She was missing something. She just had no idea what or how to find it.

Which was what kept her up at night—worrying and reading. She'd been poring over tutorials online and reading books she'd borrowed from the library, her photographic memory cataloging it all. Because she needed to stand out as a developer. And mastering the database side was how she'd do it. Being able to troubleshoot server issues and laggy SQL without a data admin's help—that would make Delia the unicorn Lucy already thought she was.

"Once we have our data from the beta test, we'll be able to finalize this slide," Lucy said, clicking through the Demo Day presentation she'd been putting together. "And you'll narrate along with the others that really dig into the code." She tapped the screen on her laptop.

"What? You mean me? Onstage?" Hives prickled beneath Delia's skin just at the thought. No one ever said anything about her having a speaking role. "Isn't Demo Day your thing?"

"Nothing about this is just my thing—"

Maddie snorted.

"We boom or bust together, ladies," Lucy continued, ignoring Maddie and what seemed to Delia the ever-present tension between the two. "And I for one need a big, bad . . ." She mimed an explosion with her hands. "An earth-shattering one."

Delia nodded, her pulse still in overdrive. "Me too."

"Uh-huh, sure," Maddie said, her stylus sweeping against her tablet as she doodled what looked like horns coming off a close resemblance to Ryan Thompson. "You both want this, so I'm in. Even though Pulse is a complete and utter crock."

"Don't start," Lucy said. "We know how you feel about Pulse."

"It's not just Pulse, it's Emma. Sadie said she was supposed to play at that stupid Pulse-a-palooza, and I checked and she's not on the lineup anymore. Even the entertainment needs to be Crushing It."

"So? Since when is Emma your BFF?"

Delia cut in. "And what about Eric? He's the one who lost a third of his team. And he needs this."

Lucy eyed her. "Not more than us, Delia. I know you guys are a thing—"

"We're not." Because Delia didn't date. (*And because Eric hadn't asked her out on one.*)

"But we have to come first."

Delia sank deeper into her plastic-coated mattress as Lucy returned to the slideshow. She knew her team came first, and she wanted to win, it was just that she wanted Eric to win too.

Lucy had designed the Lit beta test, enlisting several on-campus spots and a couple off-campus venues as their test subjects, to be rated in real time. And that was the biggest "snag"—the ratings weren't averaging fast enough. The more ratings Delia put into the app at once, the slower it worked. A lag might not be noticeable on a small scale like the beta test, but once the app hit a fully functioning market, the delay would become monumental. The judges could extrapolate as easily as Delia had. They had to fix it—Delia had to fix it.

She ran through all the possible solutions again—a recitation she'd committed to memory same as when she helped her mother rehearse. Only Delia's lines were a jumble of letters and numbers that she couldn't untangle.

A buzz interrupted. A text from Cassie. Delia picked up her phone and shot up so fast, she hit her head on the bottom of the upper bunk.

"Please tell me that's not the right time," she said, holding up her phone.

"Can't," Maddie said. "That's the right time."

Lucy placed her hands on her hips. "Painted Ladies, huh? No significance whatsoever to that being your background picture since you and Eric aren't a thing."

The mattress squeaked as Delia shoved herself off of it. She grabbed her kiosk nametag from her suitcase/nightstand and searched under her bed for her backpack. Maddie's stuff made its way into every available crevice on their side of the room, with balled-up sketches in the corners, sneakers dangling off the bedpost, and chargers dropping down into Delia's sheets. As Delia slid her backpack across the floor, it brought with it a Red Sox hat filled with pretzels.

"What are you doing?" from Lucy.

"Hey, I've been looking for that," from Maddie.

"How long has it been missing?" Lucy asked.

Maddie paused.

"Don't tell me," Lucy said, snatching the hat and dumping the pretzels in the trash.

Delia edged past her. "Guys, I'm really sorry, but I've got work."

"Now?" Lucy said. "But we planned this all week. You said you'd take tonight off."

Maddie tucked the hat low on her head. "May be boring as hell, but even I know we have to be on the same page before the beta test."

"Because," Lucy said, "if we come out on top, we have an eighty-five percent chance of winning Demo Day. *Eighty-five*, Delia."

"I know. And I want to stay, I do," Delia said. "But no one could cover for me. And I'm already late."

Lucy twiddled her fingers. "Tell loverboy we said hi."

"That's not why I'm going."

"*Right*," Lucy said.

Her phone buzzed again. This time, it was Eric.

Where are you? I'm doing my best to cover, but between the "unwrapping" and the "setting" and the fire department on speed dial, I'm afraid I'm missing something.

A grin snuck up on her, and even Maddie sounded pissed when she peered over Delia's shoulder and looked at her phone. "Eric, really? Not cool, Delia. I'm here, trying to win, for you."

Delia's smile vanished, and she stood frozen in the doorway. Her phone lit up again, this time with a phone call. Cassie. But Cassie never called—Delia wasn't even entirely convinced her friend knew her phone, despite its name, had the capability.

She shrugged an apology and answered on her way down the hall. "Is everything all right?"

"Dee Dee, it's me."

"I know."

"Good, we can cut to it then. My bus is about to leave."

"Cut to what? Wait, why are you getting on a bus? Shouldn't you be at the theater?"

"Not tonight. And not tomorrow. And not because I'm all sorts of psychic like you, but because your parents already said they canceled tomorrow night's show too."

"They what?" Delia's parents were the definition of "the show must go on." Her mom spent the first two hours of her labor with Delia onstage as Juliet. A testament to her dedication to her craft even if those last scenes had her lying on a slab, pretending to be dead.

"When was the last time you talked to them?" Cassie asked.

Delia thought. "A few days ago. I've left messages, but I know how busy they get during the season, and they're the worst texters."

"Listen, Dee Dee, Chicago's calling me, and unlike your parents, who you know I love—sometimes more than my own— I'm answering. So, you didn't hear this from me, but the theater's in a major nosedive, like snatch those oxygen masks and say a dozen Hail Marys. And now someone's swooping in, offering a parachute. I think they just might jump ship."

Delia closed her eyes. "Cassie, I live for your mixed metaphors, but I'm already late for work and . . . and these are my parents. The theater's everything to them. It's their life."

Our life.

"Some vultures want to turn your parents' theater into a multiplex. Offering big bucks."

"A movie theater?" Delia couldn't remember the last movie she'd watched with her parents. "But how . . ."

"Because, Dee Dee, the theater's not everything to them. You are."

A pickup drone-flying tournament had just ended when Delia arrived at the Hot Pocket kiosk. An actual line awaited her. She nodded to Eric, who had an equal number of customers holding drones with clipped propellers and broken camera lenses despite his being a computer repair station. Numb, she was grateful to have something rote to do. If she paused for too long, the scream simmering at the base of her throat threatened to bubble out.

Selling the theater. *Selling the theater.*

Cassie would never mess with Delia, especially about this, and still some part of Delia clung to the hope that her best friend was pulling a prank.

After her line dwindled and Eric was embroiled in what sounded like a tedious explanation of the forces of gravity, Delia called her parents. This time they answered.

"Dad, put Mom on the line too."

"I'm here, doll," her mother said. "We've been dying to hear how it's going. Sorry we missed you, but you know the summer season—"

"Are we really doing this?"

Her dad sighed. "Cassie."

"No. No sighing over Cassie telling me what you both should have." Delia took a breath. "It's not like . . . done, is it?"

"Not yet," he said. "But we're close."

"You can't!" Delia cried, and Eric looked her way.

"Delia," her mom said. "We know it's upsetting—it's hard for us too."

Her dad took over. "But sometimes life tosses a ball your way, and you just have to catch it."

"But I'm here," Delia said.

"And we're so very proud of you," her mom said.

"No, I mean, I'm here, I'm doing okay." She swallowed and touched her necklace. "Great. Doing great." Her parents had done so much to keep her dreams alive. And she was here to do the same for them. She just needed time. More time. "So you don't have to worry about me for college or—"

"Honey, listen," her mom said. "We'll talk about this when you get home. All performances suffer when you're distracted. It's why we've restrained ourselves from calling as much as we'd like."

"Twice a day," her dad joked.

"He really means three," her mom said, and Delia could imagine the smile lighting up her face. "Now, don't you worry about us. Just break a hard drive, okay?"

"And a keyboard," her dad said. "Or two."

"But—" Delia started.

"We love you! Bye-bye!" in simulcast and then *click*.

And right there, in front of the Hot Pocket microwave, Delia screamed.

Eric set two plates down on the bench outside the student center. A turkey, bean, tomatillo salsa on the right, a vegan cashew cheese on the left.

"Preference?" he asked.

"Cashew cheese."

He cocked his head.

Delia gave a soft smile. "Kind of addicting." She broke off a piece and rested it on his plate.

He tasted it. "Not bad. Though must be a real pain in the ass to make."

"Why?"

"Just think, milking those tiny cashew udders."

Delia paused, then broke out in laughter.

"And my work here is done," Eric said, a smile brightening the green flecks in his eyes. "Unless you want to tell me what that was about. Can't grow up with a grandmother who talks as fast as a coyote steals a backyard poodle and not be a good listener."

"That's not true."

"'Fraid so. Both."

"Remind me not to move to Denver and buy a poodle."

"Okay, but only on the second part of that sentence."

And that's all it took. Delia talked. Told Eric everything, about her parents, about her clearly foolhardy plan to win ValleyStart, get a job, and ease her parents' money worries. About her fears of getting that job, of living here, so far from home, but also of her desire to live here, so close to what she'd always been good at. Or was before she got here.

"No wonder you're screaming," he said. "I'm barely holding it in just listening to you. You're putting so much damn pressure on yourself. Comparing yourself to everyone else here."

"Because they have so much more, better schools and computers and programs they learned on."

"I didn't. And I'm here. Same as you. You know how much of an accomplishment it is to just be here, don't you?"

She nodded. "But I—I want more."

"Good. So do I."

"But I'm afraid to want more. Because what if . . ."

What if I let everyone down?

"What if you don't get it? You try harder." He trailed his hand through his hair, and pieces of it flopped over his eye. He tossed them back.

"Which women in tech have to do, right? Especially women of color, like Emma. Is that why she left?"

He paused before shaking his head. "I think her heart wasn't in it. Music's her thing. She only came here because her dad wanted her to. Which is cool. I get it."

"Your parents wanted you to come?"

"Not exactly." He bent over, resting his elbows on his knees. "My mom died when I was in fifth grade."

Delia reached for a curl. "I didn't know."

He looked back at her, smiling weakly. "It's okay, really."

"I'm sorry, Eric."

He nodded a thanks. "Here's the thing: my mom didn't exactly want me to come but she's the reason I'm here." He faced forward and rubbed his hands together. "See, after, my little sister had nightmares. For weeks. She slept in my room and would wake up each night like it suddenly hit her. 'We don't have a mom anymore,' she said one time. Shit, I was ten, and I didn't know what to say, so I said something like, 'I'll be such a good big brother that you won't even notice one day.' My grandma had moved in by then and my sister's crying must have woken her. She came in and said, 'And I'll be such a good grandma, that you'll notice every day your mom is gone, but some of those days, you won't notice quite as much.' And she was right." He ran his hand through his hair again. "Always felt guilty for saying that. Like a betrayal to my mom for what I said to my sister and to my grandma for her hearing it—like I didn't appreciate what she gave up to come help raise us."

"Eric, that's not . . . You didn't mean it like that. You were just trying to help."

"I know." His eyes lowered. "It's just . . . my grandma shouldn't still be clocking in every day on the pediatrics floor and my dad shouldn't be working two jobs, but they are. A couple of years ago, I looked up top-paying jobs straight out of college, and developer was one of them."

"That's why you started coding?"

"Yeah, didn't realize how much I'd dig it though. So I'm here for them, all of them, but I'm here for me. You need to be here for *you*, Delia. And you need to know that that's okay. It's the only way to push through the rest of it. Trust me."

He stood and reached for her wrist. "Come up here."

It wasn't until Eric's skin was against hers that she realized she was shaking. He pulled her close and cupped his hand around both of hers.

"I wasn't always able to talk about this stuff as easily," he said. "What helped get me here, well, I'll spare you the ones that didn't work, but my grandma sorted through her mental Rolodex until she landed on a sort of mantra that helped me keep my emotions in check." Eric stepped back and released her hands. "Now, I'm going to say it before I ask you to repeat it, so you can get your snickering out—"

"I won't laugh at you, Eric."

"Not me, this. And you better. Because if you don't, you're gonna be too close to my grandma for me to be having the thoughts I'm starting to have about you."

Delia flushed everywhere, but when she raised her head and caught Eric's small, tentative smile, she didn't mind.

"Here goes," he said. "'Breaths raise you from the depths.' *And* cue laughter."

Delia did, a little, because it was corny. But one thing Delia had learned from her dad was to embrace the corny.

Eric placed his hands on his stomach and signaled for her to do the same on hers. "Next time you want to scream and not scare away stoned summer students, breathe in, and think, 'Breaths raise you from the depths.'"

"Breaths raise you from the depths," she said.

And they did.

But so did Eric.

SIXTEEN

GOLDEN RULE • *The investor with the gold makes the rules*

LUCY SHUT HER LAPTOP and swiveled her head between Maddie and Delia. The bags under Delia's eyes were barely noticeable now that she'd allowed Lucy to apply a heavy dose of concealer, the same tactic Lucy had been employing all week to mask her own.

For days, Delia had been head down into the wee hours, immersing herself in all things database, and Lucy, feeling bad about the other night, had stayed up right alongside her. Maddie was there too; she'd stepped it up, just like she'd promised. The end result . . .

Lit looked fabulous.

Lit sounded fabulous.

Lit was fabulous.

Because Lit worked.

Worked!

Lit would kick Gavin Cox's ass.

And impress Ryan's.

Ryan.

Not his ass.

Though maybe that too.

"Enough," Lucy said, placing her laptop beside her *Teen Vogue* mug, a welcome gift from her editor after her first article. Eau de locker room in the ValleyStart headquarters made Lucy insist they work in the dorm room. She'd set a whiteboard on the desk in front of the windows with a running to-do list, had switched out the harsh white fluorescents for warmer bulbs, and played ambient music emitting "problem solving" brainwaves day and night.

While Delia and Maddie had been making sure the code and user interface worked together seamlessly, Lucy had been putting the pieces in place for their beta test, which due to its reliance on crowdsourcing presented more of a challenge in the testing phase than some of the other team projects. A challenge, but one Lucy had eighty-five reasons to master. Prevailing in the beta test gave them an eighty-five percent chance of winning Demo Day, which meant Lucy was that much closer to Pulse and to Stanford.

"That's enough." Lucy pushed her laptop to the far corner of the desk. "You know my motto."

"Quality and quantity," Maddie said.

"Style leads to substance," Delia said.

"Always detox after a full moon, not before," Maddie said.

"Never wear plaid," Delia said.

Lucy couldn't resist a grin. "You forgot the best one: work

hard, play hard. We've been doing so much of the former, we deserve the latter. Who's in?"

While Maddie and Delia went pillaging for snacks, Lucy logged in to the ValleyStart forum.

The daily message sat at the top:

ValleyStart: Week 3, Day 3. Smack dab in the middle, but don't dismiss this as drivel. We're now halfway, so there's no time to play. For we are ALREADY halfway!

Lucy snorted, copied the text, and added: "Let's prove them wrong. Party in the common room. Tonight." She then selected ValleyStart IDs and sent out her message.

The thumbs-ups and smiley faces were trickling in as Maddie returned, carrying an aluminum foil tower in her hands.

The smell permeated the room. "They were serving zucchini-flour pancakes for dinner?" Lucy asked.

"Nope."

"Then how did you—?"

"We know what we are but know not what we may be," Delia said as she passed through the open door holding plates and utensils.

A crinkle settled in between Lucy's eyes, and she scooted closer to Maddie. "She's been working too hard, hasn't she?" she whispered.

Maddie peeled back the foil, and steam swirled in the air. "Shakespeare, apparently. Girl working the pizza line's trying out for a play. Delia ran lines with her in exchange for these." Maddie bit into a pancake, and her eyes widened. She fanned her mouth and mumbled, "Can't feel my tongue, but worth it."

Lucy looked at Delia. "Shakespeare? But you said you didn't want to be onstage on Demo Day."

"*Hamlet*, specifically," Delia said. "And I'm never onstage, I just rehearse with my mom. I kinda have a good memory."

"How long has your mom been acting?" Lucy grabbed one of the extra dorm-issued sheets from the closet and set it on the floor to protect the shag rug.

Delia's face lit up. "Forever." She sat cross-legged on the sheet, untied her sneakers, and dropped them in the shoe basket. "She's been everywhere."

Maddie plopped down in front of Delia's suitcase that served as her nightstand. "So this was hers?"

"Yeah. Guess she'll need it back if they actually sell the theater."

"What? But you said they love the theater."

"They do. But this place . . . college . . . it's expensive. They think it's what I want, but . . ." Delia shook her head. "Sorry, you guys don't care about this."

"I do." Maddie bugged her eyes at Lucy, who'd yet to sit down. "*We* do, right, Lucy?"

"Of course, of course. It's just . . ." She eyed the pancakes suspiciously. She hadn't yet acquired a taste for them.

"Oh I, forgot." Maddie reached into her messenger bag and pulled out kale chips, spicy tuna rolls, and a bottle of iced coffee. "Got these for you."

Her favorites. *Maddie knew?* Lucy tried to cover her surprise as she nodded her thanks and gently sat down on the sandpaper sheet beside Delia. "You miss it?"

"The theater?" Delia nodded. "It's weird to not be there for the summer. I wish you guys could see it. See her." She paused before grabbing her phone. She swiped open her photos, showing them her mom onstage, pointing out her dad in some, Cassie in others, with Delia always behind the lens.

"I never even minded that we didn't get cable until I was twelve," Delia said. "Watching my mom was better than anything else. I slept backstage so much, I used to cry anytime I actually had to go to sleep in my room."

"And now they're selling it," Maddie said. "Sucks."

Commiserating nods made the rounds. They ate silently with Lucy trying to think of something to lighten the mood. Finally she said, "But you know who doesn't suck?" She rested her eyes on Delia. "Eric Shaw."

Delia's skin instantly turned red, and she snatched a pancake, which she mostly used to shield her face.

"Oh, come on," Lucy said. "We've seen you together."

From behind the pancake, Delia said, "We're friends."

"Uh-huh," Maddie said.

"We are. We all are."

"Maybe." Lucy fluttered her eyelashes. "But it's only when he looks at you that he turns into a total emoji with hearts where those pretty eyes should be."

Delia barely got out her mumbled denial before she was saved by a double rap on the door.

"Waiting on you, Katz!"

"Ah, perfect timing!" Lucy hopped up and rubbed the backs of her legs, which she expected to be oozing blood from the scratchy sheet. "Eric's probably here already." She reached for her lipstick.

"Eric?" Delia said. "Why?"

"Because I invited him. As you know, we're *halfway* to Demo Day." She smirked. "And you've smelled headquarters. When personal hygiene takes a back seat, it's definitely time to let off some steam." Lucy noted the shock on their faces. Like the night they went to the club, they just needed a little extra encouragement. "Just an intimate gathering." She opened the door and waved them out. "Common room. Let's go see who's here."

Lucy led the way and waited inside the doorway, assessing the intimate number that had shown up.

"There are at least thirty people here," Delia said.

"I know, but it's early." Lucy patted her arm. "Don't worry. Things will pick up after the keg arrives."

"Keg?" Delia glanced at Maddie. "I meant, there are *at least* thirty. I thought it was going to be just us, maybe Eric and Marty—"

"They'll be here, don't worry."

"But what if . . . what if we don't want to be?" Maddie said.

Lucy was taken aback.

Maddie gestured to the table being set up for beer pong. "We were having fun without all this. Weren't you?"

"I . . ." Lucy, for the first time she could remember, was at a loss for words. She thought of the past four years, when her social life revolved around parties, group dates to the movies, road trips to the beach with "friends"—half of whom weren't even contacts in her phone. And then she thought of her mom, who had no friends except those in her book club, whose meetings she missed half the time. "I guess I was."

And she wanted to keep having fun with Delia and Maddie. She opened the door to start corralling people out, but a massive keg blocked the exit. Gavin and one of his teammates hauled it into the room.

"And the party's here! Put away your knitting needles, ladies!" Gavin high-fived half a dozen male hands before turning to Lucy, Maddie, and Delia. "Oh, sorry, and girls."

"Sexist ass," Maddie said.

Lucy ducked as sleeves of red Solo cups flew around the room. Most of their incubator would be here. How would it look if they weren't? After *she* invited everyone? What if they missed something about Demo Day?

Socialize.

"Five minutes," she said. "Ten, tops. Then we go."

Delia looked to Maddie before they both nodded in agreement.

Perfect.

Someone tapped the keg, and Gavin commandeered it—doling out cups and downing a full one himself. After filling another, he jumped on top of the coffee table. He motioned for the music to be lowered and raised his cup in the air. "A toast to our host, Miss Lucy Katz. A perfect ten, in every way . . . including her app."

Soft, awkward laughs rolled into bigger ones, and Maddie clenched her fists.

"Oh, wait, sorry, my mistake, our little Lucy happens to only be a Pulse 4." He frowned. "Despite her private meetings with Ryan Thompson."

Jealous, really, Gavin?

And of what? Her being with Ryan or the other way around?

"But, dudes, her Pulse may not be a ten, but the rest of her sure is—trust me."

A gasp escaped before Lucy could stop it.

Gavin began grinding the air, and while Lucy couldn't move, Maddie did. She rushed forward and rammed her foot into the coffee table. Gavin toppled off, saved from face-planting by one of his teammates.

Line not crossed, Gavin, line obliterated.

Lucy strode up to him, opened her palm, and was about to slap him when Delia caught her.

"No uninvited physical contact, remember?" she said of the clause they'd signed as part of their acceptance into the program.

Gavin winked. "I won't tell if you do, Luce." His breath stunk of booze—deeper, harder stuff than the beer he'd consumed.

"What's wrong with you?" Lucy said.

"Apparently what's wrong is that a tie for first isn't actually first, at least according to my old man."

"Your father's an ass," Lucy said. "But this, well, congratulations on finally sinking lower than him."

They stood still, Lucy waiting for Gavin to respond. They weren't ever really a thing, but they also weren't nothing. The Gavin she'd held in her arms as his voice trembled wasn't this Gavin. She thought she was a good judge of character, but the truth was she didn't know which Gavin was the true Gavin—and feared the answer was both.

A sharp knock made Lucy turn around. The door swung open and in strode Ryan Thompson. The music stopped, Solo cups disappeared behind backs, and Lucy's heart pounded. Her mom's voice echoed in her head—the words not mattering; all that mattered was the tone she'd be using if Lucy appeared back on their doorstep, kicked out of ValleyStart. It'd be the same tone she'd used when she found out Lucy was wait-listed.

"So this is where my minions are," Ryan said. "But right now, I only need one. Lucy, would you mind?"

He crossed back into the hallway, holding the door open for her. She swallowed and stepped forward. By her second step, she wasn't alone. Delia was on one side of her and Maddie the other.

Lucy hadn't had a lump in her throat this big since she'd opened the Stanford email. "I'll be fine," she whispered, but they remained by her side until she reached the doorway.

"It was all my idea," Lucy said when Ryan had shut the door behind them. "No one else's."

"You don't think I know that?" Ryan's flip-flops clicked as he moved closer to her. "You are one hundred percent Lit and Lit is one hundred percent you. Couldn't have come from anyone else's pretty little head. Which is what I wanted to talk to you about."

"You . . . my . . . what?"

"You being the face of Lit, literally." He raised an eyebrow. "Though I think this discussion might go better with a beverage. I'm parched."

"Uh, sure, we've got some LaCroix—"

"Zuckerberg swill?" He screwed up his lips. "Yeah, I'll pass on the bubble gum–flavored seltzer financed by that poseur." He relaxed his tight shoulders. "But I wouldn't say no to something stronger. . . ."

Relief washed over Lucy, and she agreed to meet Ryan on the balcony at the end of the hall. Adrenaline still coursing through her, she ducked inside the common room and filled two Solo cups with beer from the tap. From across the room, Maddie caught her eye and lifted a hand in the air as if to ask what's going on. Lucy gave her a reassuring nod and hurried back to Ryan.

"Sorry to crash the party," Ryan said after taking a long swig.

"It's not a party."

"Just a figure of speech. I didn't *actually* see a party. A party I'd have to report," he said with a wink.

"Of course, no parties anywhere. God, this place is so dull," Lucy joked. She lifted her cup and sipped, hoping the alcohol combined with the spa-like sound of the trickling fountain down below would calm the jittery nerves that had crept up.

Ryan laughed. "You really are something, aren't you?" He tapped his cup, looking at her. He then whipped his phone out of his back pocket, and before Lucy knew what was happening, he had his arm around her waist, said "Whoops, sorry, bad angle," and slid his hand up her side as he made his way to his ultimate destination—her shoulder. "There, that's better. Now say, 'Got a Pulse!'"

He snapped a picture, and Lucy wasn't even sure she'd smiled, it'd all happened so fast, including the feel of his arm against her.

She sipped her beer and let a smile through. Because Ryan Thompson had basically hugged her.

He kept his arm around her as he played with the dozens of

heart backgrounds he explained he'd had commissioned for his exclusive use before he settled on one and showed it to her for approval. She nodded even though she wasn't sure what she was nodding to. By the time he'd posted it online, tagging her, she realized she hadn't told him what her Pulse handle was.

"This doesn't get your Pulse moving, nothing will." He lifted his arm from her shoulder and said, "Now, tell me, how it's going with Lit?"

As Lucy snuck down the hall to retrieve round three, she slipped into her room to change her shoes.

Ryan Thompson was tall.

And liked to talk. A lot. Mostly about himself. But that was okay. Because he was *Ryan Thompson*. Though she had a crick in her neck from looking up.

She slid her feet into her highest heels, kept her head down as she smuggled two new beers out of the common room, and returned to the balcony.

Ryan waved to her excitedly. "Anyone can live . . ." He dangled his phone in front of her face.

She almost dropped the drinks. He grabbed one from her, and she traded it for his phone. "But I've got a Pulse!"

Thumping. She was Thumping!

She didn't realize she was dancing in place until Ryan joined her.

"See?" he said. "Told you I could give you a boost." He pushed his cup into hers. "Cheers!"

Lucy bumped back before drinking half her beer in one gulp. She was well on her way to intoxicated, half from the beer, half from Pulse, and half from Ryan.

Wait . . .

Ryan tilted his beer toward her. "Keep this up, you'll be Crushing It by Demo Day, and we'll be fighting off VCs."

"VCs?" she asked. "You really think we could get actual funding?" She shook her head to clear it. She wanted to savor every moment of this, remember it, to tell Delia and Maddie, word for word.

"You, maybe. Me, definitely. I'm thinking a merger may be in our future. Might be time to take our little Pulse-Lit to market."

Pulse-Lit. Lucy snarfed, and beer tickled her nose. And then his words hit her. "Wait, you're serious?"

"As serious as a red screen of death," he said. "Dinner first, though?"

Lucy was desperately trying not to wipe her nose with the back of her hand. "What?"

"A business dinner? To discuss? On the down low, of course. Because . . ."

"You can't appear to have favorites. Even if you do."

"Even if I do."

"Pulse-Lit!" she cried, raising her beer in the air. She started laughing so hard, she pitched forward in her heels, toward the balcony railing.

Ryan swooped an arm around her waist. "I've got you."

Lucy clutched his hand, steadying herself, grateful. Her

head was swimming, and she knew she needed to go to bed. She stepped back, away from the railing, and Ryan, instead of letting go, pulled her toward him. Against him.

Lucy froze.

And then, down the hall, through the glass window of the door to the balcony, Maddie stared at her.

"Thank you," Lucy said with a soft pat on his hand.

Slowly he released her.

"So, Lucy, do you like Thai?"

SEVENTEEN

SNIFF TEST • *A rapid evaluation of a product or circumstance to see if it's legit*

SHE SHOULDN'T HAVE DONE it.

But she did.

She clicked.

And then Maddie cursed under her breath—a string of Irish slang and Chinese she'd learned from her parents.

The site for the virtual reality game startup had gone live that morning. The site *she* should have built—the one she would have built if her "friend" hadn't stolen the job right out from under her. Though the site looked as though she *had* built it, integrating every single one of her ideas. From the broken grid layout to the scrolling game animations, every facet of her proposal was alive on her screen.

Not as smooth as she'd have made them, but enough to satisfy the client.

Cheaters weren't supposed to prosper.

Tell that to the ten grand weighing down her "friend's" bank account instead of hers.

Maddie reached for her phone to text Lucy, who'd left while she and Delia were still sleeping. The conversation Lucy's drunken state had staved off last night needed to happen. Maddie stroked her four-leaf clover, hoping for an explanation that didn't make her regret staying on Lucy's team.

Before she could send her text, her phone rang. Though the number was unfamiliar, the *New Hampshire* underneath made her scramble to answer, spitting out a hello even before the phone reached her ear.

"Maddie Li?" a woman's voice said. "Danny Li's sister?"

"Yes, is something wrong?" Panic gripped her. "Is he hurt?"

"I'm sorry to alarm you. No, he's perfectly healthy."

The woman identified herself as Kerin Labbott, the camp's assistant director. "We called your mother first, and she directed us to you. Because Danny is, well, he's refusing to leave his cabin. He won't say why. It's quite unusual for him—he's such an active participant that his cabin counselor has to corral him back in at lights out."

"Let me talk to him," Maddie said, her pulse still quick, the tentacles of panic not yet released.

Maddie heard the creak of a door and then Kerin explaining who she had on the phone.

"Mads?" Danny said.

He sounded stuffed up. Like he had a cold. Or had been crying.

"Hey, kid, how those fireflies treating ya?" Maddie said breezily.

Silence and then a simple, nasal "I miss you."

A vise squeezed Maddie's heart. "I miss you too, Danny. So much."

"I want to go home. When you go home. When will you be home?"

"Soon," Maddie said, though she still had more than a couple of weeks left at ValleyStart. "But what's wrong? Emojis don't lie. From the ones you've been sending, you seemed the definition of a happy camper."

"Nothing. I just don't like it here anymore."

"Why? Did someone say something? Or do something?"

Silence.

"Danny, you can tell me." Maddie paused. "Please tell me . . ."

"They took my socks. They won't give them back."

His special socks—the ones he lived in until the smell made Maddie's eyes water and she begged him to let her wash them. The socks Mom and Dad bought him, together, at the opening of the Gumberoo theme park.

"I'll talk to Kerin. We'll get them back, okay? I promise."

Danny still didn't respond, and Maddie hugged her arms against her chest, wishing it was her brother she was holding.

"Danny, is there something else? Do you know why they took your socks? Did they need a wash—"

"No! I washed them on my feet in the lake like every day."

"Okay, but there has to be a reason."

"They . . . This one kid said I was a liar. But I'm not a liar."

"I know you're not, bud."

"I told everyone I knew Esmé Theot, and he called me a liar. I told them Esmé Theot read the last chapter of the first Gumberoo to me as a bedtime story, and he called me a liar. So . . ."

"So what, Danny?"

"I put a snake in his bed."

"Danny!"

"A garter snake—won't hurt him!"

"Danny, it's not right that he took something from you, but you were very wrong to put a snake in his bed." Part of her was glad Danny was standing up for himself, but she didn't want him to do it this way, like her parents would.

On her laptop screen in front of her, the available games on the VR website automatically showed a small screen of the game-play in the corner, so users could preview what the game looked like while being played. That really was one of her better ideas. Taken from her, and what did she do? She left the forum. She said nothing. She did nothing. She . . . she just let him.

She didn't want Danny to follow in her footsteps either. "Listen, Danny, kids can be mean. Say stuff and do stuff that's not nice or right, but you need to tell the counselor, not put snakes in their beds. That only makes it worse. Do you understand? You can't sink to their level. Because you have better ways to get back at them."

"Yeah, like what?"

"Like proving you were right. Hold on." Maddie swiped open the photo album on her phone and searched. She chose two images, both of Danny with his wide, crooked grin beside Esmé Theot in their house—the "Li Family" sign above their mantel clearly in the background. At the time she signed with Maddie's parents' fledgling agency, Esmé technically lived in Boston, but she was at Maddie's house so often it was like she lived with them. The publishing world was new to all of them, and they learned it together. "Check your messages. And show that kid who Danny Li is."

After talking with the camp director, Maddie hung up and texted her mother:

Get your son more Gumberoo socks.

She pulled her laptop toward her and punched in the graphic design forum site, scanning the threads. She found the one she knew would be there, a congratulations on the gaming site going live. It had always been a supportive group—they'd cheered her when she'd gotten into design school. She scrolled through the congratulations thread, taking in the confetti and champagne, but the anger that normally bubbled up was replaced with something else. She seized on the feelings of empowerment building and added her own comment to the thread: "Congrats! Encouraged to see how well you incorporated all my ideas. Next time, though, ask first."

In her profile settings, she turned the notifications back on, eager to see the responses.

A text popped up from her mom: *What size? I'll have my assistant send them.*

No, not your assistant, you. With a note. FROM YOU. SIGNED BY YOU.

She thought of Sadie.

And send a second pair here, along with a signed copy
of the series.

The full series, every single book.

Maddie closed her texts and logged in to the ValleyStart portal. The private messages section was alight with news of the party
and how "RT" showed up. "RT"—like if word leaked no one would
be able to crack the code. She scrolled back, noticing a posting on
the Pulse-a-palooza thread. Someone had asked if Emma could
get them in since she was one of the 10s playing. The last comment
read: "No dice on entry. RIP Crushing It Emma Santos. She's a
peon like the rest of us now. Comatose."

Comatose? Hadn't Sadie said she was a 4? Now she was a 1?
Maddie thought back to what Sadie had said about how unusual
it was for a 10 to fall so fast. Maddie had been so sick of Pulse and
Ryan Thompson that she hadn't wondered why. Until now.

By the time Lucy came back, Maddie was hyped up on cashew
cheese Hot Pockets and iced coffee left over from the party in the
common room.

"Look," Maddie said, shoving her phone in Lucy's hand and
forcing her to drop her shopping bags.

"Maddie, can I get in the room first?"

"You're in, now look."

Lucy looked. "YouTube. You really are getting the hang of this newfangled thing they call social media, aren't you?"

"Emma's on it."

"Along with ninety percent of the world. And I'm starting to get a complex, here, Maddie. You're more obsessed with a departed team member than your own."

"It's just that her following's pretty decent. Same as on Snapchat and Instagram and even Facebook. Her fan page has a crap-ton of likes."

"From creepy old dudes, most likely."

"Including Ryan Thompson."

"Ryan's not creepy."

"Is that what you learned last night?"

"We were just talking."

"What was that you said to Delia? 'Just talking doesn't walk you to your door'?" Maddie joked.

"He didn't."

"Close enough." Maddie eyed Lucy. "I saw you together."

Lucy moved to her side of the room and delved into one of her shopping bags. "I fell. I was in my monster heels and I tripped. Lucky he was there, otherwise I'd have gone headfirst into the quad."

"You didn't look like you were falling."

"Because he stopped me."

"If he stopped me like that, I'd report him," Maddie said.

Lucy dropped the black dress in her hands and spun around. "For saving you from, oh, I don't know, certain death?"

"For putting his hands where they shouldn't be. If you were doing more than 'just talking' then it'd actually be better. But since you weren't . . ."

"We weren't."

"You should mention it to Nishi then."

"Maddie, it was nothing. I was drinking. Three beers. I had *three* beers."

"So?"

"So stumbling's entirely my own fault."

"The stumbling, but the catching . . ."

"Maddie, it was my stumble, my catch, and my call. I sent out the message about the party. If anyone finds out . . . I can't lose this. I'm so close." Lucy reached into her purse, took a deep breath, and pushed her own phone into Maddie's line of sight. "I'm Racing. Seven, Maddie, I'm a 7. Just in time for the beta test. Do you have any idea what this means? For Lit? For us? And we have Ryan Thompson to thank."

Maddie forced a smile, except all she could picture was Emma Santos saying the same thing. Right before she went from Crushing It to Comatose.

As Lucy tried on what looked like an entirely new wardrobe, Maddie opened the Pulse app and signed up for an account.

EIGHTEEN

SWEAT EQUITY • *The equity or ownership stake gained in a startup due to its founders' hard work and perseverance*

IN ALL THE YEARS Delia had been coding—creating the theater website, adding the online ticketing system, expanding Delia's Den to include the likes of Grace Hopper and Mary Jackson—she'd never had pain in her wrists. And yet a single night where a Frisbee tournament, a skateboarding competition, and a "hottest tech gadgets of the year" convention collided threatened to sideline her. Could one possibly get carpal tunnel from jabbing buttons on a microwave?

Though it was almost midnight, light filtered out from under nearly all the doors as Delia made her way down the hall. ValleyStart teams may have been running on fumes, but they were still running. She heard a slew of curses from a room far down, smelled nachos from one near, and heard the pounding of music from another and the pounding of a fist in response next door to it. She unlocked the door to her room and kicked off her shoes. She set her backpack on the floor by her bunk and nodded to Maddie, who was still awake, headphones in her ears. Lucy seemed to be asleep in her bed, facing the Stanford pennant on her wall.

As quietly as she could, Delia downed two ibuprofen and crawled into bed. The moment the night turned to the next day, ValleyStart sent its daily message:

> **ValleyStart:** Proof comes through use. And that proof starts today. The beta test is here: hooray!

And Delia could only think of home.

Even though the shows had resumed their regular schedule, being two hours behind meant even theater folk would be asleep. Instead of calling her parents, she texted Cassie.

> **Cassie:** You know it's like two in the morning right, Dee Dee?

> **Delia:** I showed you how to set up your "Do Not Disturb."

> **Cassie:** I turned it off.

> **Delia:** Then don't complain if I wake you.

> **Cassie:** You didn't.

> **Delia:** Then don't complain.

> **Cassie:** Who said I was complaining? Just asking if you know it's two in the morning. Why are you awake?

Delia: Work. If I even smell cashew cheese again, I may hurl.

Cassie: I'm hurling just thinking about it.

Delia: And why are you awake?

Cassie: Wired after the show. You know.

Delia: So it has nothing to do with a certain usher you're crushing on?

Cassie: Please don't attempt to rhyme. But, yes, we're watching a movie together right now.

Delia sat up straighter.

Delia: In your house?

Cassie: I wish. She's in hers, I'm here. It's a tragedy.

Delia: A regular Juliet and Juliet. Did you ask her out yet?

Cassie: I will. Right after you ask the E-man out.

Delia sucked in her bottom lip.

Delia: Truce?

Cassie: Truce.

Delia: Now tell me about the multiplex.

Delia wished she hadn't asked. Because now it was two in the morning her time and despite her exhaustion, sleep refused to come. Cassie had said the past few nights were almost full and that the upcoming weekend, which preceded the Fourth of July— always a solid time for the theater—was sold out. Yet her parents were still in talks to sell the theater. And buy a Winnebago, according to Cassie.

With her head on her pillow, Delia stared at the stickers on her mom's suitcase. She'd already been everywhere. New York, Los Angeles, Las Vegas, Paris, London, even Singapore. Each sticker represented the life her parents had before it included her.

Delia leaned over the side of her bed and dragged her backpack closer. She reached into the front pocket and pulled out the San Francisco sticker she'd bought in the campus bookstore before her shift. The Golden Gate Bridge, which was red, not gold, sat atop the name of the city Delia kinda sorta loved even though she'd only caught a glimpse of it. She ran her fingers over each letter before returning it to her backpack, slipping it inside the other thing she'd picked up in the bookstore: a brochure and application to Mountain View University.

She'd never be able to afford it.

Unless, maybe, just maybe, she won ValleyStart, and it was enough to earn her one of the merit scholarships listed in the back of the financial aid section. Maybe she could even start in the spring semester.

She'd have to leave Littlewood, Cassie, her parents. She couldn't imagine that. Then again, a few months ago she couldn't imagine ValleyStart either.

Suddenly Lucy flipped over and grumbled, "Maddie."

No response.

Lucy then tossed back her covers. "Maddie!"

"Yes? Headphones, sorry."

"It's after two. Your dedication to Lit is stellar, truly, but do you have any idea how horrific blue screens are for sleep? You're keeping us up."

Maddie tapped the bunk. "Delia, you're awake?"

"If I wasn't, I would be now, but yes, I'm awake."

"Perfect." Maddie snapped on the light clipped to her bed, and Delia and Lucy both groaned. "I've been working on this all night."

"Lit can wait until the morning," Lucy said. "And if I'm saying that, even though the beta test is *tomorrow*, you know how very tired I must be. And I'm running out of concealer."

"This isn't about Lit." Maddie climbed down from her bunk and plopped herself in the middle of the room. "It's Pulse. It's Ryan Thompson. Something's not right."

Lucy put a pillow over her head, muffling her words. "I swear, you mention Emma Santos, and I'm screaming bloody murder."

"Emma?" Delia said. She and Eric had been doing a lot of their programming together. She'd always thought coding was a solo endeavor. But having someone to code alongside, to bounce ideas off of, and to brainstorm solutions with had shown her just how much she'd been missing and what she had to look forward to at a company, working as part of a team. And yet while she was able to spend time delving deeper into the complexity of database servers, Eric had been forced to learn more of the design elements. All while Emma's "family emergency" seemed to be her need to play her guitar in dive bars, at least according to her Instagram. "You're talking to Emma? The girl who left Eric's team with some made-up excuse?"

"No, I'm not talking to Emma," Maddie said. "I'm researching her. Because her Pulse shot up so fast, relatively speaking. I've compared her trajectory with a dozen others, and, Delia, I'd love your input since this is really your area of expertise, but it's just not adding up. Things that should lift aren't and things that shouldn't are and it's all—"

"A complete and utter waste of time," Lucy said, tossing her pillow at Maddie. "You're not even working on Lit? You're keeping us up all night and you're not even working on Lit? I swear, Maddie, I don't understand what's gotten into you."

"It's not me. It's Pulse." Maddie trailed her fingers through the shag rug. "You know, maybe I should reach out to Emma directly. There was this thing she wrote right after she left about Pulse having no heart or something. Sadie showed it to me. I checked her profile after I signed up for my account, but it's not there anymore. But I know it was. So, I could contact Emma, or maybe even tweet something about Ryan and—"

"What?" Delia shot out of bed. "I'm here on a *scholarship*, Maddie." She wanted to say more, that her roommates might know what that word means but not how it feels, but Delia wasn't one for conflict. And yet between her parents and San Francisco and Mountain View and her wanting this *so much*—not just for them but for herself—conflict was starting to consume her. That a ValleyStart win and maybe financial aid to Mountain View U could remotely be possible scared her like *The Shining*. It meant giving up everything she knew, all that felt right and safe, but still she wanted to *keep* it possible. She couldn't have whatever this new obsession of Maddie's was ruining it for her. "A scholarship that's sponsored by Pulse, by Ryan Thompson. And you're, like, what? Investigating him? Don't you realize how bad that'll look? For all of us?"

"And," Lucy chimed in, "if you're going to stay up all night at least you *could* be working on Lit. Remember when you told me there were more important things to worry about than Pulse? Well, right back at ya!"

"Don't yell at her," Delia said.

"Why not? You did."

"Because this affects me. And her part on Lit is fine. That's not what needs yelling about."

"Sure, her part's *fine*. She did fine. You did fine. I did fine. *Fine, fine, fine*. Fine isn't good enough. And since I'm covering your tush in the Demo Day presentation, it's up to me to make it all more than fine, to make it fan-freaking-tastic. You may think I'm over here painting my nails and flirting with boys, but instead I'm running all over campus to make sure our beta test actually has betas to test it."

And with that, Lucy yanked the covers over her head.

Delia wanted to jerk them right off and sleep under them instead of her comforter that she swore scratched her cornea the other night. Instead, she turned away from Maddie and her ginormous laptop, snatched Lucy's luxuriously soft pillow off the floor, and sank into bed. She buried her head beneath her sandpaper covers and wished for sleep.

NINETEEN

BLACK SWAN • *An unforeseeable incident often with dire consequences*

LUCY SUCKED ON THE metal straw of her smoothie and gagged. Peanut butter. She'd asked for almond butter and they'd clearly put in peanut butter. She pushed the cup aside. Even liquid food was questionable anyway thanks to the gymnastic routine underway in her stomach.

The beta test was today. And after, her dinner with Ryan. And after that, surely an acceptance from Stanford. Because Lucy planned to ask Ryan for a recommendation at dinner. How could she not leap off the wait list with a personal letter from the founder of Pulse?

Across the table in the ValleyStart headquarters, Delia tugged her hand through her hair for the millionth time, expanding her curls to doorway-blocking proportions. Hunched over and shielded by her laptop screen, Maddie let out a small huff every now and again, which was Delia's cue to check out what problem

Maddie had uncovered—problems they might have found earlier had Maddie not gotten sidetracked by her obsession with Pulse.

None of them had spoken about last night.

They'd barely spoken since last night.

At least the final touches to Lit could be done by pointing and grunting.

Fine. It's going to be fine.

She sat back in her chair and played with the straw as she assessed the competition. Gavin's eyes were rimmed with red from fatigue—or maybe from crying over unsolved bugs in his code (*hey, one could hope*). Eric and Marty appeared calm, cautiously confident. But most of the other teams were pointing and grunting too, downing energy drinks and looking in need of a factory reset. Burnout pervaded the room. She took comfort in it. It meant that her team was no different.

Lucy cleared her throat and slid her smoothie forward. "Either of you want this? Otherwise I'm chucking it."

"Wasteful," Maddie said.

Lucy forced her nostrils not to flare. "Only because they screwed up the order. They put in peanut butter, and I hate peanut butter."

Delia's head snapped up. "See? This is why Eric's app's so important. At least you won't die from that sip."

That Delia considered Lit to be frivolous wasn't news. That Maddie waxed and waned more than the moon in her feeling the same about Lucy wasn't either.

At least Lit hadn't suffered.

Lucy wanted to scoop up pom-poms and rah-rah them all

over the finish line, but she'd barely slept, and all the unknowns for tonight—from having enough users, to their app scaling if they did have enough users, to what Ryan would ask about Lit's business plan over dinner—meant she simply couldn't muster the enthusiasm or find the right words.

Instead, they spent the afternoon on Lit.

Stray booms and pops punctuated Lucy's walk around campus. It was Fourth of July eve, and students had been setting off firecrackers and sparklers all day. Events were being held all around campus, which meant more students, which meant more potential beta testers.

It was the perfect night for their test, just as Lucy had planned. Though teams could pick any day that week to run their beta test, Lucy had specifically chosen this one.

That afternoon she'd visited each venue she'd recruited to confirm their participation. These included places on campus (the food court; all the kiosks in the student center; the music hall, which had a concert scheduled; and the outdoor amphitheater, which was hosting an open mic night) and off campus (the new pizza place that'd just opened and a comedy club). Lucy had spread the word to the summer students by coordinating with the university and using its communication channels. She'd also posted signs all over campus, ensuring the Pulse logo was front and center, as big as ValleyStart. Students might not know Valley-Start, but they knew Pulse.

To reach more potential betas, Lucy had compiled a list of users who'd tagged Mountain View U on social media. She then cross-referenced that list with Pulse, categorizing users by number of hearts. She'd scheduled posts about the beta test from her personal accounts, tagging users with the highest Pulse rankings.

She'd done what she could. And now, it was up to Lit.

Lucy swung her arms to help release the buildup of nerves as she marched down the main path that led to the enclave of dorms and passed under the seventy-year-old wisteria arbor. The last remaining purple flowers from the springtime bloom dangled through the lattice, releasing the heady scent that always reminded Lucy of cat pee.

She lifted her hand to cover her nose at the same time as a figure in front of her in khaki shorts and a white tee turned around and leaned against the post at the end of the long arbor.

Gavin.

She lightened her step and tossed her hand back down to her side, but not fast enough.

He thought she was waving. And he waved back.

Lucy spun her head, searching for an out. But this path cut straight through campus with nothing but expansive green lawn on either side, dotted by a few sunbathers, Frisbee throwers, and a group playing giant Jenga. Any buildings loomed too far in the distance to get to unnoticed. She'd have to stay and walk past Gavin—the Gavin she'd yet to forgive for being a sexist ass in front of half of ValleyStart at the party in the common room. She quickened her pace and focused straight ahead.

"Hey," Gavin said. "Wasn't sure you were talking to me."

His fingers grazed her elbow and trailed down to her hand—the sensation sparking a flood of tactile memories of his arm around her waist, her cheek against his chest, his lips soft and searching against hers. His redwoods scent wafted over them, and more memories rushed to the surface—wind whipping through her hair beside him in his open-top Mercedes, snorts of laughter as he inhaled three Double-Double burgers at In-N-Out, tears wiped from his cheeks the night he told her about his father, ones coating her own the next morning when she woke up hours late for her Stanford interview.

The warmth spreading across her chest turned into a burn, and she shook him off.

"Trust your instincts," she said.

Gavin's lips parted, but no sound came out. He held her gaze, his eyes clouding with a look she recognized not just in him but in herself. It kept her feet glued in place. Finally he said, "Dad says to do the opposite. That my instincts are crap."

"But you used Swift," spilled out before Lucy could stop it. She didn't want to make Gavin feel better. But she also didn't want to make him feel worse.

He tilted his head. "Maybe. But my dad's instincts had him investing in Pulse before it was even called Pulse." Gavin tipped his chin, gesturing to the campus. "He thinks it means this is a no-brainer, but ValleyStart and Pulse aren't the same. Still, I'll be 'an embarrassment to the family' if I don't win." He used air quotes just like he had in her dorm room, just like he had in his room in high school—she'd forgotten about that.

"Everyone here's at the top of their game," Lucy said, for the first time admitting the thing that frightened her the most since crossing under the arched entrance to the hackathon.

"Which is why I have to act like the best *and* be the best to get him off my ass." Gavin slammed the back of his foot into the post. The force reverberated down the arbor, shaking free more odor of cat pee. He then grasped his curls so hard that when he released them they stood on end as if he'd used an entire container of gel.

"Fine," he muttered half under his breath. "Whatever it takes to win. That's what he wants, so that's what I'll do."

Lucy wasn't sure if he was talking to her, himself, his absent father, or all of them. She simply watched as the anger in his steps catapulted him down the path. He continued toward the dorms without looking back. Lucy hugged her arms against her chest, an unease that no longer had anything to do with the beta test billowing inside her.

She breathed in the last of the wisteria as she exited the arbor, appreciating her mom in a way she hadn't done in years.

Delia wouldn't stay still. In front of the pizza oven, she bounced from one foot to the other. Back and forth. Forth and back. Lucy couldn't take it anymore.

"Maddie's at the music hall, right?" Lucy asked, to which Delia nodded. "Then I'm staking out the student center. You stay here. Text me if anything happens."

The beta test was an hour in, and they only had a handful of reports.

It was working, just not hard enough. They needed testers.

Lucy opened her scheduling app. Another blast about participating in Lit was waiting. She hesitated and then amended each post to include the photo of her and Ryan.

Any and every advantage.

She opened Lit and marked the pizza place as "worth the trip." She then ducked into the restroom. By the time she came out, half a dozen students were in line, all on their phones. She weaved through, sneaking a glance at what was up on their screens. Lit. They were on Lit.

"Better be good," one guy in a beanie said. "I'm starved."

"No worries," the guy beside him said. "Level 10 approved. Said 'worth the trip.' So it will be."

Level 10?

Lucy slunk into the corner. No one else had marked the pizza joint as "worth the trip."

She bit down on her lower lip. Wanting to open Pulse. Afraid to open Pulse. But she did it anyway.

And, inside, she screamed.

She was Crushing It.

And soon, so was Lit.

Nothing could be more perfect than Pulse-Lit. Their beta test proved it. Because when a user with a high Pulse rated a venue, more people responded—leaving when things were dull, arriving when they were happening.

Not only did Lit work, Lit was prime for exactly what Ryan had suggested—a merger. Lucy was practically floating by the time the test ended. Officially ended, that is. Users were continuing to add ratings.

Because they loved it. And everyone at ValleyStart could see it.

Gavin could see it. And Gavin, Lucy noted when she passed

him in the quad, was worried. She didn't envy the call to come with his father. But Lucy had earned this. They all had.

Lucy, Maddie, and Delia had split up for the rest of the test, each traveling between venues to assess the traffic. They'd planned to meet in their dorm room.

When Lucy arrived, she took the stairs two at a time, anxious to put their disagreements behind them and celebrate their success—which included Ryan's interest in Lit.

When she burst through the door, the room was empty.

A tightness spread across her chest.

But she was at the student center—she was closest, right?

They're coming, they're definitely coming.

She paced the room before deciding to use the time to get dressed for her night with Ryan. She tied the belt of the black dress she'd purchased the other day.

Stylize.

But also strategize. Because the faux-wrap dress was professional. More so with the blazer she'd bought to pair with it. Yet when she slipped her arms through and looked in the mirror all she thought was *total frump*—like something her mom would wear. Lucy chose her cropped leather jacket instead and, in case they went walking after, her second-highest heels.

She then opened her jewelry case. Her fingers hovered over her Star of David necklace but landed on a strand of black beads that she thought would make her look older than she was. She hooked them around her neck just as Maddie and Delia entered the room together.

"Formal celebration, is it then?" Maddie said.

Delia unexpectedly tackle-hugged Lucy, and though Maddie

hung back, the same excitement shined in her eyes. "We're going out?" Delia said. "Yes, let's go out! But, maybe, can I borrow something?"

"Of course," Lucy said, squeezing Delia's hand. "Anything you want."

Delia's wide smile ignited a deep guilt at what Lucy had to say next. Though this was going to be good—great—for all of them.

"You two go, and I'll catch you maybe for dessert." That tightness again spread across Lucy's chest as she watched not just Delia's smile fade but the light dull in Maddie's eyes. "I wanted to wait until Lit was a success—which, of course we knew it would be." She grinned, but neither of her teammates did. "Right, but, turns out, I'm having dinner with Ryan tonight."

"Like a date?" Delia said.

"No, furthest from. He asked me because . . ." She took a deep breath and gushed, "He wants to take it to market. Lit. Funding, scaling, everything. And that was before we killed it in the beta test."

Delia's eyes widened. "Really?"

"Yeah, really?" Maddie said. "Because doesn't that go against the spirit of ValleyStart?"

"ValleyStart is an incubator," Lucy said. "Can't help it if we're ready to hatch."

"We're supposed to be learning, working hard, and making real connections," Maddie said. "Like I did with my own business. Like Nishi did. This . . . things don't come this easily."

"Easily?" Delia said with uncharacteristic irritation in her voice. "This isn't easy, Maddie, none of it. We've all worked hard.

We deserve this." She faced Lucy. "We should come, shouldn't we? We can help. That way you don't have to do this all by yourself."

Contrary to what she would have expected, the idea of not going alone set Lucy at ease. Delia could field the technical questions, and Maddie . . . Lucy thought back on every negative thing Maddie had said about Ryan and about Pulse. She could ruin the deal.

"Wait to hear from me," Lucy said reluctantly. "I'm not sure if I was supposed to say anything yet. Ryan mentioned Thai, so we're probably going to one of the places in town. If it seems okay, I'll send a Lyft for you."

Maddie rolled her eyes.

Delia didn't bother to hide her disappointment either. "Okay, yeah, text us."

Lucy held Delia's gaze. "*I will.* Promise."

These were her teammates. They'd stuck together this far. And now, they'd get everything they wanted. Lucy was sure of it.

Nerves eased, and excitement built as Lucy waited for Ryan outside the student center. The ValleyStart message board was buzzing about Lit's beta test—and about Lucy, about Lucy skyrocketing to Crushing It.

Crushing. It.

Got a Pulse?
Yeah, she did.

Her newfound status gave their test a boost, for sure.

The power of Pulse.

The power . . .

Lucy sucked in her lip.

Aw, what the hell.

She grabbed her phone, opened the Stanford portal, and sent a message. She would have an additional letter of recommendation from Ryan Thompson, founder of Pulse, the following day. She hesitated, then added that as a Level 10 she would be sure to represent Stanford well at all her Pulse events to come.

Any and every advantage, right?

Ryan soon appeared from inside the student center. He was wearing jeans, a white linen shirt, and a khaki blazer. Lucy was glad she'd dressed up—let him know she was taking this as seriously as he was.

"Now, don't you look like someone who's Crushing It?" he said.

"You saw?"

"I saw." He led her to his red Tesla convertible and opened the door for her. "Might want to put that jacket on, Lucy; it can get chilly with the top down."

"Oh, that's okay. It's a short ride to town."

"Yes, it is, but we're not going to town. I hope you cleared your calendar for the evening, because I do believe all ten of your hearts have been left in San Francisco."

"Thank you," Lucy said as the hostess switched out the white cloth napkin for a black one so as not to leave lint on her dress. She then turned to Ryan. "This is amazing. My only complaint about the Valley is that it's not right on the ocean."

Lucy had been in San Francisco a hundred times but never like this. With a waterfront table—the only waterfront table, as Ryan had bought out the entire outside patio—framing the Ferry Building's iconic tower and beautiful white clock in the foreground and the artfully lit Bay Bridge in the background. Patio heaters surrounded them, nestling them in a cocoon of warmth.

The tasting menu and wines had been preselected by Ryan.

No one carded her.

"A toast." Ryan held up his glass of champagne. "To my newest Pulse-tern."

His what? Lucy tried to cover her delight at being *Ryan Thompson*'s favorite by reaching for her glass. "I mean, sure, historically, doing so well in the beta test increases our chances, but Demo Day has at least four judges and—"

"And yet I'm the one funding the program. Don't tell me you're surprised. Though you're way too pretty to be in tech, you are. You know how this game is played."

Lucy sat back in her seat, waiting for the ripple of excitement at Ryan basically telling her she was going to win ValleyStart to roll into something greater because this is what she wanted, what she needed, for Stanford, her mom, Delia and Maddie—for herself. *Winning ValleyStart.* She wanted it. But when she sipped her drink, the bubbles slid uneasily down her throat.

Ryan asked for more details about the beta test, and Lucy obliged, transitioning into the business persona she'd seen in her mom her entire life. She extracted her notebook from her bag and flipped through, detailing her strategy and how it had played out, emphasizing all she'd done to ensure success. Ryan nodded intently as she spoke, his fingertips touching and forming a triangle in front of his mouth.

Aside from a few *hmm*s and a couple of *good thinking*s, though, he didn't say much.

Was she boring him?

The server appeared with their pre-appetizer, "the amuse-bouche"—a shot glass of soup she described as essence of tom yum goong.

Ryan swirled the glass like it was wine. "Hmm . . . Maybe we should've invited your teammates. The one could have translated for us."

Lucy's brow creased, and then it hit her. "Maddie? She's Chinese American, not Thai."

Ryan shrugged indifference and downed his soup in one long gulp, and bile rocketed up Lucy's throat.

She tried a polite sip of the soup, but the burn persisted.

"Speaking of, I think you should drop them—your teammates," Ryan said, flatly, like he was talking about changing his shirt.

Drop Maddie and Delia?

Her throat tightened, and she twisted the napkin in her lap, groping for the right words, the right way to respond to Ryan Thompson, Pulse founder, ValleyStart funder, Silicon Valley icon, who wanted to take her product to market.

She forced a smile. "Too bad ValleyStart's a team program, right?" She gave a soft laugh. "We'll be fine, though—great—you'll see when—"

He raised his hand in the air, turning away from Lucy to

signal the server, then watched as the woman poured him a refill of his champagne even though the bottle was right beside him. Eyeing Lucy's barely touched glass, he said, "And let's get this little lady something more to her liking. Lucy, what's your poison?"

"No, I'm fine. It's fine." She took a sip. "Great."

Ryan wrapped his hand around the server's forearm. "Bring her the Montrachet."

Lucy started to protest but let it go.

Once the server left, Ryan stared at Lucy. "Did you know I grew up here?"

Lucy nodded.

"Not with a water view." His smile was thin, strained. "But I have one now. The Marina District would suit you too, Lucy, I can tell."

Another gentle nod as Lucy's mind spun, trying to figure out how to transition the conversation toward her Stanford recommendation.

"Getting there," Ryan added, "getting Lit to be on the tip of everyone's tongue, will require sacrifices. Offerings to the tech gods—otherwise known as VCs." He laughed. "Yours are your teammates. Complete the program, have your Demo Day together, but when it comes to business—our business—Pulse-Lit only has room for two pretty faces on its founder's page. Yours and mine." He lifted his glass, and Lucy knew he was waiting for her to do the same. She did. "It's not the journey, Lucy, it's the destination. Know your endgame and do whatever it takes to get there. That's how I'm here. Surrounded by water views."

He clinked his glass against hers. "To the endgame."

She raised her champagne to her lips. When Ryan tipped his

back, downing more than half in one swallow, she poured some of hers into her water glass.

With the moonlight sparkling on the Pacific, the Bay Bridge soaring above them, the restaurant full of servers waiting to please and customers whispering in awe, this should be the best night of her life. It wasn't. Because she was here with Ryan Thompson.

And Ryan Thompson was an ass.

When the ninth and final course was cleared, Lucy stood.

"We should get going." Not wanting to come across as rude, she added, "Thank you, this was amazing, truly." Less so was hearing all about the computer Ryan built himself when he was— supposedly—five; listening to the tale of his first unrequited love who he'd sent a dozen black roses to when Pulse went public; and sitting through the call where he scolded the curator for bringing art pieces under a hundred thousand dollars to his home. "But Delia and Maddie are waiting for me."

Lines etched into his brow at the mention of her teammates, and Lucy silently cursed herself. She still hadn't found a Stanford opening, and this wasn't going to help.

She grabbed her notebook off the table, slung her purse over her shoulder, and plastered on a fake smile. "We have the whole car ride together, though." The whole, hour-long car ride. *Awesome.* But this was business. Business didn't care if Ryan Thompson was an ass. Neither did Stanford.

"Maybe we can get back to your ideas for getting Lit off the ground?" she said.

"Focused on the endgame. I like it."

Ryan wiped his mouth with his napkin and pushed his chair back. Immediately the server and hostess were at his side, thanking him, packing up the three unfinished bottles of wine he'd had served, and discreetly acknowledging his account would be billed.

On their way to the convertible, which they found waiting with the ignition running and a valet on either side, each holding a door open, Ryan's hand brushed against Lucy's arm.

"Goose bumps," he said. "I get them too when something this exciting is about to happen."

Lucy groaned inwardly and rubbed her upper arm before putting on her jacket. She hugged it closed, tightly against her chest, as she sat in the passenger seat, wondering what bizarre universe she'd entered.

They drove down the Embarcadero, the long avenue that bordered the water, where restaurants brimming with people intermingled with working ports and, eventually, tourist attractions like the sea lions at Pier 39, the aquarium and wax museum at Fisherman's Wharf, and the shops at Ghirardelli Square. She kept her head turned, trying to at least appreciate the view. And then Ryan started talking. Again.

"It was my mother who inspired Pulse," he said. "Not directly, of course, as she was a librarian and even now can barely log in to her Pulse account without help." He snickered, and Lucy recoiled in her seat. "But she always wanted this, to live by the water, so much that she made it my goal as well. Fortunately I had an excellent role model in my father."

The extended silence meant Lucy had to say something in

response. The notebook in her lap wouldn't help—she'd not come across anything about Ryan's father in her research. Finally she said, "He was in tech?"

Ryan grimaced. "He wanted to be. My dad was a serial entrepreneur, tossing spaghetti to the wall, trying to find something that would stick. Nothing ever did, and his failures sent us from crappy neighborhood to shitty neighborhood until we were out of the city and in Oakland with my mom commuting for hours each day and me changing schools in eighth grade. Not fun." He faced Lucy with a half smile before turning back to the road. "She never forgave him for not just getting a damn job. Even at his funeral, all she could say was what a waste his life had been. He never accomplished anything." Ryan ran his hands along the sides of the steering wheel, gripping it tight. "But she was wrong. Because everything I learned, I learned from him. My life is the opposite of his. My life is this."

Ryan flicked on the blinker.

Lucy swiveled her head and realized where they were. The Marina District. On the other side of the city from where they needed to be to get back to Mountain View.

"Uh, Ryan . . ." She laced her fingers together in her lap, listening to the *tick, tick* of the blinker, hoping with each beat he was simply turning around. "Doing a U-turn? Need an extra set of eyes?"

The instant the back bumper of the approaching car on the other side of the road passed, Ryan whipped the wheel and the Tesla tore across at such speed that it flung Lucy into the back of her seat—hard. The seat belt pulled taut, compressing her chest, and her purse flew to the floor.

"I'm all good. This baby never disappoints." Ryan stroked the dash. "You know what else doesn't disappoint?"

Lucy struggled against the constricting seat belt.

"The view from my living room." He tilted his head back and gestured to the three-story white mansion in front of them. "You said you loved the water, and this is the way to see it."

A chill shivered Lucy's spine, and she tried not to show it. "I'm sure it's lovely, it's just that I'm awfully tired." She gave a half laugh. "Food coma, and the rest of me wants to follow, so maybe we should just—"

A hand

Flattened

Against

Her

Thigh.

A hand

Not

Belonging

To

Her.

His.

It was his.

Ryan's hand.

Touching her.

Not by accident.

"Tired? But the night is young," he said, the pressure of his palm deepening.

She froze everywhere but her heart, which *beat, thudded, thumped, throbbed, raced, pounded, hammered* her chest, and all

Lucy wanted was to hit restart on this night and be in the dorm room watching Maddie inhale zucchini-flour pancakes and Delia deny she was falling for Eric Shaw.

Instead she was here, with Ryan Thompson, Pulse founder, ValleyStart funder, Silicon Valley icon, who wanted to take her product to market.

Ryan leaned in close. "The hot tub on the roof's always fired up."

But that wasn't all he wanted.

"I—I can't," Lucy said. *This is why he asked me to dinner?* Not because of her ideas or abilities or how well Lit was doing . . . She felt like a fool. "It's just, Maddie and Delia—"

"Will forgive you. Well, maybe not after you Zuckerberg them, but for this, for tonight, they'll understand." The pressure of Ryan's hand lifted, and Lucy began to shift in her seat when the pressure returned, only now, higher.

"You're Crushing It," he said. "Be nice to stay that way."

"I . . . what?" Lucy couldn't act, couldn't think. And then Ryan's hand began to move, and she kicked into gear, shoving him off and flattening her back against the passenger side door. "Maddie and Delia are waiting for me, and I'm not betraying them, and you need to take me home. Now."

Ryan's eyebrow lifted. "Aw, Lucy, you don't mean that. I thought you wanted Pulse-Lit. I thought you were all ready to get in bed together. Professionally speaking, of course." He grinned like this was funny.

This isn't funny! Nothing about this is funny!

"But synergy in all aspects can only lead to a better relationship, don't you agree? From those drinks we shared, it certainly seemed like you did. Besides, you let those nerds at the club put their hands all over you for nothing." Ryan reached across the center console. "At least mine come with, oh, how does two commas sound to start? A cool mil?"

And then one hand hit the button beside the rearview mirror and the other seized Lucy by her waist. The garage door began to lift, Ryan nudged the car into drive, and Lucy dug her Rescue Me Red nails into the skin on the back of his hand.

"Fuck!" Ryan cried.

Lucy grabbed her purse off the floor and jerked the door handle, spilling out onto the herringbone-tiled driveway as the car rolled forward and disappeared behind the garage door.

Scrambling to her feet, Lucy tore off her heels and sprinted, not pausing until she reached the crowds of Ghirardelli Square, twenty minutes later. Sweat glued her hair to her forehead as she ducked inside the ice cream shop, more than half full at almost eleven at night thanks to the summer tourists. She fell into a seat at one of the round tables in the center of the room, not realizing until she reached into her purse that the seam securing the wrap of her dress was torn. She pulled her jacket tighter around her.

A tremble commanded her hands, but she managed to open the app and request a rideshare. And then she opened her contacts and made one more call.

She told Maddie and Delia what happened while she stood outside the ice cream shop waiting for her ride. They stayed on the phone the entire trip, while the balls of Lucy's feet stung from the slap against the sidewalk, while tears rolled down her cheeks from the slap of reality of who Ryan was, of what could have happened, and of what did.

Delia distracted her by repeating textbook definitions of coding she'd had memorized for years, and when it bored all three of them sufficiently, Maddie took over, telling a story she'd made up for her little brother about a family of pterodactyls who lived on Martha's Vineyard. Then, in the Boston accent that no longer bothered Lucy, Maddie revealed what she claimed was the original ending to the first Gumberoo book.

It wasn't until Lucy heard Maddie's and Delia's voices echoing in her ear from inside their dorm room that they all hung up. The door opened, and tears she couldn't stop blurred Lucy's vision. She fell into Delia's open arms. Delia squeezed her with more strength than Lucy realized she had. Instinctually, Lucy reached for Maddie, who stood to the side, watching. Lucy's hand latched on to Maddie's wrist, and Maddie stepped forward, inching closer, tentatively, and then she became the core that held them all as one.

"No more fighting," Delia said, sniffing back her own tears.

"We stick together," Maddie said. "We're a team."

"We're much more than that," Lucy said.

The room only had the beds and one desk chair. So they simply stood. Together.

TWENTY

CO-INVEST • *When multiple investors fund a business on similar terms*

WHEN MADDIE WOKE, SHE reached under her pillow for her phone, not surprised to see it was after eleven. They'd been up until four.

They'd sat in a circle on the shag rug as Lucy recounted the story again and again. Maddie and Delia simply listened, prepared to keep listening for as many retellings as it took. Turned out, that was three. Three times, each one with more detail, less fear, and increasing waves of anger—from all of them.

Maddie set her phone down and hung her head over the side of the bunk. Delia was still buried under her covers. Lucy too.

Good.

After shutting her ringer off, Maddie propped her pillow behind her and logged in to Pulse. Comatose, Level 1, which made sense considering Maddie's meager social media presence. Except Maddie wasn't looking at her profile. She was looking at Lucy's.

Her fists clenched.

Pompous, arrogant, predatory ass.

Maddie didn't have to like Pulse to know what it meant to Lucy. She was Crushing It just yesterday. In one day, she'd become Comatose. Without being arrested.

In one day. One day where Ryan Thompson put his hands where they had no right to go. He'd been rebuffed. He must have been angry. Humiliated. Vengeful.

And stupid.

Very, very stupid.

Maddie pumped her clenched fist in the air.

Got him.

An hour later, Maddie saved the graph she'd made of Lucy and Emma's trajectories on Pulse, cross-referenced with their encounters with Ryan, as best she could estimate. Not courtroom proof, but paired with Lucy's story, enough to cast some serious suspicion.

Just as she was checking Nishi's office hours, a boom jarred Delia awake.

"Are we under attack?" Delia cried.

Maddie shifted to the edge of her bed to see out the window. "Only from jackasses looking to lose a hand. Illegal fireworks. Though considering our proximity, maybe we should duck."

Delia yawned. "Right, it's July Fourth."

"Which means Nishi's not here until after the holiday weekend." Maddie climbed down and perched herself on the desk. Her foot hit a ball of black fabric crammed into the trash can underneath. Lucy's torn dress. She pulled it out and turned to Delia. "We could try the Head of House though."

Delia sat up. "For what?"

"For reporting Ryan."

"Does she want to?" Delia whispered, pointing to the lump in Lucy's bed.

The lump that should have moved when the explosion went off. Maddie dropped the dress back into the trash and gently touched the comforter, which had zero resistance. It was soft, but not that soft. She pulled it back. Lucy was gone.

They found her in the common room surrounded by vitamin waters, kale chips, a stack of zucchini-flour pancakes, and half a dozen cashew cheese Hot Pockets. The light from a projector traversed the room, and on the screen at the front was a slide with the words "Lit: We Hook You Up" above the logo Maddie had designed.

"Finally!" Lucy cried. "Sleepyheads. If it weren't for me nudging Marty to shoot off one of his pop rockets a bit early you'd both still be in bed! Now, grab some sustenance and let's get moving. I reserved the common room for the full day, and we're going to need every hour of it to go over the beta test and start practicing for Demo Day."

Delia looked to Maddie for direction.

Maddie stepped deeper into the room. "Lucy, we don't have to do this today."

"Of course we do." She whipped out a lavender-scented sanitizer wipe and began scrubbing the table. "Now that we've got an edge, we have to build on it. Momentum is everything in diets, darts, and tech." She pulled in her lower lip. "Still working on that one. But you get the idea."

Lucy's effervescence filled the air around them, and Maddie wasn't eager to be the one to start popping bubbles, but Lucy was right about momentum. The more time that passed, the harder it would be for Lucy to come forward. Not just because outsiders might question why she waited so long, but because Maddie knew Lucy. The Lucy who planned and prioritized and pushed anything that didn't fit in her notebook out of her head. And Maddie was certain this was something Lucy wanted not just out but erased from existence.

"Lucy," Maddie started.

"In, in." Lucy waved her hand. "Sit, let me just grab my notebook."

"Lucy, wait," Maddie said again. "Let's talk."

"We are, and we will, believe me." She dug through her tote bag. "I emailed you both the agenda. Six pages. Single-spaced." A packet of sanitizer wipes flew to the ground, followed by a makeup case, three bottles of nail polish, a scarf, and a phone charger. "Oh, come on, it's not like it's invisible!"

Maddie widened her eyes at Delia and whispered, "Say something."

"Like what?" Delia said. "If she wants to work, let's work."

Delia tugged at her sleep tee and settled into the armchair across from the screen.

Lucy's head was still in her bag. Maddie walked to her and put a hand on her forearm. Lucy stiffened, and Maddie removed it.

"I'm sorry," she said. "But the presentation isn't important right now." Maddie tried to get Lucy to look at her. "Have you seen your Pulse today? It's not . . . great. But I'm pretty certain he's retaliating through it." Lucy still refused to meet Maddie's eyes, but Maddie continued. "I think Ryan's personally manipulating Pulse accounts for his own purposes."

"Well, of course he is," Lucy snapped. "How do you think I got to Crushing It so fast?"

"Wait, what?" Delia said.

"And Emma . . ." Maddie said.

"Sure, I'm sure. I mean, you should have seen them in the club." Lucy shuddered and tossed her bag to the floor, giving up the search for her notebook. "But I did. I saw them. How could I be so stupid?"

"You're not," Maddie said.

"I had drinks with him."

"So?"

"I smiled and laughed. I flirted."

"And?"

"I led him on. I—"

"Did nothing to invite him to put his hands on you—and not remove them when you said to."

Lucy's eyes were fixed straight ahead, and Maddie began to rethink her decision to approach Lucy so soon.

Eventually Lucy gave a derisive laugh. "A million. He actually offered a million dollars." She gave a weak smile. "Flattering, right?"

"No," Maddie said. "It's sick. He's sick. He's thirtysomething going on eight. This is all . . ." She drew in a breath. "Listen, when the beta test was such a success, even I wanted this. To win. But now to win what? A Pulse internship? Do any of us even want that anymore?"

Delia leaned over the back of her chair. "But Pulse isn't the same as Ryan, is it?"

"Maybe not," Maddie said, unconvinced. "But remember the lecture? The leader sets the tone. And if this is Pulse's tone . . ." Maddie paused, knowing she wasn't like her teammates. They wanted to win more than she did, they always had. And Lucy . . . who knew how long she'd had Ryan up on that pedestal. Her idol, all she aspired to be. To have him not just tumble but tumble like this, with what he tried to do—*was doing*—must have been making her question everything.

Maddie understood the feeling, even though she'd never shared it. "He can't get away with it," she blurted out. "We can't keep letting guys get away with this crap."

Delia pushed herself out of the chair. "Maddie . . . did something—"

"Not like this," Maddie said, "Nothing like this. But manipulated, used? By a guy I thought I could trust?" And now that she'd started, Maddie was gripped by the need to share the feelings she'd kept bottled up for months. "You know what sucks the most? I'd gotten to a good place, not going to college, staying home, staying with my brother." Her hand rose to her four-leaf clover. "I had my business. I'd worked hard for it. Landing a big client and my first five-digit paycheck was less about the money and more about proving I could do it." Tears pricked her eyes, and she fought to hold them back—instinctually at first and then, then because he wasn't worth it. "He stole it from me. And I didn't say anything. I should have." She stood in front of Lucy. "Ryan Thompson's a bully, a dangerous one. Nice hair and cute smile and a bank account the size of Maine, but he's a bully all the same. It's your decision, but I want you to know I'll support you no matter what. If you're in, I'm in."

Lucy was gnawing on her bottom lip like it was a chew toy. But quietly and carefully, she said, "I'm in." The two of them gravitated toward each other. They turned at the same time . . . to Delia.

TWENTY-ONE

MAJORITY • *The percentage of shareholders that must approve significant company decisions; usually greater than fifty percent*

THE AIR SMELLED DIFFERENT here. Not here in the common room but here at Mountain View U. Not exactly cleaner, not exactly what she'd had to learn was marijuana, just different. Maybe it had to do with the persistent sunshine or the sprays of wildflowers or maybe . . . maybe the way Delia breathed here was what was different.

She missed it already. They had two weeks of the program left, and she missed it already. Maybe if she didn't, this wouldn't be so hard. Because Delia believed that Ryan should be reported, that he couldn't be allowed to do what he'd done to Emma and Lucy, that no girl should ever be in the position Lucy was in last night.

Delia's stomach twisted when she imagined what could have happened, what she'd have done if it were her in that passenger seat.

Which was why she was awash in shame at the other thought she was having—that she wished this hadn't happened to a member of her team, her friend, because of what it meant for her.

For the first time in her life, Delia understood the desire to be selfish. She was so close. Not to winning, though that too. But to feeling like there was a place for her, this place, this place she didn't know how much she wanted to be in until she was actually here. To feeling like what she thought and did and had—knowledge, abilities, talent—were respected, maybe even admired. A feeling she'd seen exhibited on her mother's face her whole life. A feeling she was ashamed to want to keep.

"Delia?" Lucy said. "We don't have to. We can keep going—"

"No, not for me. That's not a good enough reason."

"Yes, it is. To me, it is." That Lucy's voice was softer than usual didn't mean it lacked strength. She was resolute when she said, "Being here was a given for me. For the prestige, the connections . . . Résumé building's kind of my thing. I didn't actually expect to learn anything, and I certainly never expected to learn what I have so far. Including what happened last night—"

"But Ryan, how could you—"

"No, not Ryan," Lucy said, her voice full of venom. "This isn't his to own." She unclenched her jaw and let her eyes travel from Delia to Maddie. "See . . ." Lucy paused to gather her thoughts. "I've always been surrounded by friends, but I've never actually had them before."

Delia felt a twinge in her chest at Lucy's words. She'd have never survived without Cassie.

Lucy focused on Delia as she continued. "I didn't realize what that meant until last night. And that when I said majority rules at the hackathon I was wrong. Because that's not how friends treat one another. If you don't want us to do this, we won't. No questions asked."

"You'd do that for me?" Delia said.

"I'd do that for us. Because if we do this, you don't have to be psychic to know our odds of winning ValleyStart will be as Comatose as I am."

"And me," Maddie said.

Delia twirled a lock of hair around her finger, picturing herself telling her parents she'd won, that she was going to work for Pulse, that they didn't need to let the theater become a multiplex and go buy a Winnebago. And then she pictured telling them why. Because she hadn't acted like the person they'd raised her to be.

"I—I don't care," Delia said. "Well, no, I do. This place . . . I wanted this. But I can live with being wronged for doing what's right." She already had. Before Lucy could finish her "thank you," Delia found herself saying, "You know the town fair I said I worked at?"

Lucy nodded. "Frying cornholes."

"Dogs."

"You fried dogs? Is that, like, legal in Indiana?"

"Illinois. And no."

"Delia," Maddie interrupted, shooting Lucy a look. "You were saying . . ."

Delia hesitated—she'd never told anyone, not even Cassie. "I worked the Ferris wheel. I took tickets and made sure the safety bar was latched. And, yes, Lucy, it was as boring as it sounds." She sighed. "It had this rickety old computer board running the mechanics, and one day, the ride just stopped with a full load of people on it. My manager tried to fix it himself, but the longer he took, the more everyone in the cars started to panic. I'd let Cassie's little sister ride alone—I shouldn't have, but I did. She was at the top, and I could pick her cries out of all the rest. I was as scared as she was. I thought I knew how to fix it, so I went to my manager, and he—"

"Wouldn't listen?" Maddie said.

"Wouldn't even let me speak. I was so nervous, I just went back to where I was supposed to be, taking tickets I couldn't take because the ride was stuck. All the while Cassie's sister was screaming for me. I couldn't let her stay up there. So I tried again, and again he waved me away." Delia started rubbing her hands together, the feeling of helplessness rising to the surface just like it had that day. "Eventually I couldn't take it anymore and pushed everyone aside and fixed it. Cassie's sister was safe. She was latched on to me when my manager walked over like I'd been the one to break the ride to begin with. He acted like this was a training exercise—like he was giving me a chance to prove myself and he was just about to step in."

"Wild guess?" Maddie said. "Never covered in training?"

"Not once. The next day I was frying cornholes. Dogs."

"Ass," Maddie hissed.

"Him or me? Because what if it happened again? I should have told someone. Instead I pretended like I loved the smell of deep fry in my hair every night." Delia picked up a Hot Pocket. "But, hey, it qualified me for this, so good for my own résumé building, I guess."

Silence enveloped the room, and they all stared at the Lit logo on the screen. They'd built something out of nothing. Something amazing. And they'd done it together.

Which was how they'd do this too.

"I'm in." Delia looked down. "Right after I put on some pants."

TWENTY-TWO

GETTING SWALLOWED BY A WHALE • *When a smaller company or startup is put out of business by a larger one that gets to market first with a similar idea*

ON THE WALK ACROSS the quad, Lucy had the unexpected urge to call her mom.

Lucy was an only child, raised by her single mother and a host of nannies. She was a surprise—what she always imagined was an unpleasant one—to her career-minded mother and the product of a business arrangement even as a fetus. Her father sent cards and stock options on her birthday and for each night of Hanukkah, and in exchange, she posed for photos with him to "humanize" him in the *Wall Street Journal*. She saw him once a year, and in truth, that was enough for Lucy. They had a cordial relationship but not a warm one. Not that her relationship with her mom was particularly warm either, but that had always been fine with Lucy.

She appreciated her mom treating her like an adult from the time she was two and would take that over home-baked cookies any day (*and her trim waistline thanked her for it*). Her mom pushed for long enough that when she stopped, Lucy pulled, the desire to excel infused into her thanks to nature and nurture.

And Lucy did. She excelled in school and tennis and marathons and did it all while living too, having fun, something her mom had long ago forgone. Serious was one thing, dull was another. *Strategize, stylize, socialize.* It was all three that led to corner offices.

Which Lucy had had her eye on since she could say the words "Silicon Valley." Which was why she'd interned at a startup in San Francisco the summer before sophomore year in high school. Which was why she'd worried she was already behind when she found a sixth grader there "shadowing" the CEO.

One night, she'd hopped on an earlier Caltrain home because her dad was visiting. She opened the door to their faux Spanish-style McMansion and heard the ice—one cube, only ever one—*tink* in her mom's tumbler before she heard her say, "She'll never be me."

The chill she thought she'd left behind with the San Francisco fog iced her to the bone. They were never the "popcorn and rom-com and cucumber facial" mother-daughter-bonding-night type (her mom would have to have been home before bedtime for that). But Lucy thought she *was* following in her footsteps. Sure, maybe she wasn't the techie her mom had been, but Lucy surpassed her mom in people skills and likability and, well, *having a life*. Which Lucy was determined to do even harder from that moment on.

And then Stanford and freaking Gavin Cox. And now Ryan Thompson.

Her mother was right about Lucy not being her. Lucy had never wanted to be.

Until now.

Lucy decided not to call her mom. She had Maddie and Delia. She had her friends.

They sat in a row of three on the couch in the living room attached to the Head of House's apartment.

A white guy barely in his twenties, the Head of House had on the Silicon Valley uniform of expensive sneakers, logo tee, and hoodie. He spent the first ten minutes talking about his days at ValleyStart only a couple of years ago. He'd won with an app that counted the number of trees in acres of forest land that he subsequently sold "in the upper two commas" to some Wall Street timber fund. Silicon Valley, the place that made you a millionaire for doing what any preschooler could do. Lucy couldn't help picturing the logo Maddie would design: a toddler counting on fingers and toes.

Though Lucy felt naked without her notebook in her hands, the image helped to relax her nerves and infuse a calm in her voice when Tim Corrio, the Head of House, finally got around to asking why they were there.

Lucy cleared her throat. "It has to do with Ryan Thompson."

"My man!" Tim clapped his hands. "Did you know the Ryeman and I—"

"No, just no," Maddie said.

Lucy widened her eyes, but Maddie simply said, "Go ahead, Lucy."

Grateful to have gone through the events multiple times with Maddie and Delia, the only part of Lucy shaking were her hands, which she easily slid under her thighs. Though her pulse was quick, her words remained level as she began. "Last night, I left campus and went to San Francisco to have a business dinner with Ryan—"

"That's it!" Tim jabbed his finger at Lucy. "San Fran! The club! I remember you from the club." He raised his arms over his head and grooved to his own "*untz, untz, untz.*"

"Uh, okay," Lucy said.

"You and my bud, Marc, were tearing it up on the floor."

Lucy pressed her thighs harder into her hands. "Sure, right."

"Marc with a *c*?" He raised his eyebrows expectantly before waving his hand. "Ah, forget it. You were trying so many on for size, how could you remember? No worries, I won't tell him. No need to crush my boy's feelings."

"Okay, yeah, thanks." She cleared her throat again. "But like I was saying, last night, I—"

"And that was you heading into the office with Ryan during our shotgunning tourney, right?"

"Yes, that was my mentor session."

"Man, he's your mentor? What I wouldn't have given to have had him as my mentor when I was here." He smirked and flung the hood over his head. "Oh, wait, probably did okay without it." He mouthed "two commas" and held up his index and middle fingers.

Maddie groaned, and Delia, surprisingly, did too.

"Yes," Lucy said. "Ryan's my mentor, which is why—"

But Tim's head was in his phone, his finger swiping up and

down. "Comatose? For the love of LaCroix, you're Comatose? I'm surprised you were even let into ValleyStart. When I was applying—"

"Counting was revolutionary?" Maddie said.

Lucy nudged Maddie's shin and sat up straighter, retaking control. "But that's part of this. I wasn't always."

Delia spoke for the first time. "Lucy, why don't you tell him about Emma."

"Oh, *r-i-i-i-ght*," Tim said. "Emma Santos. Now this is starting to make sense." Tim held up his phone, showing a picture of Emma beside Ryan. He then pulled it back and swiped, returning it to the air, this time with the photo of Lucy and Ryan. "Listen, sweetheart . . ."

Maddie moved to the edge of the couch, and Lucy put a hand on her knee.

"No shame in looking to raise your Pulse by being 'close' to my man." He put air quotes around "close" and wiggled his eyebrows. "And no doubt you're hot enough that it should have worked. But you can't come running to your elders when your 'business dinner'"—another set of air quotes—"doesn't quite yield the results you expect. Real-world tip here . . ." His lips smoothed into a sympathetic smile. "Sometimes the Pulse rubs off, sometimes it doesn't. I mean, if I had a dime for every chick cozying up to Ryan to skyrocket to Crushing It, I'd be a rich man." He pressed his finger to his lips. "Oh, wait—"

"That's it." Maddie leapt to her feet.

"Yes," Lucy said, also standing. "It is. Let's go." She tipped her head toward the pile of dirty laundry on the kitchenette counter that made Lucy wish she'd bathed in hand sanitizer before entering the room. Hanging over the edge was the tee only given to Pulse employees.

She locked eyes with Maddie and then Delia. They all saw. They all knew what this was. A waste of time.

That night, Lucy, Maddie, and Delia stood on the balcony off the common room watching the explosion of fireworks that lit up the night sky. Palms as tall as the buildings dotted the quad, and each new flash bathed the airy fronds in vibrant colors, like light reflecting through a prism.

"At least it's beautiful," Delia said.

"Nothing beats Boston's," Maddie said. "But it's all right." As the sequence of bursts transitioned from red to white to blue, Maddie faced Delia and Lucy. "That was a mistake. Mine, and I'm sorry. I thought we'd gain something by reporting it quickly, but at least we can prove we tried. We'll go to Nishi as soon as she's back. She'll believe us. I'm sure of it."

She would. Lucy didn't doubt that. And yet . . . what had she said in the club? *Different rules for the gents.* A warning. That Lucy didn't heed. She may even think Lucy had brought this on herself. Because that's exactly what Lucy thought.

"No," Lucy said. "I changed my mind. I don't want anyone to know."

"What?" Maddie said. "But we agreed. He's a bully."

"Maybe. But he's also Ryan Thompson, and I'm a wannabe. A Comatose wannabe looking to do anything she can to win the incubator."

"No, Lucy, no. You can't let Mr. Two Commas—"

"I'm not *letting* anyone or anything. I dressed up, I went to dinner, I drank champagne with him. I wore crop tops and I danced at the club and I flirted and I used Pulse to make our beta test a success. Even you can see how it looks. What's true matters far less than what people want to believe."

If this got out . . . what would her mom say? What would Stanford think?

Fear rippled through her at the thought of losing everything she'd worked so hard for. Because of what? A hand on her leg?

Ryan Thompson made news. Ryan Thompson was news. She wanted her name in a headline—but not like this.

She steeled herself and said, "I want to be known for what I do, not for what someone does to me."

Despite the concern in Delia's eyes, she said, "Okay."

Maddie's expression shifted from resistance to resignation. "If that's what you want . . ."

"It is," Lucy said. "But that's not all I want. I want us to do what we said we'd do. I want us to win ValleyStart. Not for a job at Pulse, but for us."

"I'd like that," Delia said.

Maddie bobbed her head in distracted agreement.

In front of them, the pyrotechnics escalated into the finale. Lucy stepped forward and wrapped her hands around the metal railing, watching each light tear through the sky, burn brightly, and then fizzle out into nothingness, never realizing she could have this much in common with a firework.

What am I even doing here?

TWENTY-THREE

FUZZING • *Inserting random data sets to reveal vulnerabilities or bugs in the code*

MADDIE ADJUSTED THE SHEET of paper underneath her hand, a trick to minimize the smudging that often comes when shading. Her pencil moved, filling in the wings of the pterodactyl hovering over the outline of Martha's Vineyard. She hadn't drawn anything just for fun in a while; her clients and their needs dictated the time that Danny didn't.

Three days had passed since the ass otherwise known as the Head of House had belittled Lucy, prompting Maddie to take a page out of her brother's book and google where to buy a cobra in Silicon Valley. The search came up empty, forcing her to remain on the high road she was beginning to think was as much of a crock as Pulse. Instead, she'd overnighted a new pink notebook for Lucy and a set of baby-soft cotton sheets for Delia.

Though still uncomfortable with the decision not to report Ryan, Maddie was on board with staying and finishing the program, partly because she didn't have enough of a reason to return home. But more than enough reason to make it impossible for Ryan Thompson to dismiss them and, specifically, Lit.

Nishi had led a group critique of the beta tests. Lit was the standout.

Maddie let out the barest of smiles as she once again read ValleyStart's daily message:

ValleyStart: Who enters the penultimate week with their odds of winning mightily increased? Don't you sit, let's all stand and give it up for Lit!

Which was why this week saw most of the other teams heavy in reiteration and their team like this:

Maddie drawing pterodactyls.

Delia bugging her own code.

Lucy living inside PowerPoint.

Lit worked. Maddie's part was basically done. Hence the pterodactyl. Yet as she watched Lucy silently rehearse and Delia try to hack her own code, Maddie wished it weren't. She could use the distraction.

Her phone rang, and a grin she'd missed feeling scrunched up her cheeks.

She ducked into the hall to answer. "How's my favorite brother?"

"I'm your only brother."

"So?"

"I have to be your favorite."

"Cocky, aren't you, kid?"

"*Maddie.*"

"*Danny.*"

"Did you talk to Mom?" He didn't pause long enough for her to answer. "I mean, happy birthday, happy birthday to you, did you talk to Mom?"

Eighteen. An adult—as if she hadn't been one since Danny was born.

She'd decided not to tell Lucy and Delia that today was her birthday. The mood in room 303 was far from celebratory.

"No, I haven't talked to Mom yet." Because it was up to the parent to call the kid on their birthday. Scratch that. It was up to the parent's assistant to dial and then transfer the call.

"Oh," he said.

"What is it, Danny?"

"I'm not supposed to tell."

"Which means you have to. What's up?" She'd been waiting for Danny to send a happy face emoji after receiving a package of Gumberoo socks. He hadn't.

"Mom called from New York."

Danny's voice began to shake, and Maddie's hackles rose even though this wasn't unusual. With New York City being home to most of the big publishers, her parents traveled there often.

"From . . ." Danny sniffled. "From an apartment. She said I'd like the view and that it's got great light for your drawing. Guess it's near some park."

"Central Park?"

"Yeah, I think so."

"That's not some park, Danny, that's *some* park." She laughed. He didn't. "Get it?"

He was silent.

"We've been through this," she said. "I can't see you shrug."

His voice was weak when he finally spoke. "She said it's also near my new school."

"Your what?"

"So you don't know?"

"Danny, what did she say? Tell me exactly what she said."

"I'm not coming home to Cambridge after this, Mads. I'm supposed to meet her in New York City."

"What?"

No, no, no, no, no.

"At least you can go to Maryland now," he said. "You don't have to choose between us."

"I wasn't, Danny, there was never any choice."

"She said I don't have to choose either. Dad already agreed."

Sure he did. And they both did this behind my back.

"I'll fix it," she said.

"And I can't come to your demo thing anymore. She said none of us can because of the move—"

An unexpected tightness spread across Maddie's chest. "It's no big deal. Forget it." She forced a lighthearted "Now tell me about rock climbing."

When he finally sounded more like himself, she let him go. The goodbye still hung on her lips when she traded it for "What the hell, Mom?"

"Maddie?" her mom said. "This is my private line. You never call this line."

Because you never answer it. "News flash, Mom, I'm part of your private *life*. At least I'm supposed to be."

"Does that mean you want to be? Because that hasn't always been clear."

Maddie's nostrils flared. "When were you going to tell me about New York?"

She gave an exasperated sigh. "My assistant was supposed to schedule a call. But between negotiating the office lease and educating this fetus of a designer on what mid-century modern means, I've been—"

"Did you even . . ." Maddie tried to breathe. Her birthday didn't matter. Neither did asking if this meant separation or divorce for the business, for their marriage, or both. All that mattered was what always had. "You can't do this. You can't just take him from me."

"He's *my* son, Maddie."

"Since when?" The stabbing in Maddie's chest made it hard to see straight. "Did you even send him the socks?"

"The what?"

"The socks. Socks, Mom, socks! Ridiculous, splinter-spitting, bushy-eyebrowed socks! *Socks!*"

Maddie screamed. Every. Last. Word.

Lucy poked her head into the hall. "Maddie? Are you okay?"

Maddie hung up on her mother and slumped against the wall. "I'm grand. Just grand."

"Well, in that case, would you mind taking another spin through the lost and founds?" Lucy held up the notebook

Maddie had given her. "I love it, really. It's just that I'm trying to nail this last section, which I know I'd already summed up perfectly."

Though Maddie needed one as big as Central Park, at least this was a distraction. "I'll start with the study hall."

The ache in her chest consumed her as she trudged across campus to the ValleyStart headquarters. *New York?* Her mother was moving to New York? With Danny? And her dad . . . he was just letting it happen? No one told her. How could no one have told her?

When she finally reached the study hall, the swirling in her mind stopped.

Because Sadie was talking to Ryan Thompson.

A surge of adrenaline propelled her into the room. As she got closer, she realized that it wasn't just Sadie; it was all the kids from the day camp along with their counselors.

Relief. But not enough.

Maddie strode up to Sadie. She didn't bother to hide her disgust when she looked at Ryan. But the boredom in his eyes unnerved her. Not even a hint of fear. Like he knew he'd get away with it. Because he probably already had—and not just with Lucy.

Maddie felt her smile waver, but she wouldn't give him the satisfaction. She tugged Sadie's sleeve. "Let's talk. I have some ideas about your porcupine."

Sadie's eyes widened. "Porcupine?" Her voice was two octaves higher than usual. "*Pa-leez.* That silly thing? I'm way past that." She laughed and looked at Ryan. "Way, way."

"Of course you are." He reached a hand out as if to touch Sadie, and Maddie put herself between them. He narrowed his eyes at her. "Where are you from again, Mandy?"

"You know it's Maddie. And Boston. Says so right on my application."

"Sure, but where are you *really* from?" He raised an eyebrow. "You're not Thai, by any chance? Because I happen to know a great place in the city."

Is he actually goading me? Or just this much of a prick?

Shock at his blatant insult delayed her response.

Sadie answered for her. "She's half Chinese, her dad's side."

Maddie bit the inside of her lip to keep from spitting on Ryan. "Come on, Sadie, let's go."

If this place were on Lit, it'd have Maddie's smiling silver sardine stamped across it. Every table was packed, full of teams reworking their code. Maddie grabbed Sadie's hand and weaved her way through until she found a secluded spot next to the recycling, which brimmed with empty cans of energy drinks and bottles of iced coffee. A tower of pizza boxes stood beside it, at least a couple of days old from the trail of ants heading for it.

"What, what, what, what, what?" Sadie cried, shaking off Maddie's hand. "What is so important that you're dragging me away from Ryan Thompson? *Ryan. Thompson.*"

"Stay away from him," Maddie snapped. "Don't even follow him on Pulse, okay? In fact, stop with Pulse altogether."

"Have you been smoking the wacky weed?"

"Have I . . . what?"

Sadie shrugged. "What my brother always says to me when I

do insane things like pull my friends away from Ryan Thompson. *Ryan—*"

"I get it."

"I don't." Sadie huffed and turned her back to Maddie. "And you can forget about my presentation thing too. My brother's not even coming because it's not that big of a deal, so—"

Maddie's heart wrenched at the line she was sure Sadie's brother had delivered. "I'll be there."

"Yeah, whatever." She turned and faced Maddie. "But I guess you do owe me for *Ryan—*"

"Don't say it!"

"Don't yell at me!"

"I'm not."

"Tell that to my eardrums!"

"Just . . ." Maddie took a deep breath. "Enough, Sadie, just listen to me. Stay away from Ryan Thompson and stay off Pulse and will you please take your hands off your ears?"

Sadie made a face at Maddie and stormed off in one direction, and Maddie tossed her hands in the air and stormed off in the other.

She flung open the door to the student center and jerked her head back to the ridiculously puffy clouds in this eternally blue sky.

What am I even doing here?

TWENTY-FOUR

CODE SMELL • *A surface issue that indicates a deeper problem in the code*

"UH, LIA?"

Eric had started calling her that a week ago. No one called her that. She loved that no one called her that except for him.

The beta test had secured Delia's confidence in Lit. But after what happened with Ryan, Lit needed to not just work, but to be flawless, to account for every possibility and every impossibility.

She much preferred the quiet of the library and the proximity to Eric to the chaos of all the teams scrambling to rework their code in the study hall in this last week before Demo Day. Though she found she couldn't be *too* close to Eric and still concentrate. They'd taken to sitting across from each other, laptop to laptop, where she could hide her flush every time he called her Lia. *Every single time.*

"Marty texted me again," Eric said.

"More PowerPoint trouble? Tell him to text Lucy. You'd think she invented it with the things she can do."

"It's not that."

"Then what?" Delia's grin faded when she saw the concern on Eric's face.

"First, we'll figure it out, I promise, we'll figure out what—"

"Eric? What is it? Just tell me."

"I think it's better that you see it." He rotated his computer with one hand and reached for hers with the other. Goose bumps erupted on the surface of her skin, but what she saw on the screen meant they were increasingly no longer a result of Eric.

"How . . . how is this possible?" Delia said.

She released Eric's hand and pulled the laptop closer. She read, running her finger along each line, determined to get to the end, to the punch line, to the joke this had to be. *Had to be.*

Eric pushed his chair back, circled the table, and sat beside her. "It's yours? All of it?"

Delia couldn't summon enough saliva to speak. She barely had the strength to nod. On the browser screen in front of them was an open-source coding site. Programmers and developers tossed up ideas and source code to contribute to the community, to get feedback and input, ultimately for anyone to take and use, the theory being that higher-quality software would result. Technically, open source meant anyone was free to use the code, but in the context of ValleyStart, this was strictly prohibited. It was in the pledge they'd signed. The one Delia had signed.

Yet right here on this site was the code behind Lit. Down to every letter and number. Dated two months before ValleyStart began. Before Lit began.

"How . . . how?" Delia kept reading. In the notes preceding the code was the exact description of Lit, including the potential applications to malls, amusement parks, and all the things Lucy had worked hard to bring to life in her Demo Day slides. "We didn't, Eric. I swear, we didn't steal it. Lit was ours. Lit *is* ours. It's not . . . we didn't do this."

"I know. Of course I know. You didn't think . . ." Eric tried to take her hand, but she pulled away. "That's not why I showed you. I know you'd never do something like that, Lia. But if this link is making the rounds . . . not everyone knows you as well as I do."

Delia's breathing grew rapid.

All that work! All my work!

The scream stayed inside but tore through her. Sweat broke out on her forehead, her palms, her armpits, her feet . . . so much . . . enough to drown in. She leapt from the table. "I have to go."

She had to tell Maddie and Lucy before someone else did. She whirled around, only half hearing Eric's attempts to calm her. She rushed to the nearest exit, and then, once outside, drove her feet hard into the ground, running so fast that her lungs struggled to keep up. She tore down the path under the arbor toward the dorms. She was so focused that she heard the laughter before she even realized she was on the ground. She'd tripped. Apparently eyelash glue had a shelf life. She stared at the sole of her shoe beside her as pain roared in her knees.

Gavin and a few other guys from ValleyStart were laughing. Sitting on the benches in front of the dorms and just . . . laughing. Already bright red from her sprint, heat spread deeper beneath her skin. She pushed herself to her knees, then to her feet. She bent to retrieve the torn sole and stopped, instead chucking off her broken sneaker and leaving it on the sidewalk.

Her ascent up the stairs was slow. Scrapes burned the heel

of her foot and her right knee. When she reached the door, she realized she didn't have her key. She knocked, and Lucy let her inside.

She refused Maddie's offer to wash out her cuts, didn't answer when Lucy asked if she was all right. She just walked to the desk and used Lucy's computer to show them.

Lucy's face paled.

Maddie's eyes turned cold.

No one spoke, so, finally, Delia did. "What are we going to do? Demo Day's in a week!"

No response.

"Should we report it? We should report it."

"Because that worked so well last time," Maddie said.

They both looked to Lucy. But she was staring at the floor. She mumbled something about needing air, covered her eyes with her butterfly-frame sunglasses, and headed for the door. Delia wanted to stop her, to keep her here, with them, so they could figure this out, together. But she was out the door before Delia could find the words to make her stay.

"How could this have happened?" she said to Maddie. To the Maddie who'd arrived on day one. Sullen and distant.

Without a word, Maddie lifted her bag off the top bunk and left.

Delia stood in the center of the room—alone.

She shut Lucy's laptop. She couldn't have the code—*her code*—staring at her. She spun around, not knowing if she should stay or go. Finally, she slumped onto her bed, her head sinking into the pillow that Lucy had insisted she keep. She pulled her eyes away from the Ada Lovelace quotation under her bunk and rested them instead on her mom's suitcase. Each of its stickers soon blurred as she gave in to her tears. Her body began to tremble and her head started to swim and suddenly there wasn't enough air in her bunk, in the room, not even the hall that she stumbled into.

She was suffocating, hot, burning up, spots blinking in front of her eyes. Her hearing dulled and her stomach rocked with nausea.

Disoriented, she whirled in place, searching for the right way to go, for which end of the hall led to the balcony . . . to air. On her last circle, she saw it. She staggered down the hallway, shoved the door open, and rummaged in her pockets until she found her phone. Dizzy, she gulped down air, but her heart still beat in her ears as she jammed her finger on the call button.

"Delia!" her mom crooned. "How's everything? We want to know everything, every detail. Here, I'll put you on speaker."

"Mom, I—"

"Hanging ten yet?" her dad said.

Delia had no hope of giving him the laugh he wanted. She grappled for words, still light-headed and woozy.

"Dad, Mom, I'm not sure what's happening—"

"Because we haven't been keeping in touch," her dad said. "We wanted to wait until things were final before—"

"But we should have called sooner," her mom interrupted. "We know how upsetting this is for you, but, honey, we're good. We're great. We accepted! Your father proposed an absurd counteroffer, and they said yes!"

"Still got my acting chops," her dad said. "Total poker face, though inside I was having a panic attack."

Delia's heart was exploding out of her chest and she needed them to call 911 because she thought she was having a heart attack but was this . . . that's what this was? A panic attack?

It was like she was in a free fall with nothing left to catch her. "I . . . you . . ." She pressed her hand against her chest, then gripped her necklace, hoping to steady herself. "You actually did it?"

"Done and done!" her dad said. "And we did something else—we booked our flights. We can't wait to see your production."

"Demonstration," her mom corrected.

Delia closed her eyes to combat the black spots. "You're coming? Here?"

"You have to ask?" her mom said. "We love you, Delia. We're so very proud of you."

"So proud." Her dad sounded choked up.

And Delia's heart quit racing and simply . . . broke.

She stayed on the phone for a minute or two longer before she told them she had to go. Her heart used each beat to normalize, and she stood still, waiting. She wanted to call Cassie, but what would she even say? She clung to the railing, holding it tight between her hands, the cool metal lowering her temperature, inviting her to lean her body against it, so hard and deep that she hung over the side, looking down at the fountain in the quad. She pressed her forehead to the metal, rubbing back and forth, listening to the gently bubbling water before she turned to let the coolness soothe her sweaty back—and there was Eric. Standing in the doorway, her backpack in his hand, the panic that was easing inside her written all over his face, living in his eyes, ones full of pity.

"Lia." He stepped forward.

"No," she said. "Not . . . don't, just don't."

Don't call me Lia here, now, after you saw me making out with the railing . . . after I freaked out like the geek I am and always will be. . . . I'm a fool. A complete and utter fool and this place isn't my place and isn't my home and never will be and why did I ever want it to be and how did I think I could actually be here . . . how did I think I actually belonged?

How could I give up everything I had to even try?

Humiliated, she grabbed her bag from Eric's hand and pushed past him, feeling every bit like the girl from Littlewood who should have never left.

What am I even doing here?

TWENTY-FIVE

TROUGH OF SORROW • *The period of struggle a startup faces after a significant setback, when quitting seems the most reasonable option*

LUCY'S SHEETS TRAPPED HER like a straitjacket. Instead of sleeping, she'd turned this way and that, twisting her bedding around her. As the morning light filtered through the window, she clawed and kicked her way free.

None of them had slept much. Somewhere around midnight and again at about three, Delia had tried to get them to talk about what had happened, but Maddie just hugged the wall, her back to them, and Lucy remained quiet, knowing there was nothing to say.

Nothing she could say. Because this was all her fault.

It was the username. She'd recognized it immediately. "PissingInATinCan." Aka Gavin Cox. Did he want her to know it was him? Or did he think she wouldn't remember? She needed it to be the latter. The latter meant he was using any and every advantage to win; the latter at least she could understand even if she had no idea how he could have done it. But the former, being that mean, that vindictive against her, hurt in a place so deep Lucy didn't have a name for it.

A Maddie-sized bundle lay buried under her covers, but Delia's bed was empty. Lucy set her feet on the floor and unplugged her phone from its charger.

The ValleyStart daily text mocked her:

ValleyStart: Week 5 and still alive? Then tonight you better crack the whip, for tomorrow's our Pulse field trip!

The tour of Ryan's company. Lucy jammed her finger down and deleted the text.

She then opened her email. Only one new message downloaded, the bold lettering forming a word Lucy had been able to spell since she was four. Her heart wedged itself in her throat.

Please.

Her finger gently tapped the screen, and she closed her eyes, knowing when she opened them, her world would never be the same.

She opened. She read. She kept reading. She read again. And again. And again and again and again and it never changed.

How could it not change?

She ripped off her pajamas, wanted to keep ripping, right through her skin, this skin that was being eaten alive by something devouring it from the inside, something she couldn't stop even if she wanted to. And she didn't. She didn't want to be in this skin any more than she wanted to be here in this room, in this dorm, in this life. She just didn't . . . didn't want . . . she didn't have anything left to want.

She tore the pennant off her wall, jumped out of bed, and clawed through her closet, yanking her exercise tights and tank off the hanger so hard that she fell back against the bunk bed. The thud roused Maddie.

"I'm trying to sleep," Maddie groaned.

Lucy ignored her and wrenched herself into her running gear. She rammed her feet into her limited production sneakers, opened the door, and ran.

Past the fountain in the quad.

The eagerness shown in updating your application, while commendable, ultimately called certain values held in high regard by our institution into question.

Past the student center.

Concern arose regarding the promised recommendation from Mr. Ryan Thompson that never arrived.

Past the ValleyStart headquarters.

This concern deepened as claims of social media prowess were proven to be false.

Past the library.

Misrepresentation, be it from a lack of follow-through or purposeful deceit, cannot be disregarded.

Past the computer science center.

When considered along with the unfortunate circumstances of your missed interview, which was not preceded by a notice of cancellation or need to reschedule . . .

Past the tech day camp.

. . . we regret to inform you that we will not be able to offer admission to our incoming class and your name has been removed from our alternate list.

Past and past and past.

Removed removed removed.

Lucy's arms pumped and her feet pummeled the ground.

Have a nice life, loser.

She sprinted through the park that bordered the edge of campus, her eyes zeroing in on the backless bench in front of her. She stayed her course, closing the gap, and when she neared it, sprang into the air to hurdle it. One leg stretched out, clearing it easily, but the toe of her other foot clipped the edge, and she pitched forward, plowing into the ground face-first.

The impact forced all the air from her lungs and she rolled onto her back, grappling for oxygen. Pennant still clutched in one fist, she wrapped both hands around her torso and curled her legs toward her stomach, reaching for them, holding herself, rocking, fighting the tears rising to the surface. And then, she flung her arms and legs to the side, spread-eagled on the ground, and screamed.

It wasn't until she finally stood that she saw the playground off to the side. Swings, slides, merry-go-rounds all motion-less, halted as children and parents and nannies gawked at the spectacle that was Lucy Katz.

She waved.

And curtsied.

Then plopped onto the bench that had tried to kill her, motionless herself until her last tear dried.

Now what?

She spent the morning wandering through campus, her walk as aimless as her life. She shredded the Stanford pennant as she went, dropping strips of felt into trash cans along the way until there was nothing left but bits of red fuzz beneath her fingernails.

When her eyes rested on the tall glass windows and steel frame of the computer science complex—a modern anomaly on the mostly white stucco and red tile campus—Lucy realized where she was: outside Nishi's office. Lucy was inside and knocking on her door before thinking through why.

"Lucy?" Nishi said, glancing at her phone. "I don't see you on my schedule—"

"I'm not. Sorry, I can go."

"No, no, come in. I've got some time." She sipped from a small blue ceramic mug. "What can I help you with?"

Lucy hovered in the doorway, inhaling the warm spice of Nishi's chai, unsure how to answer. Because she needed help, they all did, so much help.

"Is it your presentation?" Nishi said. "I can't imagine it's not perfect down to the fade-ins and -outs. You've been meticulous about taking notes on everything since the first session. Your notebook must be an excellent blueprint for Lit."

Her notebook. Lucy's notebook *was* an excellent blueprint for Lit. It contained everything they'd thought and done and hoped to do. And had been missing for days. Since the night with Ryan.

A shock wave jolted her.

His car.

When they'd careened across the street and into Ryan's driveway, everything she had with her was thrown to the floor. She'd grabbed her bag. She remembered grabbing her bag. And then she remembered grabbing her notebook off the table in the restaurant. She'd never put it in her bag.

Ryan had it. And must have given it to Gavin.

And it was then that she knew the answer to her earlier question. Gavin wanted her to know it was him. Same as Ryan did. They wanted her to know they did this—together. That they teamed up to destroy not just Lit but her. Because if she told about the code, she'd have to tell about that night with Ryan. And the one with Gavin. Everything would come out. And it wouldn't matter who Lucy was or wasn't; all that would matter was what it looked like. What she looked like. And that wasn't anything good.

So what? She'd already lost everything.

Nishi sat behind the desk, an increasingly confused look on her face, but Lucy was remembering a different expression: the awe she'd shown upon meeting Lucy's mother.

Which meant Lucy had just one thing left: her reputation. And Maddie's and Delia's. She had to protect all of them.

She moved into the office, her hand at her side, her fingers typing a quick text to Gavin.

Take it down. You won.

Three little dots appeared, then disappeared, then appeared again.

She didn't care—whatever he had to say, Lucy was done with Gavin. She blocked his number.

An extra layer of guilt weighed heavy on her as she sat in the wooden chair across from Nishi. She switched off her ringer and shoved her phone under her leg.

"Lit is . . ." Lucy struggled to finish her sentence. Finally, she simply told the only truth she could. "Things aren't going the way I planned."

"Is that all?" Nishi pushed her laptop aside.

"I'm sorry, but . . . what?"

"Don't get me wrong. Earthquakes, root canals, zombie apocalypse—plans have their place. But happy accidents? Why, they've given us everything from Corn Flakes to pacemakers to Post-it Notes. To me."

That got Lucy's attention.

Nishi folded her hands together, the long sleeves of her tunic, red with a small black teardrop pattern, resting against the desk. "I was an engineer. That's what I came here to do and to be. But when I got sick of crashing on my cousin Sanjay's couch and eating a diet of ramen, I took the only job I could get, which was in marketing. But it was planning three product launches, four focus groups, and my boss's daughter's wedding all in one year with inferior software that led to me creating my own."

"Your first company."

"Listen, Lucy, I just think when life hands you lemons and all you can think to do is make lemonade, you're not trying hard enough. And you've never had my mom's lemon chicken biryani."

Lucy drew in a breath.

"Sound familiar?"

"My mom. Except hers was lemon cake."

"Never had much of a sweet tooth. But the sentiment stuck. Heard your mom say it in a talk when I first moved here. You know she was one of the first women in tech to reach a C level?"

"But she's stayed there. Under three different CEOs."

"Exactly," Nishi said. "She's stayed. Under three different

CEOs. All voted out and yet the business is more profitable each year. Why do you think that is?"

Lucy had never thought of it that way before.

"Women like your mom, they give hope to the rest of us that we can be firsts too, be it the first with brown skin or a name that's hard to pronounce or whatever isn't what people expect to see on a founder's profile page. You might say she's the reason I never quit."

A hardness pressed against the sides of Lucy's throat, and she stared at the new scuff on her formerly pristine sneaker. But inside she thought, *Me too.*

"So," Lucy started, "if we needed to change Lit, could we? Could we present something else?"

"A happy accident? Sure, why not? The mentoring and beta tests are all to help teams put together the best presentation that they can. If a team wants to forgo all of it, that's their choice."

And Lucy knew, she had to find Maddie and Delia.

TWENTY-SIX

SYNERGY • *Working together so the combined effect is greater than the sum of the parts*

IT WAS THE *THUNK* that finally roused Maddie from bed. She climbed down from her bunk, smelling a bit like Danny's favorite socks. She opened the door, and a hefty overnight package fell into the room. The return address wasn't one she recognized. Unlike the handwriting on the note inside.

> *Maddie!*
>
> *Why, I wish I knew you were in my sunshine-y state before now! I'm doing the pretentious thing and "summering" in Santa Barbara. Gah! Four books in, and still I can't believe I'm one of those people using "summer" as a verb.*
> *I dare say I spit a splinter or two myself when your mom explained where you're "summering." Most impressive, Maddie! Your art of Roo still hangs above my dining room table. Still wish the powers that be would have accepted your*

version for book four. So, talent? That I knew. But I didn't know you also had an affinity for the technology world. But then, why not? Limits are only good for speed and hot peppers, I always say. Your parents must be so proud. (Don't roll your eyes at me, my dear—there are souls beneath those wireless headsets even still!)

Enclosed, find the latest prototype of Gumberoo gear—would love to know what you think! The same has been sent to little Danny. Next time, reach out to me directly.

Happy "weeding"!
Esmé

Socks, hats, tees, and the full series of books, signed by Esmé. The tee, sent in Maddie's size, would be a nightshirt on Sadie. She'd love it.

Maddie grabbed her toiletry kit and towel. Her whole shower, she replayed her argument with Sadie, knowing she needed to apologize. It was wrong to expect Sadie, who worshipped Ryan Thompson and Pulse the way Lucy had, to understand why she'd been so upset.

As Maddie returned to her room and dressed, she tried to block the image of Ryan near Sadie. The one that rekindled the urge to shop for cobras.

She reached for her messenger bag, peeled back the flap, and emptied the contents onto the desk. She stuffed the bounty of Gumberoo gear and all the books inside and began to sort through the junk that had collected in her bag since the program began. Sketches for the logo of the pet-grooming service they'd abandoned, a handful of pterodactyl drawings, flyers for their beta test and one for . . . Sadie's presentation.

Maddie brought her phone to life to check the time. She'd missed it.

She ran all the way to the day camp, her heart exploding not from the unusual physical activity but from picturing the same look on Sadie's face that she'd seen on Danny's every time their parents missed a soccer game, a music recital, or . . . dinner.

She'd slept through it.

Seriously?

She ran faster.

What was wrong with her?

Her feet kept moving and her head kept spinning and she didn't see the skateboarder veering into her path until he was right in front of her. She leapt to the side, and the weight of her messenger bag dragged her to the ground. Her left hand and knee took the brunt of it, but she hopped right up, brushing off the dirt, no time to even let herself feel the pain of it.

When she finally arrived, she caught sight of Sadie across the room in a black sleeveless dress, looking older than eleven, like a young Lucy, if it weren't for the red hair.

Shame infused Maddie's every step, and she slowed as she made her way to Sadie. She tried for a smile as she asked, "How was it?"

Sadie crossed her arms in front of her chest and shrugged.

Maddie turned to the woman beside her whose own red hair suggested she was Sadie's mom. "Hi, I'm Maddie, I've been—"

"Oh, I know," Sadie's mom said. "My monkey hasn't stopped talking about you all summer."

Sadie glanced at her feet.

"I'm Rachel, and you're really sweet for taking time to help my daughter."

"It was my pleasure. And actually, I should be thanking Sadie." Sadie looked up at Maddie from under her eyelashes. "I would have been way more homesick without her."

A hint of a smile betrayed Sadie's stoic face and pushed Maddie to again ask, "How'd the presentation go?"

"She kicked ass." Rachel side-hugged Sadie. "Tell her all about it, hon, while I go outside to call your MIA brother and revoke his car privileges for the weekend."

A flicker of hurt darkened Sadie's eyes at the mention of her brother, and Maddie promised herself that, no matter what her future held, she wouldn't ever let Danny feel like this.

Sadie's mom pecked her daughter's head. "Course then we'll be stuck with him, won't we?" She sighed but gave a little smirk. "Sometimes parenting is a no-win situation."

After she left, Maddie nudged Sadie's foot. "Kicked ass, huh? I'm just that good, I guess."

Sadie clutched her arms tighter.

"Right. Okay . . ." Maddie sucked in a breath. "I'm sorry, Sadie. Truly sorry. I messed up. I wanted to be here, I promise."

Sadie lifted her head. "Why weren't you?"

"I . . ." Maddie rubbed her hand against her shorts, trying

to ease the sting of the scrapes from her fall and from the look in Sadie's eyes. It might have been Sadie's brother and Maddie's parents, but it didn't matter; Maddie knew what it was like to be let down by those you trusted most. "The truth is, I have no excuse. I was too busy having a pity party for myself."

"Is everything okay?"

Maddie's throat went dry at Sadie's immediate concern, and she forced out a "Yeah, it's fine. I mean, it will be. You, uh, look nice, by the way. Certainly befitting a Pulse 10."

"Awesome," Sadie said with a hefty amount of snort that surprised Maddie.

"Maybe I'm the one who should be asking you if everything's okay?"

Sadie hesitated, staring at Maddie, before waving for her to get closer. Maddie did, leaning down to lessen the height gap.

"See that kid over there?" Maddie turned, and Sadie cried, "Don't look!" Sadie shielded her eyes. "But you see him?" Maddie nodded. "Okay, well, his mom's a 10. I got him to introduce me to her and I was asking her about Pulse-a-palooza and she laughed at me. Like this: '*HA!*' It's not like I was asking to go, I just wanted to learn more about it and she—"

"Was ridiculously rude. I'm sorry, Sadie."

"Yeah, well, I'm not sure I care about Pulse-a-palooza that much anymore anyway. It was cooler when I sorta knew someone who was going to be there."

"Emma would have been great," Maddie agreed.

"Her feeds were always fun, way different than a lot of the other 10s. I've been following so many, and they just started to feel the same after a while. Like . . . I don't know, like my tap-dancing porcupine. It works and looks pretty and all, but it's almost too perfect."

"Like it was designed that way," Maddie said without really thinking. But then, she started to. To think. About Ryan. And Lucy and Emma and the 10s.

"I'm all for pretty." Sadie flashed a sly grin. "But too pretty . . ." She brushed her bangs back and pointed to a couple of indents on her skin. "Chicken pox. Gives me character though, you know?"

"And makes you real," Maddie said slowly.

"Unlike the 10s," Sadie said.

"Unlike the 10s," Maddie repeated, and with each word a light bulb flickered in her brain. "Sadie, you're brilliant."

"I know."

Maddie reached into her bag for her phone, but it started buzzing with a text from Lucy before she even unlocked it.

Where are you? We need to talk about Ryan and Gavin.

Maddie typed: *And Pulse.*

This was important; Maddie knew it in her gut. Same as she knew Sadie was important. So she slipped her phone into her pocket. "Kicked ass, huh? Will you show me your presentation?"

"Can't get enough of that spiny thing, can you?"

"Nope. Pretty awesome. The only reason I keep coming around."

"*Ha!*" Sadie cried, mimicking the 10.

Maddie grinned and wrestled her bag off her shoulder. "Here. A little congratulations."

"Uh, you really need some lessons in gift giving, Maddie. That thing's nasty."

"Just take it. And look inside."

Sadie did. "You . . . but how . . . Maddie, it's . . ."

"You're welcome." A warmth spread across Maddie's chest. "I'll explain next time, but trust me, that's a much better fandom to be a part of anyway."

Sadie dropped the bag and flung herself at Maddie, giving her a hug that threw her off balance—in every way. Especially when she found how hard she was hugging back.

After walking Sadie to her mom's car, Maddie unearthed her four-leaf clover and squeezed. She'd given up a lot for Danny—and she didn't regret it one bit.

She waved goodbye and started back toward the dorms. Ryan, Emma, Lucy, Pulse, the 10s all looped in her mind. Over and over, something there but not there. Like the 10s. Surface. Fake.

She increased her pace and texted Lucy: *Pulse. It's not right. I don't know what it is, but it's not right.*

Lucy: Sure, because Ryan runs it.

Maddie: It's more than that.

Lucy's text crossed Maddie's: *Because Ryan's an ass.*
Maddie added: *And sexist.*

Lucy: And manipulative.

Maddie: And will do anything to win.

Lucy: Like me.

Lucy: It's okay, it's true.

Maddie: Was true.

Lucy sent a heart. Then ten. Then a gagging emoji.

Lucy: He flaunts it. On the first day, remember? Joking that my low Pulse must be because of a glitch in the code.

Lucy: He's the glitch.

He's the glitch, Maddie thought. Pulse is his. The leader sets the tone. Everyone follows the leader. The leader who's a sexist, manipulative, predatory, juvenile ass.

Her thoughts were so rapid fire, she couldn't type fast enough: *What if he wasn't joking?*

Maddie: What if there's an actual glitch in the code?

Maddie: What if it's not by accident?

Lucy: What are you thinking?

Maddie: Not sure. But all the 10s are so . . . so perfect.

Lucy: An advertiser's dream.

Maddie: Right.

Maddie: Like it's designed that way. Manipulated to be that way.

Maddie: Do you think

Lucy: He's

Maddie: His whole company

Lucy: Is a crock.

Maddie: Is a crock.

Their texts crossed at the same time as they both crashed into something.

Each other.

Maddie pushed herself off Lucy, rubbing her wrist, which had collided with Lucy's nose. Lucy pinched the bridge of it and jiggled her head.

They faced each other, silently piecing it all together.

Lucy spoke first. "We need—"

"Delia," Maddie finished.

TWENTY-SEVEN

BOOTSTRAPPING • *Reinvesting initial profits as the sole method of funding a company, i.e., "pulling yourself up by your bootstraps"*

DELIA CRAWLED INTO BED. She'd called in sick. All it took was two steps inside the student center and a glimpse of Eric's light brown hair shielding his face as he hunkered over a keyboard, prying off a letter to clean out the caramel mocha latte, bison burger, or pot brownie crumbs stuck underneath, and she knew she couldn't do it.

She couldn't spend the afternoon across from Eric after he'd seen her meltdown. She couldn't spend the afternoon punching buttons on a microwave for ten dollars an hour that didn't matter now that her parents had sold the theater. She couldn't spend the afternoon pretending that her life hadn't imploded all around her.

So she didn't. She sank her head into Lucy's pillow, made softer thanks to the gift of Maddie's plush sheets, and opened Delia's Den.

She'd been adding functionality to Ready for Hedy, a

torpedo-based coding game that paid homage to the 1940s Hollywood actress Hedy Lamarr. Her beauty supposedly inspired Disney's Snow White, but she was also an avid inventor, with her work leading to the development of wireless technology used in everything from Wi-Fi to GPS to Bluetooth.

Wanting to help the Allied cause in World War II, she focused on torpedoes, powerful weapons that, she reasoned, could be better controlled if they were radio-guided. But radio signals could be jammed. Along with her co-inventor, Lamarr came up with the idea for frequency hopping, a way of moving around on radio frequencies to avoid a third party jamming the signal. Skeptical, the military didn't use it then, only integrating it after. Decades passed before she was recognized for her revolutionary work.

The game was quickly becoming Delia's favorite.

She was lost in it when Maddie and Lucy charged through the door.

"We know what he's doing," Lucy said.

"Ryan," Maddie said. "With Pulse. It's—"

"Manipulating—"

"Everything—"

"We're sure of it—"

"We just need to prove it."

Lucy stepped deeper into the room. She crouched at Delia's bedside. "We need *you* to prove it."

Delia's head was spinning from Lucy and Maddie being so in sync as much as from what they'd said about Gavin and Ryan and Lucy's notebook and Pulse. The evidence was circumstantial. Yes,

Lucy and Emma's rankings shot up and down quickly—quicker than most? Delia wasn't familiar enough with Pulse to know that. And Lucy and Maddie had no way to support their theory that Emma had brushed off Ryan's advances, causing him to retaliate through Pulse in the same way they were convinced he had with Lucy. Still, there was the discrepancy in Emma's social media feeds—that all her likes and favorites and everything were still high but her Pulse was Comatose. So . . . maybe?

But the 10s? That everyone Crushing It was *put* there? Because beautiful faces, skinny waistlines, six packs, and pearly white teeth were coveted? Because who you knew, not what you knew, mattered most? That it all led to an endless loop of more likes and favorites and followers and popularity that drew advertisers like bees to pollen? That in turn meant Pulse drew advertisers and investors and enough cash to buy every theater in the country if Ryan wanted? Fund thousands of scholarships every year? Give him his hot tub and surround him with water views?

That couldn't happen because Ryan was manipulating individual accounts on a whim. It had to be in the code. In Pulse's code. It had to *be* Pulse.

"I don't know," Delia finally said.

"But it's possible?" Maddie asked.

"Anything's possible," Delia said. "It's just so . . ."

"Slimy?" Lucy said.

"Fraudulent?" Maddie said.

"Wrong." Delia moved her aging laptop to the end of her bed. If she were a 10 she would have had the newest one on the market. "It's wrong."

But how could Ryan have done it? Delia ran through what she knew of Pulse—some of which was the same as Lit. The rankings had to be determined in real time by the app based on data from the user's social media accounts. There was no hard-coded number associated with an account that could be changed with a stroke on a keyboard. The rankings would be regenerated any time someone loaded their Pulse account.

So could Ryan hack it? No. But then again, he wouldn't need to hack it. He controlled the source code. And the databases.

Delia sat up straighter. *Of course!*

The very thing she'd been immersing herself in for weeks. If Ryan was doing this . . . if he was manipulating Pulse rankings not just for himself but for all of Pulse in order to give advertisers what they wanted—*or maybe even what they asked for?*—he'd do it using the database. He'd need to have his own private list—a table in the database that only he could access. If the table had the person's name and a rating that Ryan could change at will, then the code would have to do what? Somehow override the automatically generated ratings. So the code would need to have a function that would check this table first to see if a user was in it. If a name was there, then the code would tell the program to display Ryan's chosen rating. If not, then the normal calculated rating would appear. An extra step. One that could be done quickly enough. One that would change a person's rating. For better or worse. Just as he'd done with Emma and Lucy. Just as he could do with anyone—*for* anyone. Anyone who offered him something in return.

"Delia?" Maddie said with concern. She bent down at her bedside next to Lucy. "I know we're asking a lot. And I don't know how we'd even start proving it. But I think we have to."

"And not for me," Lucy said. "This is bigger than me and Emma. Pulse changed the world. What everyone who comes here wants to do, and he did it. But what he's changed it into is . . ."

"Twisted," Maddie said. "It's bad enough that he makes eleven-year-olds anxious about their likes, but this, perpetuating the idea that beauty, that perfection, is everything? For profit? I can't just let him. If we're right, people have to know."

Lucy looked at Delia. "I know you're here on scholarship and—"

"It doesn't matter. Not anymore. I was doing this for my parents—so they wouldn't have to worry about putting me through college, but now . . . they sold the theater. I don't need to win ValleyStart and work at Pulse for them."

"Oh, Dee, I'm really sorry," Lucy said.

"I can't believe they actually did it," Maddie said.

Moisture glistened in Delia's eyes. "It seems to be what they want."

Lucy put a hand on Delia's. "And what do you want?"

Her eyes traveled between Maddie and Lucy. She knew. She'd always known. Guilt weighed heavy on her chest because her parents selling the theater meant she was free to have it. "To be here. One day. Not at Pulse, but here, doing something good."

"Showing Pulse as the scam it is wouldn't hurt," Lucy said. "Think of it—if you could hack into Pulse's code . . . only a unicorn could do that."

"Pink and blue and swirly," Maddie said. "Or whatever color you want it to be."

"*We* want it to be." Delia inhaled a deep breath.

Breaths raise you from the depths.

And then she stood. If she could hack into the Pulse database and find the secret table, then they'd have real evidence. Usernames and ratings compiled outside the normal system? It'd launch a formal investigation. Into Ryan and Pulse. Would she make enemies?

Maybe. But she cared more about her friends.

"I'll try," Delia said. "That's all I can promise. I'll start at the Pulse field trip tomorrow . . ." She stopped herself. "But wait . . . can we go? We can't use Lit anymore. We don't have an app. Can we even stay here? If we're not presenting at Demo Day?" Delia's shoulders slumped. "Which my parents are coming to. They booked tickets already, and all they'll see is me sitting in the audience beside them."

"Mine aren't coming," Maddie said matter-of-factly. But her eyes lowered when she added, "At least Danny won't be here to see me sitting in the audience beside you."

Delia glanced at Lucy. "And yours . . ."

"I'm not sure what my mom is planning to do. How sad is that? I never invited her. That's sadder, right?"

No one responded, not because the answer was clear, but because the answer was complicated. Like everything for all of them right now.

Lucy sighed as she sat on Delia's bed, shifting the computer to make room. "Hey, what is this, Dee?"

"Nothing, it's silly, don't even—"

"I didn't know you were into playing video games."

"It's not a video game. Not exactly. It's just something I work on sometimes."

Lucy set the computer on her lap. "You created this? Hedy

Lamarr? The actress who had something to do with creating Wi-Fi, right?"

"Ultimately, yes," Delia said, feeling increasingly self-conscious as Maddie perched herself beside Lucy. "The graphics aren't great. It's more what elements of the coding it's teaching."

"This teaches coding?" Maddie said. "Is this the kind of stuff you did to learn on your own? So cool."

Delia's cheeks burned, and she moved to take the computer. "We should really get back to Demo Day."

Lucy scooted deeper into the bunk. "We are."

"No, we're talking about my silly game."

"One and the same. Because this . . ." Lucy tapped the screen. "This is how we stay in it. We pivot, just like Nishi did when she had to plan her boss's wedding."

"What?" Maddie said.

"Never mind. Point is, we need an app for Demo Day. We have one. Right here."

"But the games aren't fancy or anything. And they're based on female coders and mathematicians. Hedy Lamarr and Grace Hopper and Dorothy Vaughan and Joan Clarke. Women who did amazing, smart things that most people know nothing about. People won't care."

"You do," Lucy said.

"But I'm into this stuff. Because I've got some robot brain or something."

"Robot?" Lucy tapped the screen. "Uh, no, I don't think so. This whole thing is super creative."

Delia could only think of her mom onstage. "No, it's not. It's just code."

"Made fresh and fun. That'll appeal to kids. We both know how rare that is, Delia." As Lucy paused to gather her thoughts, she looked up at the bottom of the bunk. She read the Ada quotation as she removed it. "'Imagination is the Discovering Faculty, preeminently. It is that which penetrates into the unseen worlds around us, the worlds of Science.' If this is your goal, this is how we achieve it. Together. Because including women? Historical women? Who are total badass screen queens? I could pitch the hell out of this." Lucy ratcheted her enthusiasm down a couple of notches, turning more serious. "Which isn't why I'm saying this. It's just a great idea."

"Teaching kids how to code," Maddie said. "That's perfect. And kicks that tap-dancing porcupine's ass."

Delia sat at the desk, a mix of fear and excitement bubbling inside her. "You really think we could do this? In a week?"

"The games are already there," Lucy said. "And, really, we only need one to be fully functional for Demo Day. Which means you can mostly focus on Pulse."

"Maybe . . . but . . ." Delia faced Maddie. "It'll mean a lot of work on your end to make it look remotely professional."

"Excellent. I've been bored out of my gourd."

"And you'll have to redo the presentation," Delia said to Lucy. "Without a beta test."

"Heard it right from the ass's mouth: all I need to do is own the room." She smiled her most confident smile. "Got it covered."

Delia thought of how much she'd have loved games like these as a kid—after all, that's who she'd always been designing this for: her younger self. "You really want to do this? Because if you do, I'd like us to try. And not just so we don't have to leave the program."

"Because this is important," Maddie said. "Like Eric's app."

"It could be. I wish I'd said something sooner."

Lucy waved her off. "I probably wouldn't have listened. But I'm listening now. And, actually, there's so much potential—"

"Lucy," Maddie warned.

"No, I'm serious, because this would be perfect for an underserved market." She got out of the bunk and spun around, like she was already on the Demo Day stage. "Girls."

"I like that," Delia said.

"Sadie would love that," Maddie said, a spark in her eye that had never been there when they talked about Lit.

Lucy's excitement matched hers. She swung the printed quotation in her hand and then faced the door, still covered in old Lit logos. She tore them all down and pressed Ada's words dead center. "And that's just the beginning, ladies."

Maddie sat on the corner of the desk, Delia stayed in the chair, and Lucy paced the room, her ideas flying even faster than they did when she'd proposed Lit. And this time, she paused to hear everyone's suggestions.

Maddie: Offering bite-sized daily games and larger ones to attract all types of users from the casual to the more dedicated.

Delia: Committing to free intro-level games, the rest at a low price with discounts for coding groups, schools, libraries, to encourage girls to work as teams.

Lucy: Including free and paid tutorials run by women in tech, from high school students to C levels like Nishi and her mom.

Maddie: And not just women in tech; talks about working hard by successful women like Esmé Theot.

"Right," Lucy said. "Like we can just call up Esmé Theot and ask."

"You can't." Maddie swiped at her phone and held the contact up for them both to see. "But I can." Lucy's jaw fell open, and Maddie said, "Why, I think I just impressed Lucy Katz."

She had. And as the afternoon turned to evening turned to early morning, and they'd all impressed one another more times than they could count, Delia took a deep breath to steel herself and texted Eric.

Delia: I'm sorry about last night. I was scared.

Delia: I still am.

Eric: Glad I'm not the only one.

Eric: Got plans for breakfast?

A quickening of her pulse preceded Delia's grin, and Lucy said, "Excellent! I like it too."

"Wait, what?" Delia had missed whatever Lucy had said.

"So you don't like it?"

"Like what?" She tried to hide her phone and then just admitted it. "Sorry, I was texting Eric."

Lucy sighed. "Total code crushing."

"I—" Delia just shrugged. She was. They were. And she couldn't have been happier.

"It's cool. I'm just mega jealous." Lucy winked, then held out both hands. "So, here it is, our app name: Girl Empowered. What do you think?"

"Don't answer yet," Maddie said. She flipped to a new page

in her sketchbook, wrote the words at the top, and Delia watched, amazed, as an image formed underneath. A computer monitor at the bottom with three lines coiling up.

"Power cables," Maddie said, but didn't need to.

Attached to each cable, the outline of a girl morphed into shape, then lines connected them back to the computer in a continuous loop. On the screen, at the bottom, she filled in something, barely readable unless you knew what you were looking for: 303. Their room number.

Delia took in the rainbow of colors on Lucy's bunk bed turned closet, the crumpled pile of clothes and papers spilling over the end of Maddie's bed, the San Francisco sticker peeking out from under the pillow of Lucy's that was now hers, and then, the scuffed knees on all three of them. They were pretty badass screen queens too.

"It's perfect," Delia said. "Now let's go break a keyboard."

TWENTY-EIGHT

DATA SMOG • *An overwhelming quantity of information, often as a result of an Internet search, that serves to confuse the user instead of helping one understand*

THE VIBE WAS DIFFERENT. And not just for Lucy.

The first field trip, everyone was high on the newness of ValleyStart, the energy of what was to come, the buzz of a private night at the city's hottest club—not to mention the cooler of alcohol.

This time, as the bus veered down the hills of San Francisco toward Pulse's headquarters, the only thing high was the stakes. Demo Day had everyone heads down in laptops, bleary-eyed, exhausted from days and nights of prep that no amount of caffeine could combat.

Lucy kept her eyes glued to her PowerPoint slides most of the ride. But when the bus hit the Embarcadero, she looked up. She waited for it to come into view. The circular drive where valets helped her in and out of the Tesla, the walls of glass enclosing the indoor space, the patio at the back, barely visible from the street but vivid in Lucy's mind. It was where her teammates were insulted, where her ambition was used against her, where she was treated like a commodity that could be bought with champagne and views and charm that proved to be as fake as Pulse.

He thought it would work. The Lucy he saw made him think it would work. Was the fault in his interpretation or in Lucy's reality? The question had been gnawing at her ever since that night. She still didn't know the answer. She wasn't sure how to find out—or if she really wanted to.

"Lucy?" Delia said. "Everything okay?"

Maddie turned to see what the bus had passed. "Is that where . . . ?"

Lucy nodded. "I just realized I haven't seen him since."

"You don't have to," Maddie said. "We can get a rideshare and go back."

Lucy breathed in, feeling incredibly lucky to have been assigned to room 303. "No. What we're doing is more important. Besides, I have to see him eventually. Better that I'm not alone." She felt the tears welling up, and she let them. "And even better that I'm with you guys."

Delia draped her arm around Lucy's shoulders and squeezed.

Lucy gave her a thankful smile but said, "Back to work. We may be on each other's side, but time isn't."

Hesitantly, Maddie and Delia returned to the app, and Lucy placed her hands on her keyboard. Her fingers spread out across the letters, her bare fingernails stark against the black keys. Last night she'd tossed every bottle of nail polish in the trash. Trophy Wife and Gold Digger and Ditzy Blonde and all the ones with names no self-respecting woman—no Girl Empowered—should let define her.

Today she was simply Lucy.

It was the lending library that surprised her the most. The ping-pong tables, yoga studio, fancy tea makers, espresso machines, on-site bicycle repair—even the free beer garden on the roof. Status quo for an elite tech company like Pulse. But the library . . . floor-to-ceiling mahogany shelves lined the perimeter of the room, wooden ladders hung on rails across the top of each, the collection ranged from children's books to mysteries to cookbooks to nonfiction everything, and, of course, an entire wall dedicated to technology: hardware, software, manuals, biographies, how-tos, and more.

And then she remembered that Ryan's mother was a librarian.

The contradiction filled her not with confusion but disappointment. Because he had it in him to be a better person than he was.

Then again, who didn't? Some people's gaps were just much wider than others.

Which became clear when they entered Ryan's "Be VIP or Be RIP" room. An entire room of Ryan. Photos with every A-list female actor, model, and pop star, and in each and every one, a hand hidden from view, sometimes in seemingly innocuous places, most times not. Not enough to notice, unless you were looking for it, unless you were trying to discern a pattern. A pattern that continued with the photos of Ryan with tech movers and shakers. All men. Not a single female founder, CEO, CIO, CTO, VP, VC, or otherwise in the frames.

As they lined up to exit the room, Maddie and Delia huddled together, whispering, but Lucy hung back, taking a final look at the only photo of Ryan by himself, circa age five, a grin as wide as his current ego, filled with pride as he leaned over a homespun-looking computer.

Sadness for him, for her, for everyone in the photos hanging on the walls and for everyone behind the desks contained within this building with its nap pods and wellness center and executive chef. Sadness for what Pulse could have been, for what Ryan Thompson could have done, and for what he chose to do instead.

When she finally exited the room, he was there. Shaking every ValleyStart student's hand, personally welcoming them to his home away from home. She couldn't avoid him.

She waited until the end, watching his fake smiles, head bobs, and words of encouragement. Gavin was up next. He donned a conspiratorial grin, broadened his chest, and put his hand up for a high five. But it stayed there. Because Ryan barely glanced at him before moving on to the next student in line. Gavin shrank before her.

As he continued past Ryan, Gavin turned and caught Lucy's eye. They held each other's gaze. She wasn't sure what he saw in her, but she saw everything Gavin was—arrogant enough to do what Ryan asked and naïve enough to think it meant something more. Because he wanted—needed—it to mean more.

Lucy was the last in line. She pushed herself forward and stood before Ryan.

His face exuded warmth, but the tilt of his head and the slow travel of his eyes scanning every inch of her iced Lucy to the bone. She refused to let him know.

"Miss Katz? I'm surprised to see you here," he said. "I heard you were having some trouble with Lit."

"We were," Lucy said breezily despite the clawing beneath her skin. "Which is why we switched apps. Fortunate to not be a one-hit wonder when it comes to ideas, don't you think?"

Ryan's face fell but recovered quickly. "But that must go against the rules. To switch just because you hit a road bump?"

"Less of a bump and more of a grenade tossed straight at us."

"But you can't—"

"They can," Nishi said, coming up beside them. She turned to Lucy. "If anyone can come from behind it's you, but I am sorry Lit didn't work out."

"I'm not. This is way better."

Ryan's lips thinned.

"Really?" Nishi said with interest. Today she was wearing a deep blue scarf with a tiny undulating pattern that reminded Lucy of the way the light shined on the Pacific. "Care to give a hint?"

"Sorry, but I think we need to keep this one to ourselves."

Nishi nodded. "Like any good startup should."

Ryan cleared his throat. "Right, well, if you girls will excuse me, it's time for the *pièce de résistance*."

Ryan brushed past them, and Nishi snorted.

"Oh, sorry," she said.

"Don't be. He really is full of himself."

As they walked down the hall, they passed a room full of egg-shaped woven chairs hanging down from the ceiling, employees cocooned inside them, plugged into laptops and headphones.

Nishi paused at the doorway. "After I sold my first company, Ryan tried to get me to work for him. None of this was here. *Here* wasn't even here. He built all this after. Guess he's got reason to be full of himself, doesn't he?"

"Does he? You're not."

"I'm not nearly as successful. Yet," Nishi added.

"You're nothing like him, and you won't be even when you are as successful. More."

"When? Not If? You remind me of your mom."

"Yeah?" Lucy's heart beat a little faster—this time, in a good way.

"Yeah," Nishi said, and Lucy wanted to tell her everything—about Girl Empowered, about the night with Ryan, about Emma and the fraud they thought Pulse was. But if they were wrong and they involved someone else . . . someone like Nishi who had everything to lose if—no, *when*, definitely when—Ryan hit back . . . That gap between the person Lucy was and the one she wanted to be would stretch wider than she could live with.

Nishi leaned into Lucy. "Now, not even a hint . . ."

"Just one. It was inspired by you. Speaking of, do you think you could direct me to the source for some of those stats you were quoting at the women in tech talk?"

Nishi's eyebrow lifted. "I'm going to like this, aren't I?"

"If we pull it off, you're going to love it."

"When. *When* you pull it off."

"When." And Lucy couldn't wait.

TWENTY-NINE

STEALTH MODE • *A startup operating in secrecy, not revealing what it actually does in order to stave off competition*

MADDIE HELD HER BREATH, trying not to release the venom she longed to spew at Ryan Thompson. Must have been all those cobra pics she'd viewed while online shopping. People seriously Pinterested everything.

"Tell me," Ryan said. "Can you stand here and not be wowed?"

The view from Ryan's wraparound office—five times the size of their dorm room and easily fitting the sixty-plus of them—inspired awe. Like a postcard of San Francisco with windows on three sides showcasing the icons of the city, from the soaring pyramid of the Transamerica building to the glimmering blue of the Pacific Ocean, to the arching Golden Gate Bridge, to the mounds of green mountains in the distance beyond.

"Because if you can, then Pulse needs new headquarters." Ryan chuckled. "Every day I step into this office, take in the view, and am full of—"

"Shi—" Maddie started under her breath.

Delia bugged her eyes at Maddie.

"Adrenaline, thanks to my Pulse—both of them," Ryan finished. "Now, since I've got you all captive here, let's revisit how Pulse became Pulse."

Murmurs covered Delia's whisper. "Let's go. Now."

"Don't you think we should hear this?" Maddie said.

"Nothing he's going to say isn't in his PR packet." She hiked her backpack higher on her shoulder. "We need the actual truth, not the one Ryan's probably gotten so used to saying he actually believes it."

"Huh." Maddie started behind Delia, who was inching her way to the door while everyone was occupied with Ryan and the view.

"What?"

"I know you think you're just a girl from Littlewood, but whatever Littlewood's doing, it's doing it right." They spilled into the hall, and Maddie let Delia take the lead. "Remember when you said you'd follow me? Well, I'll follow you anywhere, Delia Meyer."

The expression on Delia's face was one Maddie was familiar with, and so before Delia could brush off the compliment, Maddie said, "But, uh, where is that, exactly? Right now, I mean. Literally. Not figuratively."

"Wait a sec," Delia said, tapping out a text to Lucy.

Cover for us.

Secret spy stuff? Danny would love this.

Maddie trailed behind Delia, down the hall and into the

wide atrium they'd passed through earlier with plants cascading down from living walls, one side groomed into the shape of ten hearts, the other spelling out *PULSE*.

"I never thought I could feel so sorry for plants," Maddie said.

Delia stifled a laugh and pushed forward through the wide space, kicking into a higher gear and gesturing for Maddie to keep up. They passed the Pulse Lounge with its blood-red walls and heart-shaped beanbag chairs and hit a four-way intersection. Without a pause in her stride, Delia turned left.

"How do you know where we're going?" Maddie asked. "And where *are* we going?"

"Developer space," Delia said. "Remember?"

"I remember being there, I would have just never found it on my own."

They rounded the corner and passed two white guys in nearly identical hoodies, Pulse tees, and jeans.

Delia and Maddie kept walking.

"Oh, man," one of the guys said from behind them. "I never get tired of the views around here."

"Gotta *love* Pulse-terns," the other one said.

Maddie's heart hammered her chest, and she whirled around.

"Maddie," Delia whispered, closing the gap between them. "Now's not the time. Just keep moving."

Though she clenched her fists, Maddie did as Delia asked. "Only for you, Dee."

Still hanging on to Maddie's sleeve, Delia said, "What an ass."

Maddie stopped, and a smile usually saved for her brother broke through. It was the first time she'd ever heard Delia curse.

"They work here. What do you expect?" Maddie said. "Now, let's do this . . . whatever this is."

"Right. Okay." Delia pushed her shoulders back, inhaled, and whispered something about the depths before marching into the developer space and swiveling her head from side to side. She landed on a young white girl with a mass of brown curls who was wrestling her hand through them, repeatedly. Delia spread her hands through her own spirals, growing them wider, pulled her laptop out of her backpack, and approached.

"How's it going?" Delia asked, nerves causing her words to run into one another. "What are you working on?"

"Complier errors. Lots and lots and lots of them."

"Yeah, uh." Delia slowed herself down. "I'm on some too."

Maddie raised an eyebrow, and Delia mouthed, "back me up."

"You're new too?" Maddie said.

"Obvious much?" The girl's whole body deflated. "It's my second week. But my first was all HR and training and, oh God, I'm going to be sent back for more training, aren't I?"

"Is that, like, possible?" Delia said.

"I don't know. Is it?" She tugged her hand through her hair. "Maybe we should go ask—"

"No!" Delia cried. "I mean, no. . . . What's your name?"

"Natalie."

"Of course, Natalie. Well, Natalie, I can't go ask anyone anything because . . . because . . ." She held up her laptop. "I can't log in remotely, and it's like my third time having a problem, and if they find out . . ."

"Hey, don't worry. Grab a chair and let's figure it out together."

"No," Maddie said. "She can't. She doesn't have time."

"I don't?" Delia said. "Right. Time. I don't have time. I have all this work to do. Pulse work. But I have to be home in like . . ." She looked at her wrist, which had no watch. "Fifteen minutes. Home in Stinson Beach."

Eric had said that was where Emma was staying. But he never said exactly how far it was.

"Stinson? You'll never make it!" Natalie looked around, panicked. "Listen, that's your laptop?"

Delia nodded.

"Here, give it to me." Natalie grabbed it and quickly connected to the Wi-Fi. "You don't even have the remote program downloaded?"

"I did, but then it kept crashing, and so I—"

"No matter. We'll get you there." Natalie's fingers moved at the speed of Lucy's lips, and while she downloaded the program that would allow remote access to the Pulse server, she and Delia spoke in a language foreign to Maddie but that still fascinated her. Not because of the content but because of Delia.

Natalie closed the laptop. "Okay, so you're logged in as me, Natalie Travest, for now, just so you can work today."

"You're a lifesaver, Natalie," Delia said.

"Ah, we newbies have to stick together. In fact . . . maybe we could have lunch one of these days?"

Delia sucked in a breath. "I'd like that."

Natalie sighed in relief.

Maddie watched, remembering how she hadn't wanted to be paired with Delia or Lucy at the start of the program. Now she couldn't do this without them—and wouldn't want to. It was a feeling she hadn't had about anyone other than her brother in years.

Lucy texted Maddie: *You both have food poisoning from that ostrich sashimi they served.*

A bit of bile rocketed up Maddie's throat.

Maddie: I thought it was chicken. And cooked.

Lucy: So East Coast. Meet us in the parking lot. I got you covered. Can't wait to see you guys.

Maddie: 👍

Maddie couldn't wait either.

THIRTY

DISRUPTING • *When a product services a market that couldn't be reached before; it's nearly impossible for an existing company to respond to a disruptive product*

"I NEED A HOTSPOT," Delia said as soon as they crammed onto one long bench on the bus. Her head was bursting with what they'd managed to do. She flipped open her laptop and started pounding the keyboard. "Come on, come on."

Lucy scrambled to turn on the settings on her phone that would allow Delia to connect to Wi-Fi. "What happened? What did you find out?"

"Shh . . ." Delia needed to concentrate. Compressed between Maddie and Lucy, she scooted forward for more space. She hunched over her computer, her fingers jamming letters and numbers, hoping the access would be enough to allow her to hack deeper.

Maddie leaned around her and said to Lucy, "She's in."

Lucy's eyes widened. "She's actually *in* in?"

As Maddie began to explain to Lucy, Gavin leapt up the steps and onto the bus. He placed a hand on the back of the seats on either side of the aisle and swung his legs forward, landing beside them.

When Maddie quickly slapped the laptop closed, Delia snapped her head up. "Maddie, I'm—"

"Taking a break. Really, you work too hard, Dee."

Delia took in Gavin's narrowed brow and slid her computer into her backpack. "Yeah, you know what, I do. Especially since things couldn't be more on track."

"*R-i-i-i-ght,*" Gavin said in a spot-on impersonation of Ryan. Delia felt Lucy tense beside her. Gavin continued. "D-Day's coming, and you chicks aren't the Allied forces or the Germans. You're the beach."

He high-fived his teammates, who seemed as dumbfounded as Delia. "What does that even mean?"

Lucy looked disappointed and then said through gritted teeth, "It means we have to succeed. In all of this."

"We will." Though the queasiness in Delia's stomach seemed less sure. The confidence fueling her inside of Pulse petered out the more she thought about what she'd done and what she was about to do, which she was pretty sure was illegal no matter the intention behind it.

She switched seats with Maddie, who'd begun filling Lucy in, talking softly to her in the French they both knew, while Delia watched San Francisco pass on by. She wanted to be here, she wanted to succeed, but like this?

Ryan, Gavin, the guy who betrayed Maddie, the boys who insulted Delia for years, they were bullies; they didn't care who they hurt.

Delia leaned forward to face both Maddie and Lucy. "This

girl . . . Natalie. Natalie Travest." Delia picked up her phone, found her on Instagram, and followed her. "I don't want her to get in trouble. I'll hack in as far as I can and make a copy of everything I can find, but I won't log in again."

"What?" Maddie said. "What if you don't have everything? We just stop? We're so close."

"I know," Delia said. "It's just . . . Girl Empowered. It's not just a name to me."

"Me neither," Lucy said, surprising Delia.

Lucy looked around the bus. "It might have been . . . before all this. But now . . . it's different. We have to be different. Change comes from us, right?"

Maddie hesitated. "Most people wouldn't care. Not if we get results."

"We're better than most people," Delia said.

"Or we're trying to be," Lucy said.

Delia wasn't sure she could do it, not because she didn't believe in herself but because confidence and arrogance were two very different things, something personified by Gavin and Ryan. "I'm going to ask Eric for help. You can trust him because—"

"You do," Lucy said.

"When will you get started?" Maddie asked.

"Tonight," Delia said.

"How can you possibly carry that much weight?" Eric asked, four days later.

Delia plunked half a dozen books down on the library table, the noise loud enough to draw looks from their neighbors.

"Oh, of course," she said. "I forgot how soft you city people are. See, we Midwesterners can carry a cow into the barn while we're milking it."

"You have a barn?"

"No. But that's what you ask? Not if we have a cow?"

Eric grinned, and Delia's only thought was how glad she was that her parents were coming to Demo Day. She wanted them all to meet. Because it felt strange that the people she was closest to didn't know one another. And she was becoming closer and closer with Eric.

Operation Flatline, aka take down Ryan Thompson, meant they were spending every minute they weren't spending on Demo Day prep together. At this point that was about twenty-four hours a day because their work on each of their apps was done. With the presentation in two days, it was now up to Lucy for Delia's team and Marty for Eric's.

Which wasn't to say that Delia and stress were unacquainted. They were besties. Because she and Eric had yet to find anything to prove her database theory.

Delia opened a book on SQL and read the first line. "Oh, right, I already read this one." She closed it.

"The whole book?"

"Most of it."

"And memorized it?"

"Most of it."

"And to think I almost chose a different incubator because I wanted to be on the East Coast . . ."

"A different incubator? . . . Different . . ." A page from the book flashed in Delia's mind. She dove into her laptop, muttering to herself.

"Uh, Lia?"

She didn't look up. "That could be . . . it might be . . ." Keystrokes flew without a pause. "We've looked everywhere in the database for this table. We can see the name of it in the code, so why can't we find it? But if the table's in a *different* database . . ."

"What are you talking about?" Eric said.

Delia pushed the book toward him. "Check the index."

Eric flipped to the back, then to a new page, and started reading. "This way no one would even know the table exists?"

"Except for Ryan. If I can access the objects that hook into it, I can find . . ." Delia kept working, her brain connecting faster than her fingers could move. She dug in, seeing it all so clearly, knowing it was there, if only she could find . . . if only it were . . . *Oh, come on.* And then, her jaw slackened. "Uh, Eric . . ." She lifted her head. "I think . . . I think maybe I found it."

He put the book down. "Found what?"

"It. I found *it.*" A rush of adrenaline shot Delia out of her seat. "The table. Ryan's secret list!"

"Delia! Are you sure? That's amaz—"

"No, no, wait." Her brain wouldn't slow down. "The table . . . so it exists . . . but is that enough?" She sat back down and extended her fingers across the keyboard. "We still have to access it, get inside, and show the connections between—"

Eric placed his hands over hers. "Hold on, one thing at a time because . . . *you found it!*"

The guy at the next table shushed them.

But Delia ignored him, taking in the pride on Eric's face. She pushed herself back in her chair. *She found it.*

A lightness buoyed her and she reached for her phone. Somehow, she'd missed a text from Maddie.

Natalie posted a pic on Instagram. Carrying a box and waving at the Pulse building with "Bye-bye Pulse" scribbled across it. And her Pulse is Comatose.

Delia's stomach dropped.

"No!" she cried, drawing rabid shushing from half the room. She squeezed her eyes shut against the sting of hot tears.

This isn't fair!

When she opened her eyes, a blurry Eric was standing before her, reading the text on her phone. He wrapped his hand around hers and led her outside.

"We have to tell," she blurted out. "We can't let her be fired because of us."

"Okay, just take a breath, Lia."

"No matter what it means." She paced the sidewalk outside the library. "We can't . . . it's not right."

"Lia—"

"She's innocent. I used her. I did this. I did—"

"Lia," Eric said again.

"*This*. It was my idea and now . . . now . . ." Delia raised her hands to her temples, pressing against the pounding erupting on either side of her head. Sweat prickled on the surface of her skin, and her vision clouded. *No! Not again, not again, not again.*

"Lia!" Eric cried. "Breathe, just breathe."

The panic in his voice ignited more in her chest and her hearing went fuzzy and she found herself reaching out, for something, anything, to stop this, to stop her body from betraying her again, like this, in front of Eric. She sank to the ground, her hands leaving her head and pushing into the concrete, the tiny pebbles of the sidewalk digging into her palms, the pain keeping her here in the moment.

She closed her eyes tight against the world, silently repeating, "Breaths raise you from the depths," over and over until . . . they started to. When flashes of light began to infiltrate the abyss she'd descended into, she opened her eyes.

Not to the world.

To Eric.

Before her.

Kneeling on the ground, his arms outstretched as if to catch her if she fell.

"Lia. Lia, what can I do?"

The tears that had ebbed began to gather once again. "Exactly what you're doing."

"But I didn't do anything."

"You were here."

"Did you think I wouldn't be?"

Delia's smile was weak. "No. Hoped, maybe, but no."

"Hoped? But why . . ."

"What girl wants the guy she's desperately falling for to see her having a panic attack?"

"You . . . what?"

"A panic attack. At least I'm pretty sure. It was the same as the other night."

"That's not the part of the sentence I meant."

"Oh." Delia blushed, and a tingle spread beneath her skin.

He flipped his hair out of his eyes, and pink colored his cheeks too. "Because I'm not falling."

"Oh," she said again, wanting to crawl inside herself and hide.

"I already fell."

Eric's eyes met hers, penetrating deeper than anyone ever had, and her instinct was to look away, but she held his gaze right back, and suddenly that wasn't the only thing she wanted to hold.

Her hands were around his back and her lips were on his and her knees were screaming from the way she'd dragged them against the concrete to reach him, but all she could think was, *Oh.*

And a bit of, *Wow.*

And, *I have no idea what happens now.*

But finding out, well, she couldn't wait.

THIRTY-ONE

COPY AND CRUSH • *Setting your sights on a competitor with the goal of eliminating them from the market; often spoken of in relation to a dominant organization like Facebook*

"FOMO!" LUCY CRIED. "MADDIE, FOMO!"

Maddie leaned over her bunk. "Perpetual fear of yours, I know, but is this prompted by something in particular?"

Lucy jutted her hip. "I do not have a fear of missing out."

"Uh-huh."

"I don't. Because there's nothing to miss if I'm not there." She smirked. "In this case, it's a club."

"You want to go out? Tonight? I've just about got your presentation memorized from listening to you run through it nine million times, so I know you haven't forgotten that Demo Day's the day after tomorrow."

"It's for the presentation."

Maddie seemed unconvinced.

"No, it is." Lucy summoned a bit of the courage she was going to need to go through with this. "Do you trust me?"

Maddie pushed her laptop aside. "Yes."

"All right then. FOMO it is."

Maddie climbed down. "I should change."

Lucy eyed her Gumberoo tee and worn jeans. "It's in San Jose. You'll fit in just fine."

"But what if . . . maybe I want to?"

A bounce. Just one. That's all Lucy would allow herself. She nodded to her bunk closet. "My shirts will be crop tops on you, but that's so in right now. Grab whatever you want."

Maddie riffled through the stacks, and Lucy tried not to cringe (*too much*). Maddie pulled out a striped scarf, and Lucy helped loop it around her neck.

A hint of a smile broke out on Maddie's face before she reached into her front pocket. "I almost forgot. Picked this up for you at one of the kiosks."

A bottle of nail polish. A deep mauve.

Lucy felt herself blink, not because the color was such a sharp contrast against her bare fingernails but because of the gesture itself—and that it was from Maddie. "Thanks, but I'm not so much into it anymore."

Maddie's grin widened as she flipped one end of the scarf over her shoulder. "Look at the bottom."

Lucy paused, then turned the bottle upside down. The words *Girl Power* on the label had been embellished with the letters *em* crammed in before *power* and *ed* after in red ink.

"Girl Empowered," Lucy said, her own smile as wide as Maddie's. "Maddie, I—"

"Just do me a favor and open a window when you use it. Almost passed out from the fumes last time."

Lucy resisted the urge to hug Maddie and simply said, "You got it." She then slid the end of the scarf Maddie had flung over her shoulder back to the front.

Maddie rolled her eyes. "So should we text Delia?"

"Not yet." Lucy grabbed a pair of skinny jeans. "She and Eric need all the time they can get." And Delia needed to check on their surprise for Maddie—a belated birthday gift. It was just like Maddie not to tell them; Lucy only found out when she noticed the deflating balloon next to Maddie's handle on Pulse, the sign of a recent birthday. Superior as Lucy's organizational skills may be, even she was impressed that the surprise had come together so fast—just in the few days they'd realized they could actually be a part of Demo Day.

Lucy crammed one leg in her jeans, realizing this meant she and Maddie would be going to the club alone. Sure, they'd been spending more time together in the room while Delia was with Eric, but this was different. Was that why she'd asked?

"It's okay, right?" Lucy said, trying to sound nonchalant. "That it's just us?"

Maddie flipped the scarf back over her shoulder. "Yeah, it's okay."

"Cool, then."

"Uh-huh. Cool."

A little awkward maybe, but, yeah, cool.

Janky.

The club wouldn't make any *must do*s in Silicon Valley. Between the grime on the walls and the cockroaches scurrying into the corners, it was the definition of janky.

Lucy didn't need her Pulse tee to get in here. They just walked through the door. The bartender barely looked up from his phone when they asked which way was backstage.

They didn't knock. Because there was no door. They entered the dark room with concrete floors, a couch in need of a case of her lavender-scented wipes, and the stench of old beer and decomposing fruit or rat or both.

Maddie came to a halt when she saw her. "This is why we're here?"

Lucy nodded and moved deeper into the room, watching Emma Santos. She sat on a wooden chair (*good call*), her eyes closed (*ditto*), her fingers strumming a guitar (*impressively*), and her voice working through a warm-up.

She was good. So good that Lucy stopped and just listened. She hadn't slowed down since the night with Ryan. She'd been in overdrive, body and mind, because there was so much to do, so much to fix, to forget, to fight for. Here she hit pause. Listened. Breathed. Disappeared. When the music stopped, Lucy opened her eyes. And met Emma's.

And the pause was over.

"Hey," Emma said. "Thanks for meeting me here." She stood, set her guitar on the chair, and walked to Lucy and Maddie.

"Sure, course," Lucy said. "This place is . . ."

"A dump. But it's one of the few that'll let me play."

"Because of your Pulse," Lucy said.

"Most venues don't care about anything else when they

book you. I could show them a million followers on Twitter or Instagram and still they'd only look at Pulse."

"That sucks," Maddie said. "Nothing should have that much power."

Emma pushed her dark hair over her shoulder, revealing a newly dyed blue streak. "Was okay when I was at the top though. I'm a hypocrite if I say otherwise."

"Is that why you didn't write back until now?" Lucy said.

Emma shrugged.

Lucy felt Maddie's eyes on her. She hadn't told her or Delia that she'd reached out to Emma. Because if they asked why, Lucy didn't have an answer. She wasn't sure what she wanted from Emma. Not until this moment.

Here in this toilet bowl of a club that Emma was in because of Ryan.

Here feeling his fingers pressing against her.

Here brimming with fear of where they'd go next, how she'd stop it, what she'd do if she couldn't.

Here because Ryan Thompson assaulted her.

And people had to know.

Lucy studied Emma's stoic face. Her pulse rapped against her veins like her body was demanding her attention, but it was her mind that was in control, and her body would just have to find a way to deal with it.

"I understand why you might not want to be reminded of ValleyStart. Why I might not be the person you'd want to talk to if you did. We weren't really friends. I'm not even sure what we'd have in common if we tried to be." She stepped closer. "Except for one thing."

Emma looked Lucy straight in the eye, took a deep inhale, and said, "Ryan."

"Freaking Ryan Thompson."

"I thought it was harmless at first," Emma said. "I totally knew he was one of those dudes looking to get off on being around the beautiful and the famous. I may not be in the music industry yet, but I know what to look for. And Ryan Thompson all but had a siren rotating on his head. But, see, well, the thing is . . . I'm not in the music industry yet. And he is Ryan Thompson."

"He offered to help?" Maddie said.

"Not directly. But, still, help in the form of my Pulse rising came, then he took credit for it. I thanked him, and he did it again. Each time my Pulse ticked a bit higher, and I was getting so many new followers and clubs were finally returning my calls, and so, hell, if Ryan wanted to talk to me for forty-five minutes about the girl who dumped him in junior high, it was an okay tradeoff."

"That's all he wanted?" Lucy said tentatively. "To talk?"

Emma's head tilted to the side. "Come on, you're not that naïve, are you?"

Lucy stared at her. "No, I just—"

"I knew he wanted more the first time his hand trailed across my lower back like that was a normal *'Hey, how you doing?'*"

The hackathon. He'd done the same to Lucy at the hackathon.

"But he was like an oversexed fourteen-year-old. I could handle him. And he made it easy. At first, I really did think, along with the obvious, he actually did have an interest in music, in *my* music. Maybe he did and maybe he didn't. But eventually it didn't matter anymore. He was done talking. And Pulse or not, I wasn't doing anything more than talking."

"Did he . . ." Lucy started, knowing how to finish but unable to say the words.

"Nothing happened. He invited me to a show. Gave me a ticket to meet him there."

"That night at the club in San Francisco. I saw him hand you something."

"Ticket to Fungus. *Fungus.* Sold out for months, and this was a front-row seat. But the strings it came with were attached to a spiderweb. I knew what he expected after. My dad was the one who wanted me in ValleyStart, not me. So I left and sold the ticket for enough to buy me a Gibson." She pointed to the shiny guitar on the other side of the room. "Asshole," she muttered.

"Yeah," Lucy said. How had she missed the strings for so long? Was she as arrogant as Gavin? "But I'm afraid he's much more than that. Which is why we can't keep quiet."

"Lucy," Maddie said. "I thought you didn't want anyone to know."

"I didn't. A lot of me still doesn't. But I can't be that selfish, not about this. If I say something, maybe he can't do it to someone else."

Lucy held Emma's gaze until finally Emma sighed. "Fine, yeah, whatever you're doing, you need me, I'm there. Girl power and all."

"*Empowered,*" Lucy said.

* * *

"Where have you guys been?" Delia said, her curls springing with twice their usual volume.

Lucy's mind still deep in the idea she'd proposed to Emma and Maddie, running through all that needed to be done the next day, she did a double take when she entered the room and saw Eric sitting on Delia's bed. "Uh, hey, Eric."

"Eric?" Maddie said, twisting around Lucy. "Oh, right. Hey, Eric."

"If we're interrupting, we can go grab sushi," Lucy said.

"Interrupting?" Delia swiveled her head, and a curl hit Lucy in the nose. "No, we're not . . ."

"Lia, breathe," Eric said.

Lucy raised an eyebrow at Maddie and mouthed, "Lia?"

"Okay, okay. I've just been waiting for you. I texted you both a bunch."

"We had our ringers off because we were—"

"Doesn't matter! Whatever you were doing doesn't matter because we're done."

"Done?" Lucy's eyes widened. "You cracked the code?"

"Oh no, we're the ones who were cracked. Bye-bye, Natalie means bye-bye, hackers and hello, police. They're probably coming for us right now."

Eric stood. "She's exaggerating. Probably."

"Probably?" Delia said.

"We were only in the one time. And we covered our tracks, Lia. Even if they knew something was up, they wouldn't know what or where it came from."

"And if they do? If they find out? It's all on our computers!"

Eric smoothed the front of his shirt. "Fortunately, orange is my color. And always been partial to jumpsuits."

"This isn't funny!" Delia cried.

But Maddie couldn't hold in the laugh Lucy heard bubbling up. Lucy couldn't join—as cute as Eric may be. Because everything hinged on this. She needed this. She didn't realize how much until they'd started making plans with Emma.

"So that's it?" Lucy asked. "We have no proof?"

Eric reached for Delia's laptop. She tried to stop him, but he opened it anyway. "We do, actually. All thanks to Delia and her cow-benching muscles."

"Cow-benching?" Maddie mouthed to Lucy.

She shrugged.

"I can trash everything," Eric said. "Make sure there's no trace of it. Or we can keep going. Take what Delia found and re-create what we think Pulse is doing—not on a grand scale, but enough to show what Ryan would be capable of. With all the other evidence you have, it'll paint a pretty damning picture to get someone who can do something more interested. Your choice."

"And what if my choice is for you to stay out of it?" Delia asked.

"Ooh, yeah, I'm sorry," he said. "There are only two bubbles on this multiple choice."

Delia's grin was as wide as her hair. "You are amazing, Eric Shaw." And then she flung herself around Eric's neck and kissed him.

And all the strategizing whirling in Lucy's brain ceased.

Happiness for Delia overtook everything to come. She hugged her arms around her chest and sighed. "Well, how about that. Our Littlewood girl's all grown up."

Lucy and Maddie watched until it got . . . creepy.

Then, Lucy clapped her hands together and pointed to the Ada Lovelace quotation on the back of the door. "Okay, team, contrary to the vibe in the room right now, can we use our powers of imagination to dive into the sciences and get back to Operation Flatline?"

THIRTY-TWO

VULTURE CAPITALIST • *Investor who takes advantage of struggling entrepreneurs by buying their companies for less than what they're worth and selling them for a profit*

ValleyStart: And so we are here. Beside those we hold dear. With Demo Day about to begin, the only question left is . . . who will win?

Maddie stood next to the fountain in front of their dorm while Delia's parents embraced her. They'd flown overnight to be there in time. Inheriting the curls from her dad and the blonde from her mom, Delia was the perfect blend of her parents, same as Maddie was. Though without her parents there, no one would know.

Delia introduced Claire and Jeffrey Meyer to Maddie.

"Nice to meet—" Maddie's greeting was interrupted by Claire's arms, which encircled her with a flourish and filled the air with the scent of lilac. Maddie stiffened, but Claire only squeezed tighter.

When they parted, one hand remained on each of Maddie's shoulders. "Why, you are simply astonishing! Delia gave us a sneak peek of your logo, and with that alone you sealed this, my dear."

Jeffrey bobbed his head. "No matter what those judges say, you three should be taking your bows."

The smile Maddie gave Delia's parents was bittersweet. She never really expected her parents to come; she didn't need them to. They'd only exchange toxic glares and snipe at each other, and Maddie would be trying to cover as usual. The day would be about them, not about her.

Claire and Jeffrey Meyer hugged their daughter again.

And a hot prick in Maddie's eyes betrayed her. Because, sure, she didn't *need* her parents. But want was an entirely different thing.

Delia brushed against Maddie's shoulder, nudging her gently as they started to walk to breakfast. Lucy, though she wouldn't admit it, was a bundle of nerves and had gone for a run instead of eating.

None of them had slept.

The presentation for Girl Empowered had ruled the night—both rehearsing it and adding to it. Because it now included the results of Operation Flatline. They'd call Ryan out in person in front of the entire Demo Day crowd. This time, they'd be heard.

Lucy had shared everything with Emma, and the two had been messaging nonstop. Though Eric and Delia hadn't been able to open Ryan's secret table, they were able to animate a slide to show how it could be used to override the main code and change Pulse rankings. And Maddie had memorized the coding portion of the presentation. The portion that should have been Delia's to deliver, but she was too uncomfortable with the idea of being onstage. Not that any of them were comfortable with this—not even Lucy. At least Maddie would have Sadie with her.

Sadie didn't jump, she catapulted at the chance to come to ValleyStart for the afternoon. Maddie had cleared it with her counselors, who'd cleared it with Sadie's mom. That morning, Lucy would meet Sadie at her day camp, and the two of them would then hook up with Delia and Maddie to run through the presentation one last time.

When Maddie, Delia, and Delia's parents reached the glass door of the student center, they were stopped by Tim Corrio, the Head of House.

"You three." He jutted his chin. "Oh, you two. Where's the little cutie?"

Claire's eyes widened.

"Guess you two will do," he said. "The Rye-man needs to see you before the gig starts."

Though empty, Maddie's stomach roiled. "Why?" she asked as defiantly as she could.

Tim shrugged. "Just the messenger, man."

"Surely this can wait until we've gotten some grub," Delia's dad said.

"No can do, Pops. Just like nature, when Ryan Thompson calls, you answer."

Delia's mom looked ready to scold Tim, and Delia said, "It's fine. Mom, Dad, try the zucchini-flour pancakes and head to the auditorium without us. We'll catch you after the presentation, okay?"

"If you're sure . . ." Claire said skeptically. Her face then shifted into a proud smile. "Well, then—"

"Break a keyboard!" Jeffrey said.

Tim snorted, and Maddie clenched her jaw, holding herself back from saying something that would only make things worse.

Delia's parents hugged her goodbye before embracing Maddie too. Maddie could still feel the strength of Claire Meyer as she and Delia trailed behind Tim.

"It's nothing," Maddie said to reassure Delia, whose bottom lip quivered. "I'm sure it's nothing."

Beside her, Delia nodded.

They both knew Maddie was lying.

And the moment they crossed into the office in the computer science building that Ryan used while on campus, they knew it wasn't just something, it was something big.

Because even Ryan Thompson had never looked this smug. It hung thick in the air, so dense Maddie could hardly breathe.

"Girls, girls, come in. But we are missing a girl, aren't we?"

Maddie mustered a half shrug, half nod.

Ryan pursed his lips. "Ah, well, you two have the starring roles anyway."

Delia shot Maddie a panicked look.

With an exaggerated sigh, Ryan continued. "Still, a shame not to see Lucy's reaction when she learns you've gotten her kicked out of ValleyStart."

"Kicked . . . kicked . . . what?" Delia struggled. "But today's Demo Day."

"Sure it is, but not for you. Unless, of course, you want to proceed after this. It's entirely up to you, really." He turned his laptop around. "Here, see for yourselves."

An image of Delia and Maddie filled the screen. A pause button covered the middle, but Maddie knew exactly what they'd see underneath. Or rather, who.

"Alrighty, let me." Ryan hit play.

And there was Natalie. At her desk, accepting Delia's computer and logging in to Pulse.

"All the tech we have, and turns out, security cameras are the simplest yet most effective. We canned this little lamb when my IT staff got notice of a double login. Logged in at the office and an unknown remote location at the same time. It happens, but this time, her explanation didn't compute. She was helping another Pulse employee? One whose description matched no one on staff? Imagine my surprise when we reviewed the security footage. Solid gold handed right to me."

The video rolled, and Maddie felt sick. As much for what they'd done as for being caught.

"You're disqualified, girls. Which you should have been the instant it was revealed that you'd stolen Lit."

"But we didn't—" Delia started.

"Revealed how?" Maddie interrupted. "What would you know about stolen Lit code that no other ValleyStart administrator knows?"

Ryan simply smiled, and Maddie searched for a hint of something beneath his bravado. Was he really so arrogant that he wasn't even a little afraid of what they might have uncovered?

"Now," he said, "you can go ahead and give your half-assed

presentation on whatever sorry app you've come up with in the past five minutes, and I'll have the police officers waiting in the wings to escort you when you're finished. Or you can leave quietly, no fuss, no muss."

Maddie slid closer to Delia and took her trembling hand. This was why he wasn't afraid. "You're blackmailing us?"

Ryan clasped his hands behind his head and propped his feet up on the desk. "Yes. Yes, I am."

THIRTY-THREE

WALKING DEAD • *A company not yet out of funding but that clearly won't become successful, making it unattractive for buyers*

AGAIN. AGAIN, AGAIN, AGAIN.

It was happening again.

A fist tight around Delia's throat.

Strangling her every breath.

Dark spots in front of her eyes.

Obscuring her vision.

A sledgehammer pounding her temples.

Making her feel like she was dying.

She wasn't dying. She knew she wasn't. That didn't make it any less terrifying.

She pressed her hands flat against the concrete wall of the building, raised her eyes to the blue sky, and focused on a cloud—one, just one, shaped like the Hot Pockets she'd been reheating for weeks. Which made her think of Eric. Which called up his "Breaths raise you from the depths." It began to loop in her mind, and she kept it going, silently repeating it with each prolonged inhale and each extended exhale. With Maddie at her side—the warmth of her hand penetrating the linen tank Delia had borrowed from Lucy—Delia's vision began to clear. Her heartbeat began to regulate. Her muscles relaxed and her mind focused on regaining control, calming the anxiety that held her body hostage, commanding it at will.

"Dee?" Delia had never heard Maddie sound so afraid. "Are you okay?"

"Physically," Delia said, though a throbbing still beat beneath her ribs. "I—I'm getting there. But that . . . Maddie, it's over, everything, and it's all my fault."

Maddie shook her head. "We did this."

"Didn't you see that video? It was me. I gave her my laptop. It was my idea. It's my fault."

"No. No way, Delia."

The voice came from behind. Delia spun around to see Lucy with Emma and Sadie.

"I texted them," Maddie said.

"Then they know what I did." Delia tried not to let the tears welling up spill. "Lucy, I'm so sorry. It's all my fault."

Exhaustion weighed down Lucy's eyes, but what Delia expected to see—anger, fear, sadness—none of that was written across Lucy's face. What was there was what had been there since day one. Determination.

"You're not taking credit for this," Lucy said. "We took him on together."

"But—"

"No," Maddie and Lucy said at the same time. They looked at each other, Maddie giving a short laugh while Lucy grinned.

Something that would have never happened on day one.

Sadie cleared her throat and stepped forward. "And now . . . ? What?" She placed her hand flat against her jutted hip. "We just give up? Go for sushi?"

The panic attack had ebbed, but the feel of it remained in Delia's mind. She didn't want to invite another, and yet she also didn't just want to go for sushi or pizza or frozen yogurt or anything else. She didn't want to give up.

"I should have said something." Delia spoke softly. "Told him we knew about the secret table—that we knew what he was doing."

"It's a good thing you didn't," Emma said. "He'd go for the jugular."

"I almost forgot," Maddie said. "What you wrote about Pulse not having a heart? He made you take it down?"

"Oh no, no way," Emma said sarcastically. "Ryan only *suggested* that if I didn't want my dad to hear about how I'd been hitting on the founder of Pulse to win ValleyStart that maybe I should consider changing the caption on my profile."

Lucy's jaw clenched. "She's right. No matter what you said, Delia, he'd have talked his way out of it and then definitely have had you arrested. Probably thinks we were fishing. He'd never believe we could *actually* have something on him." Lucy's voice got sharper, angrier, and Delia realized just how much Lucy had been keeping inside all this time. "He thinks if he threatens us, we'll back down."

"Is he right?" Maddie asked.

"Do we want him to be?" Lucy said.

Delia let her eyes focus on each of them, then stepped back until she saw them together. The image was so much stronger.

"I don't," Delia said. "I wouldn't do it alone, but with all of you . . . well, as my mom would say, the show must go on. She didn't let childbirth stop her, so what's the threat of a little jail time?"

Lucy sucked in her lower lip, moving forward to narrow the distance between them. "And who knows . . . first all-girls team to—"

"Win," Delia said.

"Accessorize with handcuffs," Maddie said.

"Kick Ryan Thompson in the bal—" Emma said, stopping when she laid eyes on Sadie. "Backside. In the backside."

Sadie groaned. "I'm eleven, not five."

They all drifted closer, forming a tight circle and leaning in.

"So we're actually doing this?" Delia said. "Consequences be damned?"

Lucy looked at each of them. "Do you trust me?"

A chorus of yeses and Maddie's "uh-huh" sent a shiver down Delia's spine.

"Then we're presenting, no matter what," Lucy said. "I just need to make one call."

"To who?" Sadie asked.

Lucy locked eyes with Emma. "My editor at *Teen Vogue*."

Sadie's hand slapped her hip. "Yowza. And to think you're no longer a 10. Pulse doesn't know what it's missing."

"It's about to," Lucy said.

A ding sounded on Delia's phone. She checked it and motioned to Lucy. The others began talking, and Delia and Lucy slipped to the side.

She showed Lucy her phone. "Do you think we should still do *this* too? Because, well, I was just wondering—"

"No. No, no, no." Lucy shook her head. "You've got to stop with the *just*s. We all do. Me, you, even my mom. We can't 'just' wonder. We have to stop 'just' checking in. No more 'I hope it's okay, but I just needed to know . . .' No more couching. No more being afraid to say what we mean. To ask for what we want. Not anymore." Lucy opened the contacts on her phone. "Now, I do think we should still do this—all of it. But say the word, and we're going for sushi."

"No," Delia said. Lucy's face fell. "I mean, no, I don't want sushi—kind of ever again. But I do want to do this. Dial." That Lucy's resulting nod had a slight hesitation in it made Delia feel better, not worse.

Lucy hit the call button, and Delia texted Cassie back: *Go straight to the theater. See you soon.*

Cassie: 👍

Delia: 🤞

THIRTY-FOUR

MOONSHOT • *Investing in a risky area with the hope that it will be incredibly successful, i.e., "reach the moon"*

THIS. IS. IT.

Everything. Not just for the past few weeks but for the past few years. More.

A current powered by fear and disbelief and the chutzpah she'd inherited from her mom flowed through Lucy as she tucked her legs underneath her on the seat between Maddie and Delia at the back of the auditorium.

If only she didn't have to sit through everyone's presentations to get to "it."

Truth? Lucy was impressed by what most of her classmates had done. The acceptance rate at ValleyStart was two percent, and this was why. Creative, innovative, ambitious, far-reaching, many of the projects would have a good shot at attracting investors if this were that type of program.

They'd slipped in after it started, after Nishi had sent an email asking what happened, why Ryan had just told her that Lucy's team had been disqualified for violating the morality clause of the contract they'd signed. Lucy wrote back, asking for Nishi's cell number, saying she'd be in touch shortly.

Shortly was now. The final team was concluding its presentation. The next-to-final team.

"Go ahead," Maddie whispered.

Lucy drew out her phone and texted Nishi: *Someone dumped a whole cart of lemons on my doorstep, and I promise not to make a single glass of lemonade. But I need a favor.* She paused and then added: *Ryan won't like it.*

Nishi: Good. What do you need?

Lucy: Don't let things end. Announce that there's one more team left.

Nishi: Only if it's yours. Starting to feel like curiosity's not just terminal for cats.

Lucy whispered, "We're a go," and her stomach twisted into a dozen knots as Nishi walked onstage.

She did exactly as Lucy asked, and Ryan leapt from his seat.

Nishi laughed heartily into the microphone. "Well, someone's as excited as I am, it seems. But, please, Mr. Thompson, take a seat before whispers of favoritism ripple through the crowd."

Ryan's cheeks puffed like a blowfish as Lucy climbed the stairs to the stage. Her hand rose to her neck, centering the Star of David necklace she'd chosen that morning, the gift from her mom that had been a gift to her from her own mother—passing through from generation to generation. As important to her now as Delia's and Maddie's pieces had been to them all along.

Delia and Maddie used the side entrance to go backstage and upload the PowerPoint presentation to the projector.

In the few seconds of delay, a silence descended on the room. Lucy lengthened her torso and teetered on tiptoes, but even in her wedges, she couldn't reach the mic. She unclipped it from the stand and held it in one hand. She scanned the audience, her heartbeat echoing in her ears. The confidence she'd never once been without seemed to elude her.

And then she saw Gavin off to the side. He mouthed something Lucy couldn't understand. Then he did it again: "Tin can. You got this."

"You don't have to be the best, you just have to act like you are."

Freaking Gavin Cox.

But, damn straight, Lucy was the best. No acting required. She clutched the microphone in her hand, stepped forward, and tried to steady her rapid pulse by focusing straight ahead. On the woman smiling at her from the front row. Abigail Katz.

She came?

She came.

The Girl Empowered logo, all pink and blue and swirly with enough white space to fill in with whatever color one desired, blazed on the screen behind Lucy, and an energy ricocheted through her.

She pushed aside thoughts of Gavin and Ryan and Stanford and everything that had gone wrong.

Then stopped.

And pulled them all back in.

Because ignoring the pieces that had gone wrong meant ignoring the pieces of herself that had changed because of them. Happy accidents. And unhappy ones.

She channeled Nishi's warm smile and her mom's authoritative tone and her own mix of brains and charm that had gotten her this far and concentrated on something she hadn't fully believed in until meeting Maddie and Delia: a support system.

One the women featured in Girl Empowered needed then, one the girls they hoped would be using the app needed now.

"Girl Empowered," she began, raising a hand to the screen. "Our app is like every app—made up of numbers and letters, programs and code, and hoping to attract users in an underserved market. But it's more personal than that, because that market is us."

Lucy spent most of her introduction describing the app, ending with the talks they hoped to incorporate by successful women. Which led her to her mom.

"I was fortunate to grow up in a place that values the changes technology can bring to the world and in a home with a parent who was striving to do just that. My mother sent me to tech day camps. She set an example for me every day. She showed me a world I may not have found on my own. But the truth is, most kids aren't me, especially most girls. The majority of schools in this country don't teach computer programming, a deficiency seen across communities, but even more so for minorities, especially black and Latino children. And yet tech jobs are the fastest growing in the country. Who's filling these jobs? Who's going to fill them in the future? Right now, fewer than one in five computer science graduates are women, and the number of female computer scientists is actually falling, down double-digit percentage points in the past ten years. If we don't act now, women will phase out of computer science entirely, doing a disservice to the women who pioneered in the field."

Lucy began to move to the side of the stage. "Women like Ada Lovelace, credited with being the first computer programmer. Her theories in the 1840s were a precursor to machines that had yet to be built. Our app celebrates women like Ada, introducing them to the next generation. Why? Because we need to get girls engaged and excited about computer science. We need to show them role models who look like them and make them understand that there's a place for them, if they want it. Early on, it seems both boys and girls have that bug—pardon the pun." Lucy winked. "But studies show that interest in computer science drops as girls age. Our goal with Girl Empowered is to capture those girls and offer educational coding games and programs entwined with compelling stories of historical women that will age with them, fueling their interest before it flames out."

As Lucy passed the microphone to Maddie, she noticed Ryan had relaxed. Whatever he'd thought might happen hadn't.

Yet.

Maddie accepted the mic from Lucy, and her "nailed it" crossed with Lucy's "good luck." Not particularly afraid of public speaking, Maddie didn't delight in it the way Lucy did either. Fortunately, Maddie wasn't speaking alone.

Sadie zoomed onto the stage on a scooter. Maddie set her

laptop on a table Delia had stealthily carried onto the stage while Lucy was speaking. Maddie attached her computer to the cable coming up from the floor to sync it with the screen. As Sadie circled her, Maddie opened Girl Empowered. A tingle spread beneath her skin at the logo that had been confined to her laptop screen projected for all to see.

"What's that?" Sadie asked, doing a figure eight on the stage.

"An app of games."

"Computer games?"

Maddie nodded. "About coding."

Sadie scrunched up her face. "*B-o-r-i-n . . .*" She dropped her head and mimed snoring. Everyone laughed. "You want my brother, not me."

"Yeah?"

"Yeah."

"Okay then." Maddie moved her finger along the trackpad, showcasing the easy-to-navigate menus leading to games, build-your-own apps, programming tutorials, and lectures. Pride built as she talked of color theory and how the palette she'd chosen—bright but sophisticated—would appeal to tweens and teens, un-like so many of the programming games on the market that were currently targeting younger kids.

She opened Ada's Alley and began to use the drag-and-drop components to create code, code that began to play a song, for among Ada's writings was the possibility that the device that would one day become the computer could compose music and be integrated into the arts as well as the sciences.

"Hey, hold your hat," Sadie said. "That's not coding, that's music."

"One and the same. If you know how to do it."

"Will you teach me?"

"No, but you can teach yourself." Maddie gave Sadie her seat. "Now, tell me, Sadie, have you ever played this before?"

"Nope."

"Perfect. Then see what you can do in the next couple of minutes while I talk to these nice folks."

"How do you know they're nice?"

"Just play."

"Okey dokey, but if you need backup, you know where to find me."

More laughs, and Maddie once again was grateful that Nishi had sent them to the day camp. What she'd said to Sadie was true. She'd have missed Danny even more than she already had without her.

Maddie crossed to the center of the stage and launched into her prepared talk on how she made the design simple enough to be accessible to girls of all skill sets, yet aesthetically pleasing, increasing in sophistication as the games and programs progressed from beginner to advanced.

"Much like the Gumberoo series," she said, "Girl Empowered grows along with our user."

"Roo!" someone cried out.

Maddie looked out into the crowd and did a double take. *It couldn't be.* But it was. He was sitting in the third row in between Delia's parents. Danny.

Danny.

But how . . . ?

Her chest tightened as she recognized the girl beside Claire from Delia's photos. Cassie, her best friend. Danny high-fived her and waved to Maddie. Maddie could barely wave back.

Paralyzed onstage, she couldn't remember what she was supposed to do next. The part that followed hers was Delia's.

Delia's heart lodged in her throat the moment Maddie laid eyes on her brother. It had been Lucy's idea. On top of everything else, Lucy had handled the logistics: reaching out to Maddie's parents and the camp and arranging the unaccompanied minor status. Delia's only contribution had been Cassie as an escort from the airport.

But it had all worked. Same as this was. With the minor hiccup that Maddie had stopped speaking. From the side of the stage, Delia watched Sadie swivel her head, waiting for Maddie to kick back into gear, to finish the design section before Maddie moved on to the coding. The clock was ticking, and yet Maddie simply stood, staring at Danny, stroking her four-leaf clover.

Delia turned to see Lucy, who was further backstage, deep in conversation with Emma, both of them checking their phones. She'd yet to realize anything was wrong. Delia had to tell her. She took a step and reached for a lock of hair, winding it around her finger, remembering the day she left Littlewood. The day her father told her she'd eventually find what she could do, not what she couldn't. Because there was a role for every actor and for every actor a role. And right now, Delia's role was that of friend.

She gulped down enough air to last her the next two minutes, steeled herself with a brief closing of her eyes, and walked out on-stage.

"Sadie," she said, her voice shaking more than she'd hoped. "What do you think?"

Sadie raised an eyebrow, looking from Delia to Maddie, then eased back into her performance, same as Cassie and her mom had done.

"You tell me!" Sadie hit the trackpad, and a recognizable "Who run the world?" refrain reverberated through the room.

"Does that mean you like it?" Delia asked as Maddie jolted back to life.

"Like it?" Sadie tapped her finger against her lip. "Let's just say . . . I'm in!"

A look of panic consumed Maddie's face, and Delia smiled to set her at ease.

Sadie hopped on the scooter, and with a final circle, veered offstage.

Maddie moved closer to Delia, who reached for the mic in her hand.

Before letting go, Maddie mouthed, "you sure?"

Delia nodded despite the butterflies dive-bombing in her stomach. She knew what she'd written out for Maddie to say about the code, about how Delia had designed the games to work, how they progressed in level of difficulty both as a game and in the code being taught, but none of that seemed important anymore. Not as important as what Delia really wanted to say.

She rolled the microphone in her hand and brought it to her lips, which felt so unnatural. A barrier between her and the audience that her mom would never allow. Delia hooked it back onto its stand and stared at her feet. She pressed her heels into the bottom of the sandals she'd bought at the campus bookstore to replace her sneakers, *Mountain View U* written across the straps. Despite everything, maybe because of everything, she still wanted it. Because she believed in moonshots.

"I didn't grow up like Lucy." Delia rocked back and forth on the balls of her feet. "I didn't have a mom or dad in the tech world. They were—they are—the best mom and dad anyone could have—I could have." She let herself steal a glance, one, quick, and broke away, because too long and she'd lose her nerve. She would picture how poised her mother would be doing this and she'd never continue.

"I just—" She caught herself. "I loved computers. From the time I could sit in front of one. I did anything I could on them, even if it was paying my parents' bills."

"And there were a lot of 'em!" her dad cried, and the audience gave an uncomfortable laugh.

"But I wanted to do more. I wanted to not just pay the bills but pay them better—faster, easier. I wanted to be on the other side. But my school didn't teach coding; it didn't even have a club for it. I mastered the free games and apps online pretty quickly, ran through what my library had, and was left with nothing but myself and a stack of coding books. They were dense. Designed for adults, not kids my age, and definitely not girls. If it weren't for my mom encouraging me, I would have given up long ago. But now I'm here. At ValleyStart. With the most talented people I've ever met." She looked at Nishi. "Ones I could only hope to become one day. I know what it's like to want something so much you can't breathe. It's a wonder I'm alive considering it's been five weeks of me doing just that."

The ripple of laughter spurred her on.

"We want girls to learn, we want them to have fun, we want them to be empowered, to realize they can be a part of a world like tech that maybe they can't see themselves in as easily as other fields." She rested a finger on the gift her dad had given her the day she left home. "A world that uses marketing copy to advertise something like this—this pendant I'm wearing that's a piece of a circuit board—as perfect for fathers, sons, and your favorite tech lover. Not girls."

The audience was silent, listening, and so she continued. "It's how we got here, with girls thinking math and computer science aren't for them. When home computers hit stores in the mid-1980s they were marketed as toys—for boys. In one commercial, half a dozen guys are having a blast using a computer. The only girl is shown in a bikini, diving into a pool. We like to think these images don't matter. But when they're reinforced by ads and TV and movies, over and over, they tell a narrative. One that doesn't include us. *That's* why our app is for girls. And that means all girls. Girls like me who couldn't afford to buy programs and attend expensive camps. Girl Empowered fills this void by including free daily games, so there will always be a portion of the app open to everyone. We would offer more complex games at a low cost, with discounts for schools and libraries. We'd seek sponsorships from businesses and organizations for users, in the hopes that more girls like me would be able to do what they love."

Her eyes traveled from Nishi to Eric, to Cassie to her mom

and dad, to little Danny between them. They were all beaming, and finally, Delia understood how her mom must have felt every time she took the stage, her words and actions making others feel the passion she did.

Delia pushed her shoulders back, pointed to the logo on the screen, and said the words Lucy had written to close out the presentation. "Now let's get those girls empowered."

The applause started slowly. Jeffrey Meyer's hoot could be heard ringing through the auditorium followed by Danny's imitation. By Eric's whistle. By Cassie's *woot woot*. But Lucy, Maddie, and Delia barely heard it. Because the second Delia exited the stage, their ears were covered by arms and shoulders and necks and chests as they collided in a group embrace.

"We did it," Delia said.

"Together," Maddie said.

"But we're not done yet," Lucy said.

THIRTY-FIVE

BIG HAIRY AUDACIOUS GOAL • *A startup founder's grand vision to change the world*

LUCY STRAIGHTENED HER DRESS, a simple white shift with blue embroidery across the hem, befitting who she was now and the founder she was on track to become. *Strategize, stylize, socialize.* She still believed it—so long as it was on her terms. She walked back onstage.

"Thank you," Lucy said to the auditorium. "I know we've likely hit our time limit, but we wanted to take a moment to focus on this program. Because what has happened here, with us, at ValleyStart is exactly what we hope to replicate with Girl Empowered."

Delia and Maddie joined Lucy onstage, hanging off to the side.

Lucy motioned for them to come center stage. As they did, Lucy continued, "Delia mentioned part of our business model, but we also want to foster girls working together, having Girl

Empowered be the staple for coding clubs that already exist as well as encouraging girls to team up and form their own groups." Lucy found Nishi in the audience and smiled. "Because collaboration yields excellent results. And Silicon Valley will continue to be a boys' club only if we let it. Or don't start one of our own—a girls' club."

Emma walked onstage and stood beside Lucy. Together, they looked at Ryan. His head rocked back, and he adjusted the collar of his button-down.

The Pulse logo appeared on the screen. Controlled by Sadie in the back, who'd done as Lucy had asked and attached her phone to the projector, the images flipped from Pulse 10 to Pulse 10.

"A generation of kids—my generation—has been obsessed with our ratings, posting more, trying harder and harder every day to be the funniest, hippest, strongest, smartest, *est, est, est* in a desperate attempt to be Crushing It. For all the perks that come with it. But who's actually getting those perks? Is it these people?" Lucy gestured to the rotating faces on the screen. "These incredibly picture-perfect users, or are they, are we all, actually being used? Because who's really benefitting? The people getting new barbecues and bicycles and tickets to Fungus . . ." Lucy checked out Ryan and his quickly paling face. "Or the ones paying for it—the advertisers? Paying Pulse for product placement. But that placement . . . it's better if it's with people who look like all these 10s, right? Thin, young, athletic. But how could it be possible that all of the most popular Pulse users look the same? How *is* it possible?"

Lucy nodded to Sadie, and Eric and Delia's slide appeared on the screen. An animation of how 10s would appear in Ryan's secret table beside Delia's rendering of how it would work in the code.

"Something like this, perhaps?"

Murmurs spread through the audience as those who knew coding began to run through what they were seeing.

Ryan shot up out of his seat. "This is absurd!"

Nishi rose with him, Lucy's mom just a second behind. The look on her face . . . she knew.

"Where did you even get—" Ryan cut himself off and balled his fists. But then his tone shifted, and he laughed with contempt. "Creative, I'll give you that, girls. Though I doubt this is even your idea. Can't trust a team who steals apps right off the Internet and tries to pass them off as their own. A competitor put you up to this? I hope they paid you enough to make it worth denigrating what all of these brilliant students have spent their time doing this summer. Now off my stage. You're done."

Ryan began to head for the stairs, but Nishi and Abigail intercepted.

Speaking quickly, Lucy continued. "This is an approximation, but it's enough to show it could be done. The why is easy. Money, power, prestige. But the motivation, something like this, well, the leader sets the tone."

Lucy whispered, "Emma," to Sadie, who logged back in to Pulse and pulled up Emma's profile.

"Take Emma here," Lucy said, turning toward her. "She tore up the scale at a rapid pace this summer. From a 5 to a 7, and then soon, she was Crushing It, and just as fast—"

"Faster," Emma said.

"She was Comatose. Yet she never lost fans. All her likes and favorites on all the sites feeding Pulse remained at the same level as before."

"Higher," Emma said.

"The same happened to me. I was Crushing It just in time for my ValleyStart beta test."

"Mine was in time to play at Pulse-a-palooza," Emma said.

"Coincidence? None of us are naïve enough to think that." Lucy pointed to the screen, now showing how the table Delia found would look with the 0s and 1s at the top, with Emma's and Lucy's names highlighted. "And yet the only thing Emma and I have in common is—"

"Enough!" Ryan shouted.

"Exactly," Lucy said.

Sadie poked her head onto the stage. "It's live!"

This wasn't what they'd originally planned. How they intended to do this piece of it. But Ryan's threat against Maddie and Delia changed things. Lucy suspected he was bluffing, but she'd misjudged Ryan before. She wouldn't be surprised again.

"Put it up," Lucy said, loud enough for everyone to hear. "If this interests you, if you're concerned about businesses and business leaders taking advantage of their position, you can read all about it." The banner for *Teen Vogue* filled the screen, and underneath, an essay with a joint byline by Emma Santos and Lucy Katz.

Abigail gasped as she read the headline.

PULSE FOUNDER RYAN THOMPSON GIVES NEW MEANING TO "PAY TO PLAY"

Everyone started talking at once. Heads bent over phones, searching for the article, someone yelled, "Link through Twitter," and Ryan spat a string of expletives through clenched teeth.

But that was as much as Lucy saw, because then her mom had her by the elbow and was dragging her backstage.

Tears sprung into Lucy's eyes, the exhaustion of the past few days mixing with the adrenaline of being onstage and all of it coated with the trepidation of what her mom would say about everything.

Yet Abigail Katz said nothing. Abigail Katz simply pulled her daughter into her arms and wept right along with her.

When they both stopped shaking, Abigail breathed into Lucy's hair. "We don't talk. We never have. But we need to start." She pushed herself back. "I want to start." Her lower lip disappeared into her mouth. "But, Lucy, I need to know . . . did he . . . did something happen?"

New tears trickled down Lucy's cheeks as she shook her head. "I'm fine."

"Are you sure? You'd tell me if you weren't?"

"I may not have told you before, but I would now. Because I didn't understand—before this, I didn't get it. You've dealt with this your whole career, haven't you?"

"Dealt with what?"

Lucy watched as behind her mother, Delia's parents rushed to her, bringing Danny with them. He collided with Maddie with the force of a bulldozer.

Emma had Sadie beside her. Lucy caught Emma's eye and

tipped her head toward the exit. She and her mom then moved from the auditorium to the benches outside, and as they sat, facing each other, Lucy told her mom everything. It was the first time she'd ever seen her mom simultaneously cry, threaten a lawsuit, and wonder how much a hitman cost.

She was kidding on that last one.

Lucy hoped.

(*Only a little.*)

"I've underestimated you, Lucy," her mom finally said. "Putting this all out there for the world to read. I'd have never done it at your age. Or my age."

Lucy fixed her gaze on her fingernails, coated in Girl *em-Power-ed* mauve. "Because of what everyone will think of me. That it's my fault."

"No, Lucy, don't you even think—"

"I don't. Not now. But I did. At first. You always said how important it was to present myself a certain way and now this . . . it defines me."

"Only for them. And maybe that's a good thing." Abigail clasped her hands in her lap. "It shows you're the kind of woman who won't put up with bullshit. All I could think of were the repercussions for speaking out at the Women in Tech talk, but what I've put up with, Lucy . . . what I've donned a smile as fake as all the VCs in this place combined and sat back and allowed to happen, be it jokes about colleague's breasts, or the 'oopsy' brushing of them, or listening to the sports reports on the radio so I could have something to contribute to the conversation at lunch . . . or pretending I was as happy to be working late and missing putting my child to bed as they were."

Lucy looked at her, surprised.

"I never was—happy, that is. But to show it was to be weak in the eyes of people I put too much stock in. At the expense of the one person whose stock mattered most."

Lucy slid her hands forward, wedging them between those of her mom. Only their hands were together, but she hadn't felt this close to her mom in years.

"I didn't think much about being one of only a handful of women doing what I was doing when I started out," Abigail said. "I was young and smart and too headstrong not to just dive in and do the work. Back then, the company needed to survive before it could even hope to thrive. It needed great programmers, period. And I was great. I was a rising star. I mean, why else was someone at my level being brought to company dinners and investor meetings?"

"The double X factor," Lucy said softly.

Her mom's brow creased before she began nodding. "Right. Me and my C cup were proof that the company wasn't a boys' club. But it was, just like all the others. The first time an investor's hand mistook my leg for his, I told my boss. He said the right thing— how sorry he was—and then casually added how everyone at the company did things they didn't want to do for the greater good. If the company succeeded, we all succeeded."

"Mom, I'm—"

Abigail squeezed Lucy's hands between hers and kept talking. "I stayed silent after that, smiling while getting their coffee and taking their lunch orders, but I was no longer playing their game. I was playing my own. Because every meeting where I was the token female was a meeting I was able to attend that my colleagues weren't. I learned things that would have taken me years. And so I kept on playing, tagging along to the strip club buffet lunches so as not to miss out on discussions of whose product line was the next to be funded. Not participating in late nights of drinking had career ramifications, but sitting at the bar had personal ones." Abigail, who had been speaking at a rapid clip, slowed, her voice now almost hushed. "One night, things got out of hand with a senior male programmer and a younger woman. Fortunately I was there with another female colleague, and we stopped it. The young woman wanted to report the incident, and we agreed to go to HR together the next day. But I was held up by an emergency meeting. By the time I was out, word of a firing was spreading. Not the male employee, the young woman. The colleague that backed her up resigned a few days later after receiving a negative performance review."

"And you?" Lucy asked, knowing the answer.

"The only change I effected was extracting myself from the scene." She lowered her head, resting her eyes on their entwined hands. "I'm not proud of myself. Of some of the choices I made— for both of us . . . I was hard on you, I know I was."

"Right back at ya."

Her mom smiled weakly. "I wanted you to be like me—able to just keep your head down and put up with all the crap coming your way. But I knew you weren't me."

"She'll never be me."

"And that terrified me. Because I also knew what was waiting for you. But I was wrong, Lucy. I was giving you a shield when what you really needed was a sword."

"Ah, well, neither would have gotten me into Stanford."

"Screw Stanford."

Lucy rocked back, raising her eyebrows.

"Sorry," her mom said. "Yes, I did want you to go, but not for you—for me." She sucked in her bottom lip. "I'm so sorry you inherited this from me. The truth is, I loved it here. You could be really happy at Mountain View, Lucy. After such a large high school, you might find the closer-knit community inviting. And if not, well, there's UC Berkeley and Rice and NYU and Wellesley College—anywhere *you* want to go across the country. Though part of me hopes you won't do that."

"What?"

"Go across the country." She skimmed her finger along Lucy's necklace. "Not now that we're finally figuring out how to do this."

"And by this you mean . . ."

"Be a family."

Of all the reasons to pivot, Lucy thought that sounded like a pretty good one. Besides, NYU, Boston? She shivered just thinking of the snow. She didn't look good in parkas.

(*Oh, who am I kidding? If anyone can rock a parka, it's me.*)

THIRTY-SIX

FRIENDS AND FAMILY ROUND • *A startup's first round of capital, usually from "investors" who are family and friends*

"GUMBEROO'S LOOKING GOOD ON you, kid," Maddie said.

Danny was wearing every piece of gear Esmé had sent.

"And smelling even better. Why, if I didn't recognize these freckles . . ." Maddie leaned down and pinched his cheeks. "I'd swear a pterodactyl had flown off with my little brother. Though of course she'd drop him the second she got a whiff of those stinky socks."

"Hardy har har," Danny snickered. "What makes you think the pterodactyl would be a she, anyways?"

"What makes you think it wouldn't be?"

"Okay," Danny said.

"Okay," Maddie said, hoping such an acceptance never became more difficult for him.

They were almost to the end of their campus tour, and she still couldn't believe he was actually here—and that it was all because of Lucy and Delia, though Delia had given Lucy all the credit.

Maddie shouldn't have been surprised. With everything that had gone on the past few days, nothing should surprise her anymore.

One thing definitely didn't: Sadie's initial cold shoulder upon meeting Danny, which was entirely in character. As was Danny's reaction: that crooked grin that no one could resist.

Sadie was with Emma, having successfully begged her to play a couple of songs during the last few minutes of tech day camp. Maddie hoped Sadie just really liked Emma's music, but she'd gotten to know Sadie better than that. You could take the Pulse away from the girl, but you couldn't so easily take away what the Pulse had done to her.

The thought of leaving in a couple of days, before she got the chance to wash off the stench of Pulse—worse than Danny's old socks—saddened Maddie.

As did the thought of New York. And the realization that Danny didn't feel the same.

"And there's a zoo, right in the park. How bonkers is that?" he said.

"Pretty bonkers."

"And Mom said there's a rock climbing wall right in my school's gym. And my room is bigger than yours."

Maddie stopped walking. "I have a room?"

"Well, duh!"

A room. For her. Her mom was giving her a room even though she hadn't asked for one—hadn't wanted one. She felt a sinking in the pit of her stomach as she remembered something her mom had said during their fight about Danny's socks. She'd questioned whether Maddie wanted to be a part of her life. It barely registered at the time because Maddie always thought it was the other way around. That the distance between her and her parents emanated from them. But did her focus on Danny exclude them? Did she focus on Danny *to* exclude them?

Suddenly she realized she'd done the same thing to Delia and Lucy when she first got to ValleyStart. If it hadn't been for Delia asking her to go to the club and Lucy dragging her on to the dance floor, would the rest of it have happened? Picnicking on the floor of their dorm room, creating a killer app, showing the world what Pulse really was?

Guilt crept in at the edges. Consciously or not, she was starting to think that she played a role in what had become of her family.

Well, duh, indeed.

Maddie took Danny's hand—that he let her proved how much he missed her—and they walked into town. Lucy had made a reservation at her favorite Thai place because, in her words, one, it killed it on the pad thai, and two, no one, especially not Ryan Thompson, was going to dictate what she would eat. Though she said she'd likely shy away from the soup, for reasons she hadn't told Maddie but that Maddie was certain would only bolster the feeling she had that Lucy might be the strongest person she knew.

The article in *Teen Vogue* had been trending all day.

Her story in print for everyone to see. To judge. Things that should make Lucy Katz go into overdrive trying to compensate. But when Maddie and Danny arrived at the table with every seat filled but two, she found Lucy commanding it, impersonating

Tim Corrio. She raised her hand in the air and fist-pumped "the Mad-woman!" when she saw Maddie.

She grinned. Maddie grinned. Delia grinned. Danny cocked his head and gave his crooked grin, and Maddie rested a finger on her four-leaf clover. Faith, hope, love, and luck. One for each of them.

Maddie believed it.

Claire and Jeffrey told stories of Delia, like how she'd hacked into the local newspaper to retrieve the rash email her dad had sent in response to a particularly harsh review. Then Cassie told them all how she'd learned that skill: retrieving an email Cassie had sent to her crush when her cold feet had set in. Sadie stood and imitated her tap-dancing porcupine, inciting Danny to race to her side and imitate her, the two of them having a dance-off in a bid for Maddie's attention that made her both embarrassed and a bit proud at the same time. She'd rarely been anyone's center of attention. Lucy's mom talked of her days at Mountain View U with several not-at-all subtle hints as to why Lucy may find it the perfect home for the next four years. And where would Maddie's home be? Her answer had always been wherever Danny was. But was that the right answer? Would her mom be more of a mom if Maddie wasn't?

Nishi arrived just before dessert from the Demo Day party they'd decided to skip. She asked to meet privately with Lucy, Maddie, and Delia.

As they stood outside the restrooms, Lucy asked, "Is this an official ValleyStart visit?"

"No, personally sanctioned," Nishi said.

"What about showing favoritism?" Delia said.

"*Pfft.* You three have been my favorites since the moment I decided how to assemble the teams. Couldn't resist the chance to have the first all-girls team win ValleyStart."

Maddie's heart skipped a beat. "Do you mean—?"

"No," Nishi said. "You didn't win. Your presentation was excellent, the idea for your app even more so. But the bottom line is you did violate the morality clause. Even if it was ultimately for the greater—and personal—good, we can't give you the win."

Lucy glanced in her mom's direction. "I get it. I don't like it, but I get it."

"Yeah," Delia said.

Maddie nodded, more than a little disappointed at not getting to spend the rest of the summer at an internship with Lucy and Delia. *Though the internships . . .*

"Did someone win?" she asked.

"Of course. Everyone worked their tails off, and we're not going to let Ryan Thompson mar ValleyStart. He's already been removed from the program. As for the incubator, the winners will be announced shortly, though they'll likely be disappointed. We can't have them go to Pulse, not with all you've uncovered. They'll have to be satisfied with an internship at my company."

"Then we lost more than I thought," Lucy said softly.

Nishi put her arm around Lucy's shoulders. "You were incredible, Lucy. What you did, what all of you did . . . But I can't help thinking that I failed you. Why didn't you come to me sooner?"

None of them spoke. Finally Lucy said, "I was ashamed. And I thought I could protect us, our place in the program, in everything that would come after."

"You wanted to protect your friends?" Nishi said.

Lucy could barely look at Maddie and Delia, but she nodded.

"Well," Nishi said, "seems to me you've all won a lot more than ValleyStart. How I love it when I'm right. Anyway, I wanted to tell you how proud I am of each of you." She pressed her hand to her stomach. "And get something edible. Mountain View U catering tastes as bad as the dorms smell."

They pulled up another chair for Nishi, and the stories continued, Danny beginning by telling them all about the pterodactyls on Martha's Vineyard. As he spoke, Maddie uploaded the Girl Empowered logo to be the first image in the portfolio on her website.

She looked around the table, thinking of what waited at home in Boston. Not just the cloudy skies and snow to come. But the absence of this.

Family.

Because family wasn't just the one you were born to. It was the one you made for yourself.

And remade. As new people came into your life and old ones returned. The room in New York City might have just been extra square footage, but Maddie chose to believe it was an olive branch. One, despite the people around this table (*and, fine, the infuriatingly wonderful sunshine*), she was ready to accept, not for Danny but for herself. So welcome back, rain and sleet and snow.

(*After all, who worries about snow when they've got a kick-ass parka like mine?*)

THIRTY-SEVEN

ANGEL INVESTOR • *One who invests in small startups and entrepreneurs early on to help founders through the hardest stages*

THEY DIDN'T WIN. DELIA knew they couldn't, they wouldn't, and yet all through dinner, she couldn't help the nagging inside—not that she'd disappointed her parents. She'd wiped her mom's lipstick off her cheeks enough times to convince herself of that. But that she'd disappointed herself.

Because Girl Empowered was good and having a ValleyStart win wouldn't just validate it but her. That she still needed such a thing bothered her, but after what happened with Lit, after she was the one who violated the morality clause, she needed it. Right or wrong, she needed it.

"You've been holding out on me, Dee Dee," Cassie said.

Delia exited the bathroom stall and washed her hands at the sink. "How exactly?"

"Fearsome stage presence. Not that I'm surprised, considering your mom."

"Really? I was okay?"

Cassie scoffed. "If anyone's gonna tell you the truth, it's me."

"And I wouldn't have it any other way." They exited the restroom, and Delia asked, "So you and the usher . . ."

Cassie held up two fingers.

Delia's eyebrows lifted. "Two dates? Awesome, Cass!"

"Oh, in that case, three."

"Then what's two—wait, forget I said that."

Cassie winked.

Delia took a breath, knowing she couldn't stop the blush that always did and would come. It was who she was.

"You sure you don't want to come back to the room for a bit?" she asked. "Maddie and Lucy would love to have you."

"Nah, I'm good. Got a date with Danny at the hotel. I offered a video game matchup, and he said he wanted us to call Esmé Theot. Kid's a bit out there, right?"

"Oh, right." Delia attempted a poker face, picturing Cassie when the call actually went through.

When they arrived back at the table, Nishi was talking with Delia's parents. Everyone else had already said their goodbyes and made plans for breakfast the next day.

Delia retook her seat, and Nishi slid a letter across the table.

"What's this?" Delia asked.

"Open it, darling," her mom said, with a lilt to her voice.

Delia did, reading while Cassie read over her shoulder.

"Hot damn!" Cassie exclaimed.

"This is . . ." *What is this? A job? An actual, real, no joke, serious job at Nishi's company?*

"Amazing, isn't it?" Claire said.

"Couldn't happen to a better daughter of mine," her dad said. "Oh . . . wait . . ." He winked and reached for Delia's hand, which was trembling right along with the offer letter.

A job. As a programmer. In Silicon Valley.

Delia had done exactly what she'd hoped to do: go to ValleyStart and leave with a job at a tech company, with just a high school diploma, without going to college, without making her parents spend money that could go to the theater on her.

But she was too late.

"Nishi, this is . . . thank you, but—"

"But nothing, Dee," her dad said.

Delia could barely look at her parents. "But I failed you both. The theater's gone." She faced Nishi. "This is amazing. I'm . . . wow, honestly, it's just . . ." She dropped the "just" and forced herself to turn to her mom and dad. "I wanted to save the theater. I wanted you to not have to worry about me."

Claire stood and wrapped her arms around her daughter. "That is one thing you can never ask of a parent. We will always worry about you."

"That's not what I meant," Delia said, breathing in her mother's lilac perfume.

Claire crouched in front of her. "Our decision on the theater wasn't for you or us, it was for all of us. Your dad and I want new adventures. And since you'll be off having your own . . ." Her mom tapped the letter. "Your own incredible ones, then we decided we're ready for ours too. The next phase. And once we get that Winnebago, we can park right outside your doorstep for as long as we like!"

Cassie said, "Nuh-uh, Mrs. M. Not cool."

"No," Delia said, standing to hug her mom and bring her dad into it. "It is. It totally is."

Delia had convinced herself that saving the theater was for her parents, but it was as much for herself as it was for them. A safety net she'd thought was tied to a place. But it wasn't. It was tied to people all along.

When they all sat back down and Cassie had thrown napkins at the three of them to dry their eyes, Nishi spoke.

"This is because I recognize talent when I see it. You coded two fully functioning apps, both of which surpassed the programming skills of every other project at ValleyStart. My company needs talent. But we need talent that will grow and learn. So my hope is you'll consider a part-time schedule. One that will allow you to enroll in a college close to our offices."

"Like Mountain View U?" Delia asked.

"Exactly."

"But I didn't apply. . . . I'm not sure I can start in the fall."

"I may not be the founder of Pulse—"

"Thank goodness," Delia said.

She smiled. "But these are strings I can pull. Oh, and after breakfast, I'd like you and your cohorts to meet me in my office. I can't shake the feeling that Girl Empowered deserves some serious consideration. Never been an investor before, but maybe it's time to add another line to my résumé. What do you think?"

"Oh, she thinks," Cassie said, and for the millionth time in her life, Delia was grateful to have Cassie as her best friend. Cassie always had her back. And then Delia remembered Natalie.

"Uh, Nishi?" she asked. "If you're looking for programmers, I have someone I'd like to recommend. I wouldn't be here without her."

"Well, can't get a better recommendation than that. Send her my way."

The night had left Delia without words. All she had left were emotions. So many that after parting with her parents and Cassie, on her walk back to the dorms, she had to fight the ballooning in her throat. And then, a text came through, and she gave up the battle.

Eric and Marty had won ValleyStart.

Her heart exploded. She couldn't have been happier than if her team had won. And maybe, maybe not even *as* happy. Because this meant Eric was staying in the Valley. Just like she was.

She'd miss her family, but she was starting to have one here too.

She wouldn't be going back to Littlewood.

(*Good riddance, parkas.*)

THIRTY-EIGHT

IN THE WILD • *When a new product is finally out in the real world*

FOUR.

Still.

Four ValleyStart teams commanded the balcony at the end of the hall. Lucy had been pacing in front of the door, waiting for them to leave for the past twenty minutes. She'd poked (*jammed*) her head in twice (*okay, four times*), her arms full of the comforter from her bed and the bag of junk food (*fine, kale chips and wasabi peas and free-trade organic chocolate*) she'd picked up (*looted*) from the ValleyStart snack center after her mom had dropped her off. She'd already texted Maddie and Delia to meet her outside after saying goodbye to their families for the night.

The Demo Day party must have ended early. And now four teams were on the balcony that was supposed to be theirs. She'd been subtle. (*Subtle-ish.*) No more.

She dropped her blanket and tote and pulled out her phone,

determined to find the longest, most graphic YouTube video on menstruation she could when someone said, "Hey, Luce."

Not someone.

Freaking Gavin Cox.

"Missed you at the party," he said.

"Uh-huh." Lucy kept swiping.

"Saw your mom came. That's cool. Mine, well, you know. If we'd won, that'd be different, but—"

"What do you want, Gavin?"

He pushed a loose curl behind his ear. "Can't we just talk? Like we used to?"

"No, we can't."

"Fair enough."

Lucy lowered her phone. "Huh."

"What?"

"Wasn't sure that word was in your vocabulary."

"Which?"

"Fair."

"I deserve that."

"And a hell of a lot more," she muttered. But the torrent of anger she expected to be swirling inside her wasn't. All she felt was sad. "What made you do it?"

Gavin couldn't look at her. "He promised me the win. You'd have done the same."

"Probably. Which sucks. I don't want to be that person."

"No, trust me, you don't." When his eyes again met hers, they were awash in regret. "But, hey, the new app? Even cooler. So in a way you have me to thank."

"In a twisted, disturbing way, but, yeah, I guess."

"Listen, if I'd have known . . ."

"He covered well."

"He can't anymore. Not with all the comments on your article."

Her pulse quickened. "Trolls are out already?"

"Some. But most are from people who have stories like yours. Pulse board already tweeted something about an investigation into him and the company."

Everything had moved so fast, Lucy hadn't had time to think about what would happen after. This was what she'd have hoped, right? Validation for everything. And yet all Lucy could feel was intense sorrow for everyone else, for the women Ryan targeted, for the ones speaking up and the ones not, and for everyone who might lose their jobs, the ones building a company on a foundation they'd had no way of knowing was a fraud.

"Will I be seeing you at Stanford?" Gavin asked.

Lucy shook her head.

"Too bad." He tucked his hands in the pockets of his gray jeans. Paired with his white oxford, his clothes might have fooled Lucy that they were back in high school. But one look in his eyes, and what they'd been through let her know they weren't in high school anymore.

Gavin started to leave and then spun back around. He slipped his backpack off his shoulder and dug out a bottle of champagne.

"Turns out, my celebration's off." He handed her the bottle and pointed toward the opposite end of the hall. "Stairs to the roof. Not a bad view." He gave a half smile. "Assuming you already have company?"

Lucy slipped on her butterfly-frame sunglasses. "Tonight, Silicon Valley is a girls' club."

Like on day one, Maddie arrived first.

She and her brother shared the same constellation of freckles, the ones that had never lifted as high on Maddie's cheeks as when she'd seen Danny in the audience.

Lucy handed her a plastic cup.

Maddie lifted her aviators to her head and eyed the bottle of champagne. "Your mom?"

Lucy snorted. "We're not *that* close."

Yet.

"Gavin," Lucy said.

"Uh-huh."

"No, really. He apologized. Sort of. Ryan used him too."

That didn't mean she'd forgiven him. Even if some part of her wanted to.

An explosion through the doorway drew their attention, and in came Delia in her round sunglasses, body bouncing as much as her curls.

Lucy put a cup in her hand, and Delia's shoulders dropped. She removed her sunglasses. "Oh, I wanted to be the one to tell you."

"About Ryan?"

"Ryan? No, me. And Nishi. She offered me a job. Here. Can you believe it? I can stay and work and go to school at Mountain View U and . . . oh, oh . . ." Delia's eyes widened. "You guys . . . you're both . . . I couldn't have done any of this without you and

Nishi knows . . . but I mean, I'm sure she just needs programmers, and if—when—she needs—"

"Delia." Lucy wrapped her hand around Delia's wrist. "It's okay. I'm happy for you."

"Yeah?"

"Yeah."

"Yeah," Maddie said. "You deserve it. You kicked major ass. This whole time. Especially during your part of the presentation. Sorry I choked, by the way."

"I'm not," Delia said. "I'd have wondered 'what if' every day if I hadn't gone onstage. I'll take being scared over regrets."

"Sounds like a toast," Maddie said, reaching for the bottle.

"Uh," Lucy said, watching her grasp it by the neck without placing a hand over the top. "Have you ever opened one of those before, because—"

Maddie rolled her eyes and twisted too fast and the cork shot out of the bottle with a thunderous *pop!*—soaring into the sky and plummeting into the fountain below.

"Duck!" Maddie cried, peering over the edge.

"A little late with the warning, isn't it?" Lucy said.

"No, because it's for us—I'm pretty sure that's a campus cop down there!"

"A what?" Delia cried, and Lucy dragged them both down onto her comforter where they all devolved into hushed laughter as they tried to catch the cascade of bubbly spewing from the bottle.

As Delia sat cross-legged, she stroked the blanket.

"Good enough to nap under?" Lucy said, raising an eyebrow.

"It was once," Delia said, sheepishly.

"Twice," Lucy said.

"It looked lonely?"

Maddie poured champagne into each of their glasses. "If napping under this means she can code like that, well, give her the damn thing." Maddie raised her glass in the air. "Now, what first?"

"To Delia," she and Lucy said at the same time.

Lucy propped herself up on her heels. "To Delia. Who brought so many things to life—from Lit to Girl Empowered to—"

"Us. She wouldn't let us quit," Maddie said.

Their plastic cups may not have made a sound when they touched, but it didn't matter, because each of their hearts was beating loud enough.

They sipped. Delia hiccupped and lifted her glass. "And to both of you. I may have been able to do this on my own, but I wouldn't have wanted to."

"Me neither," Maddie said.

"Well . . ." Lucy started, and they both shot her a look. "Kidding, just kidding." She took another sip. "So, Delia's staying, but I'm curious . . . Madeline, have you been drawn in by our sunshine too?"

"Rain makes things green, you know," Maddie said.

"And wet."

"And lets you take a shower longer than three minutes."

"Huh," Lucy said, "you got me there."

"There's much to like here," Maddie said, quickly glancing at each of them. "But I think the East Coast is calling me. Maybe

NYU. It's a great school and the city's full of artists and museums and—"

"You're a good sister, Maddie," Delia said. Maddie shrugged uncomfortably, and Delia changed the subject. "What's next for you, Lucy?"

Lucy had been thinking a lot about that, but for once she wasn't jumping to make concrete plans. Everything seemed open to her—something that hadn't been the case since she was Maddie's brother's age. She wanted to enjoy it. Or try to anyway.

"My mom's got a business trip to London coming up. I'm thinking I'll go. Spend time with her and see my dad, and then, well, I'm still weighing my options. One thing I was kicking around was asking Nishi if she'd be interested in sponsoring an incubator for girls next summer. I'd kill it organizing that."

"You may kill everyone else while doing it," Maddie said. "But, yeah, you would."

Lucy felt herself getting choked up.

Was this it?

"Oh!" Delia almost dropped her drink. "I can't believe I forgot! Nishi wants to invest in Girl Empowered! If we want to actually do it."

"Do pterodactyls fly?" Maddie said.

"And she said we didn't win." Lucy snickered. "Sneaky, real sneaky, Nishi." Lucy poured out the rest of the champagne. "Good thing when your toasts outlast your bottle, right?"

"You do know who we're forgetting though?" Maddie said.

"Don't say anything about Ry—"

"No," Maddie said. "Older than that. Way older."

Delia grinned. "It's time she got her due. All of them. The first screen queens."

And then Lucy realized who they meant. She held her glass high and said, "To Ada."

"To Ada," they repeated.

Because that was how they were all related. The women that came before, the women of now, and the ones to come.

All empowered.

For the future they'd create.

ACKNOWLEDGMENTS

Bringing a book to life is much like founding a startup. The first thing that's required is an unwavering belief in the idea. And that I have been lucky to find with my editor, Jessica Harriton. One look at the number of smiley faces and exclamation marks we've exchanged while working on this book together is proof enough of your unbound enthusiasm, for which I am eternally grateful. Thank you for your constant support, encouragement, and sharp editorial eye.

Thank you to everyone at Razorbill and Penguin Young Readers for helping *Screen Queens* to "go public," in start-up lingo, and for making me feel so at home, especially Casey McIntyre and Ben Schrank (emeritus!). I owe my gratitude to Krista Ahlberg for her stellar copyediting skills and Vivian Kirklin for her strong proofreading eye. To Mallory Heyer, thank you for your beautiful cover illustration that perfectly captures each girl's personality and strength. Thanks also to Theresa Evangelista for the impeccable jacket design and Corina Lupp for making Pulse feel like it was ripped out of an app store! My appreciation to Kaitlin Kneafsey for all her publicity magic.

To Katelyn Detweiler, my deepest gratitude for, well, everything. Your editorial insights make me a better writer, and your warmth, optimism, and steadfast belief make me an indebted one.

I appreciate all that you and everyone at Jill Grinberg Literary Management do every day on my behalf.

Many startups owe their success to a "friends and family round" and so do I. This book wouldn't be here without the help of Pamela Ardila, Jen Brooks, Lee Kelly, Chandler Baker, Kelly Loy Gilbert, and especially Natalie Mae, whose previous life as a programmer ensured the accuracy and authenticity of both the coding and the experiences of the women in this book. You are all wildly talented—the embodiment of "girl empowered"—and your friendship and support mean everything to me.

I wouldn't be in this career without the love and understanding of my family—my parents, Denise and Frank, in-laws, Martha and Steve, and the Marangos and Goldstein families. Thank you especially for putting up with my deadlines!

On the subject of those deadlines . . . writing would not be my version of startup's "big hairy audacious goal," without one particular person. Thank you, Marc, for reading every word, and for letting me know the ones that need to change and the ones that make you laugh and cry (*sorry!*). Thank you for always being my angel investor.

This book is about taking chances. Like the ones taken by the pioneering women in this book and by the women today who are forging new paths in STEM and making their voices heard in the #metoo movement. Thank you to all the women who are standing up, often in the face of discrimination and seemingly insurmountable odds, to empower the next generation. As much as I hope Lucy, Maddie, and Delia are role models for girls pursuing interests in STEM, I also hope they represent the other key tenet of this book: the power of friendship.

RESOURCES

Thanks to the following online sources for the background that informed the definitions used in the chapter titles: Silicon Valley Dictionary, Investopedia, Funding Sage, Techopedia, Cambridge Dictionary, Martin Fowler, *Wired*, Medium, and TechCrunch.

While I have previously worked in IT publishing, many sources contributed to the base of knowledge for the experiences of women in tech, notably Emily Chang's *Brotopia: Breaking Up the Boys' Club of Silicon Valley* and *The Atlantic*'s "Why Is Silicon Valley So Awful to Women?" Statistics and facts cited in the book come from the following: the Department for Professional Employees' "The Professional and Technical Workforce"; Boardroom Insiders' "2018 State of Women CIOs in the Fortune 500"; *The New Yorker*'s "The Tech Industry's Gender-Discrimination Problem"; Microsoft's "Closing the Stem Gap"; *The Atlantic*'s "How Self-Tracking Apps Exclude Women" and "Are the New iPhones Too Big for Women's Hands?"; *Fortune*'s "The Number of Women in Computing Has Plummeted"; NPR's "When Women Stopped Coding"; and Catalyst's "Women in Science, Technology, Engineering, and Mathematics (STEM)."